AMERICAN SCHOOL TEXTBOOK
VOCABULARY KEY

GRADE **2**

Michael A. Putlack

FÜN學美國英語課本
各學科關鍵英單 二版+ Workbook

MP3

寂天雲 APP

如何下載 **MP3** 音檔

❶ 寂天雲 APP 聆聽：掃描書上 QR Code 下載
「寂天雲－英日語學習隨身聽」APP。加入會員
後，用 APP 內建掃描器再次掃描書上 QR
Code，即可使用 APP 聆聽音檔。

❷ 官網下載音檔：請上「寂天閱讀網」
（www.icosmos.com.tw），註冊會員／登入後，
搜尋本書，進入本書頁面，點選「MP3 下載」
下載音檔，存於電腦等其他播放器聆聽使用。

U0033908

FÜN 學美國英語課本 各學科關鍵英單 GRADE 2

AMERICAN SCHOOL TEXTBOOK
VOCABULARY KEY

二版

作者簡介

Michael A. Putlack

專攻歷史與英文，擁有美國麻州 Tufts University 碩士學位。

作　　　者　Michael A. Putlack
　　　　　　Zachany Fillinghan / Shara Dupuis（Workbook B 大題）
編　　　輯　鄭家文／丁宥榆
翻　　　譯　鄭家文
校　　　對　丁宥暄
封 面 設 計　林書玉
內 頁 排 版　林書玉／丁宥榆
製 程 管 理　洪巧玲
發 行 人　黃朝萍
出 版 者　寂天文化事業股份有限公司
電　　　話　+886-(0)2-2365-9739
傳　　　真　+886-(0)2-2365-9835
網　　　址　www.icosmos.com.tw
讀 者 服 務　onlineservice@icosmos.com.tw
出 版 日 期　2023 年 8 月　二版二刷（寂天雲隨身聽 APP 版）

Copyright © 2017 by Key Publications
Photos © Shutterstock Corporation
Copyright © 2023 by Cosmos Culture Ltd.
版權所有　請勿翻印

郵 撥 帳 號　1998620-0 寂天文化事業股份有限公司
‧ 訂書金額未滿 1000 元，請外加運費 100 元。
〔若有破損，請寄回更換，謝謝。〕

國家圖書館出版品預行編目資料

FUN 學美國英語課本 Grade 2：各學科關鍵英單 .（寂天隨身聽 APP 版）
= American school textbook : vocabulary key. grade 2/ Michael A.
Putlack 著；鄭家文譯 . -- 二版 . -- 臺北市：寂天文化，2023.08
　　面；　公分

ISBN 978-626-300-205-0（平裝）

1.CST: 英語 2.CST: 詞彙

805.12　　　　　　　　　　　　　　　112012143

American School Textbook
Reading Key – Preschool

The Best Preparation for Building Basic Vocabulary and Grammar

The Reading Key — Preschool series is designed to help children understand basic words and grammar to learn English. This series also helps children develop their reading skills in a fun and easy way.

Features

- Learning high-frequency words that appear in all kinds of reading material
- Building basic grammar and reading comprehension skills to learn English
- Various activities including reading and writing practice
- A wide variety of topics that cover American school subjects
- Full-color photographs and illustrations

The Reading Key series has five levels.

○ Reading Key **Preschool 1–6**
a six-book series designed for preschoolers and kindergarteners

○ Reading Key **Basic 1–4**
a four-book series designed for kindergarteners and beginners

○ Reading Key **Volume 1–3**
a three-book series designed for beginner to intermediate learners

○ Reading Key **Volume 4–6**
a three-book series designed for intermediate to high-intermediate learners

○ Reading Key **Volume 7–9**
a three-book series designed for high-intermediate learners

Table of Contents | Preschool 2 **Adjectives**

Components Workbook for Daily Review · Answers and Translations

AMERICAN SCHOOL TEXTBOOK

VOCABULARY KEY

Workbook

GRADE **2**

Michael A. Putlack

FÜN學美國英語課本

各學科關鍵英單 二版

Unit 01

Listen to the passage and fill in the blanks.

121 | **Kinds of Communities**

People live in many different places. Some like big cities. Others like living in the 1._____. And others like neither place. They prefer small cities or towns. Big cities are 2._____ communities. Some cities have 3._____ of people. People in big cities live closely together. They often live in apartments. They might use the bus or subway very often. Rural 4._____ are in the countryside. They have small 5._____. Farmers live in 6._____ areas. People live in houses and often drive cars. Suburban communities are small cities near big ones. Many 7._____ live there. But they might work in a big city. They might drive or take buses and subways.

B **Read the passage above and answer the following questions.**

_____ 8. Which sentence from the article is closest to the main point?
- a "Some cities have millions of people."
- b "People live in many different places."
- c "Farmers live in rural areas."
- d "People in big cities live closely together."

_____ 9. Which of the following statements is TRUE?
- a People in rural communities live closely together.
- b Many families live in suburban communities.
- c People who live on farms take buses and subways.
- d Farmers live in urban communities.

_____ 10. "And others like neither place." What does "neither place" mean in the sentence?
- a Not one place or the other.
- b Only one place.
- c One place more than the other.
- d Both the places the same.

Unit 02

A Listen to the passage and fill in the blanks.

🎧 122 **19th Century American Immigration**

In1789, the United States became a country. It was a huge land. And the country 1._____ and got bigger. But, at that time, few people lived in the U.S.

The country needed 2._____. So, during the nineteenth century, millions of people 3._____ the U.S. Most of them were from Europe. They also 4._____ Ireland. They came from Germany. They came from Italy, Russia, and other countries. Millions of them came to America. These immigrants worked hard. But they often 5._____ little money. Yet they slowly 6._____ their lives. And they helped the U.S. become a great and 7._____ country.

B Read the passage above and answer the following questions.

_____ 8. Which statement is closest to the main idea of the passage?
- a Immigrants in America helped to make it a great country.
- b Life was difficult for immigrants in America.
- c Americans treated new immigrants badly.
- d Only people from certain countries can immigrate to America.

_____ 9. "Yet they slowly improved their lives." The opposite of the word "improved" is _____.
- a lengthened
- b worsened
- c delayed
- d occupied

_____ 10. Which of the following statements is TRUE?
- a Immigrants made the United States grow into a huge land.
- b Millions of immigrants came to the United States in the 18th century.
- c High-paying jobs were given to immigrants when they arrived in the United States.
- d Immigrants worked hard when they arrived in the United States.

3

Unit 03

Listen to the passage and fill in the blanks.

🎧 123 | **Different Kinds of Jobs**

After people finish school, they often look for 1._____. There are many kinds of jobs people do. But there are three main 2._____ of jobs. They are 3._____ jobs, manufacturing jobs, and professional jobs. People with service jobs provide services for others. They might 4._____ the mail or food. They often work in restaurants. And they work in stores as salespeople and 5._____. People with 6._____ jobs make things. They make TVs, computers, cars, and other objects. People with 7._____ jobs often have special training. They are doctors and 8._____. They are 9._____ and teachers. They might need to attend school to 10._____ their skills.

B **Read the passage above and answer the following questions.**

_____ 11. Another good title for this passage would be _____.
- a The Wide World of Jobs
- b Why We Work
- c When We Work
- d How to Find a Job

_____ 12. Which of the following people has a professional job?
- a A waiter.
- b A factory cleaner.
- c A lawyer.
- d A car salesman.

_____ 13. "They might need to attend school to learn their skills." Which of the following has the same meaning as the word "skill"?
- a Education.
- b Ability.
- c Parents.
- d Mail.

Unit 04

Listen to the passage and fill in the blanks.

🎧 124 | **American Geography**

The United States is a huge country with 50 states. Each 1._____ in the U.S. has different 2._____ features. The Northeast is the New England area. It includes Massachusetts and Connecticut. The land there is 3._____. The Southeast is another region. It includes Alabama, Tennessee, and Florida. It has some low 4._____. There are many rivers and lakes, too. The 5._____ is a very flat land. There are miles and miles of farms. Iowa and Illinois are 6._____ there. The Southwest is hot. It has some 7._____. The Grand Canyon is located there. The 8._____ Mountains are also there. The West includes California and Washington. It has both mountains and big 9._____.

B **Read the passage above and answer the following questions.**

_____ 10. What is the main point in this article?
- a The U.S. has geography unlike anywhere else.
- b The U.S. has lots of different geographical features.
- c The U.S. is only mountainous along the west coast.
- d The U.S. has areas with both mountains and forests.

_____ 11. According to the article, the United States is made up of how many states?
- a 50
- b 51
- c 52
- d 30

_____ 12. The article says that the Midwest is a very "flat" land. A word with an opposite meaning to "flat" is _____.
- a low
- b hard
- c dangerous
- d hilly

Unit 05

Listen to the passage and fill in the blanks.

🎧 125 | **State and Local Governments**

The 1._____ government in the U.S. is very important. It is the 2._____ government of the U.S. But every state has its own government, too. And cities have governments also. Every state has a 3._____. A governor is like the president. The governor is the most powerful person in the state. And every state has a 4._____. There are many members in these legislatures. They 5._____ small sections of their states. They pass the bills that become 6._____ in the states. Cities have governments, too. Most cities have 7._____. Some have city managers though. A city manager is like a mayor. And the city 8._____ is like a legislature. But it usually has just a few members.

B **Read the passage above and answer the following questions.**

_____ 9. According to the article, which of the following is almost the same as a mayor?
- a A governor.
- b A central government.
- c A city manager.
- d A city council.

_____ 10. "The governor is the most powerful person in the state." The word with the same meaning as "powerful" is _____.
- a strong
- b old
- c small
- d political

_____ 11. What is the main point of the passage?
- a Governors are very powerful in the U.S.
- b City councils are just like legislatures.
- c Cities in the U.S. sometimes have several mayors.
- d There are many levels of government in the U.S.

Unit 06

🎧 126 | **How Native American Tribes Came to America**

The first people to America 1._____ Asia. They crossed a land bridge, a narrow strip of land that connected Russia and Alaska. It was just ice that connected the 2._____ across the sea. Then, they traveled down into the land from North to South America. They became 3._____ Americans. In the area that became the United States, there were a large number of 4._____. Some were very powerful. Others were not. All of the tribes lived off the land. Some were 5._____. They followed herds of 6._____ all year long. Others lived in small groups or villages. They knew how to farm. They grew various 7._____. And they also 8._____ and fished.

B Read the passage above and answer the following questions.

_____ 9. This article is mostly about _____.
- a Native American religious beliefs
- b the first people in the Americas
- c the importance of buffalo hunting
- d a land bridge between Asia and America

_____ 10. Which of the following is TRUE?
- a All Native Americans were nomads.
- b The first Americans crossed the sea on boats.
- c Some Native Americans fished.
- d There were no powerful Native American tribes.

_____ 11. The article says Native Americans followed "herds" of buffalo. A herd is a(n) _____.
- a group of animals
- b dangerous type of animal
- c adult animal
- d endangered animal

7

Unit 07

A Listen to the passage and fill in the blanks.

🎧 127 | **Three Great American Empires**

The first Americans from Asia 1._____ in North and South America. As they learned to farm and made their homes, they 2._____ towns and cities. Some of these people made great 3._____. The first were the Mayans. They lived in Central America. They lived in the 4._____. But they had a great empire. They were very advanced. The Mayans knew how to write by 5._____ pictures. They were also good at math. They built many amazing 6._____ and other buildings. The Incas lived in South America. They 7._____ much land there. And they built cities high in the Andes Mountains. The Aztecs lived in North America. Their capital was in modern-day Mexico. They were very warlike. They fought many 8._____. And they often 9._____ their enemies.

B Read the passage above and answer the following questions.

_____ 10. Which statement below best expresses the main idea?
- [a] There were three great empires in the Americas.
- [b] The Aztecs were a war-like people.
- [c] The Mayans were far more advanced than the Incas.
- [d] It was difficult for people to live in the Americas.

_____ 11. Which of the following is TRUE about the Mayans?
- [a] They were a war-like people.
- [b] They ruled over North America.
- [c] They were able to write by drawing pictures.
- [d] They built cities in the mountains.

_____ 12. The article says the Mayans were very "advanced." The word "advanced" means _____.
- [a] they had lots of technology
- [b] they believed in many gods
- [c] they did not know how to fight
- [d] their culture was very new

Unit 08

A Listen to the passage and fill in the blanks.

🎧 128

The Europeans Come to the Americas

After Christopher Columbus, many 1._____ sailed to America. Portugal, Spain, France, and England 2._____ 3._____ to find a 4._____ to Asia. Spanish explorers went to present-day Florida. They went to Mexico and other places in 5._____ America. And they went to South America, too. The Portuguese mostly went to South America. They 6._____ colonies in Brazil. The French soon followed. They 7._____ present-day Canada. The French 8._____ very large areas of land in Canada and 9._____ there. The English went to present-day Virginia.

B Read the passage above and answer the following questions.

_____ 10. This article is about _____.
  a history and geography
  b native cultures
  c European ships
  d Florida

_____ 11. According to the article, the Portuguese founded colonies in _____.
  a Mexico
  b Brazil
  c Canada
  d Virginia

_____ 12. "The French claimed very large areas of land in Canada . . ." This means _____.
  a they said the land belongs to them
  b they said they don't want the land
  c they said the land was unusable
  d they said the land was very special

9

Unit 09

A Listen to the passage and fill in the blanks.

🎧 129 | **The English in America**

The Spanish came to the New World for 1._____. But the English had another reason to go there. They wanted 2._____. The English 3._____ in North America. They started many colonies. Two were Virginia and Massachusetts. The first English colony was Jamestown. It was in Virginia. Life was very hard for the 4._____. Many died of 5._____ and disease. But more and more people came from England. Many of them wanted new lives in America. They came for 6._____ freedom. That was why the Pilgrims and Puritans came. They 7._____ colonies near Boston. They lived in Massachusetts.

B Read the passage above and answer the following questions.

_____ 8. Which sentence below best expresses the main idea?
- a The English started a colony in Virginia.
- b The first English colony was Jamestown.
- c The Puritans settled in Boston.
- d The English wanted colonies in the New World.

_____ 9. Many of the early English settlers came to the New World looking for

_____.
- a gold
- b religious freedom
- c an easy life
- d good weather

_____ 10. "The English settled in North America." The word "settled" means _____.
- a wrote histories of all the people living there
- b went and lived in a particular place forever
- c could not find it for a very long time
- d invited people from North America to England

Unit 10

A Listen to the passage and fill in the blanks.

🎧 130   **The Colonies Become Free**

After the first English 1._____ arrived in Jamestown, more and more people moved from Europe to America. They lived in places called 2._____. As the years passed, there were 13 colonies. These colonies were 3._____ by the king of England. But many colonies did not want to be ruled by England. They wanted to be 4._____. On July 4, 1776, many leaders in the colonies 5._____ the Declaration of Independence. In the 6._____, they wrote that Americans wanted to be free and start their own country. The colonies 7._____ a war with England. The war lasted for many years. George Washington 8._____ the American 9._____ and led them to victory. After the war, the colonies became a country. The country was called the United States of America. Today, American celebrates 10._____ Day on July 4.

B Read the passage above and answer the following questions.

_____ 11. Another good title for this article would be _____.
- a The Life and Times of George Washington
- b How the United States Became a Country
- c The War of 1776
- d The First Independence Day Celebration

_____ 12. "In the declaration, they wrote that Americans wanted to be free and start their own country." A word with a similar meaning to "declaration" is _____.
- a question   b secret   c agreement   d statement

_____ 13. According to the article, when did the colonies become a country?
- a On July 4th, 1776.
- b Shortly after the war began in England.
- c After the 13 colonies won the war.
- d When the king of England signed the declaration.

Unit 11

A **Listen to the passage and fill in the blanks.**

🎧 131 **Living Things vs. Nonliving Things**

Everything on Earth is either living or 1._____.

A living thing is 2._____. A nonliving thing is not alive. Both animals and

3._____ are living things. Rocks, air, and water are nonliving things.

There are many kinds of animals and plants. But they are similar in some

ways. All of them need 4._____ to survive. They also need food and

water. When they eat and drink, they get 5._____. Nutrients provide

energy for them. Most plants and animals need 6._____, too. Living

things also can make new living things like themselves. Nonliving things are

not alive. They cannot move. They cannot 7._____. They cannot make

new things like themselves.

B **Read the passage above and answer the following questions.**

_____ 8. What is closest to the main point the author wants to make in the article?
- a Living things are more important than nonliving things.
- b Everything in the world can be labeled as living or nonliving.
- c Living things have existed longer than nonliving things.
- d Scientists are still discovering the secrets of nonliving things.

_____ 9. Which of the following is an example of a living thing?
- a Water.
- b Air.
- c A rock.
- d A horse.

_____ 10. "Everything on Earth is either living or nonliving." The word with the
same meaning as "nonliving" is _____.
- a large
- b rocky
- c dead
- d difficult

Unit 12

Listen to the passage and fill in the blanks.

🎧 132 | **How Are Animals Different?**

There are five types of animals. They are 1._____, birds, 2._____, amphibians, and fish. They are all different from each other. Mammals are animals like dogs, cats, cows, lions, tigers, and humans. They give 3._____ to live 4._____. And they 5._____ their young with milk from their mothers. Birds have 6._____, and most of them can fly. Penguins, hawks, and sparrows are birds. Reptiles and 7._____ are similar. Both of them 8._____ eggs. Snakes are reptiles, and frogs and toads are amphibians. Amphibians live on land and in the water. Fish live in the water. They lay eggs. They use 9._____ to take in oxygen from the water. Sharks, bass, and catfish are all fish.

B **Read the passage above and answer the following questions.**

_____ 10. Which sentence best expresses the main idea of this article?
- a Animals are divided into five different types.
- b Animals can be either reptiles or amphibians.
- c Animals can sometimes be very dangerous.
- d Animals can live in many different places.

_____ 11. According to the article, a frog is a(n) _____.
- a reptile
- b mammal
- c bird
- d amphibian

_____ 12. "They give birth to live young." The word with the opposite meaning of "live" is _____.
- a scared
- b old
- c strong
- d dead

A Listen to the passage and fill in the blanks.

🎧 133 | **The Life Cycles of Cats and Frogs**

Every animal has a 1._____. This is the period from birth to 2._____.

Cats are mammals, so they are 3._____ alive. Baby cats are called kittens. A mother cat takes care of her kittens for many weeks. The mother cat 4._____ her kittens with milk from her body. As the kittens get bigger, they become more independent. After about one year, they become 5._____ cats, and they can take care of themselves.

Frogs have different life cycles. Frogs are born in eggs. When they 6._____, they are called 7._____. Tadpoles have long 8._____ and no legs. They use gills to breathe in the water. Soon, they 9._____ legs and start to use 10._____ to breathe. Later, they can leave the water. When this happens, they become adult frogs.

B Read the passage above and answer the following questions.

_____ 11. What is closest to the main point the author wants to make in the article?
- a The life cycles of animals can be very different.
- b A cat's life cycle is the same as a frog's.
- c Mammals have the longest life cycle of any animal.
- d A tadpole grows into an adult frog.

_____ 12. Which of the following is TRUE about frogs?
- a Tadpole is the last stage of their life cycle.
- b They have no lungs and can't breathe.
- c They are all born from eggs.
- d They have four legs as a tadpole.

_____ 13. "When they hatch, they are called tadpoles." The word "hatch" means _____.
- a to lay an egg
- b to come out of an egg
- c to leave your parents
- d to build a shelter

Unit 14

A Listen to the passage and fill in the blanks.

🎧 134 **The Life Cycle of a Pine Tree**

Every plant, like pine trees, has its own life cycle. A pine tree's life cycle begins with a 1._____. Adult pine trees have pine 2._____. Inside the pine cones are tiny seeds. Every year, many pine cones fall to the 3._____. Some of them stay near the pine tree, but, other times, animals 4._____ them up and move them. The wind and rain might move them, too. Sometimes, the seeds 5._____ out of the pine cones and get buried in the ground. They often start to 6._____. These are called 7._____. These seedlings get bigger and bigger. After many years, they become adult pine trees. Then they too have pine cones with seeds. So a new life cycle begins again.

B Read the passage above and answer the following questions.

_____ 8. This article focuses on a pine tree's _____.
  a growth   b leaves
  c seeds   d trunk

_____ 9. Which of the following statements about pine cones is TRUE?
  a They never move from the base of the tree.
  b They are the last stage of the pine tree's life cycle.
  c They are extremely heavy.
  d They contain pine tree seeds.

_____ 10. The article mentions that when pine cones get buried, they start to "sprout." Which of the following is something else that can "sprout"?
  a A highway.
  b A person.
  c A seed.
  d A computer.

A Listen to the passage and fill in the blanks.

🎧 135 **The Food Chain**

All animals must eat to 1._____. Some eat plants. Some eat animals. And others eat both plants and animals. The 2._____ shows the 3._____ of each animal to the others. At the bottom of the food chain are the 4._____. They are often 5._____ animals. They are usually small animals like squirrels and rabbits. Sometimes they are bigger animals like deer. Animals higher on the food chain eat these animals. They might be owls, 6._____, and raccoons. Then, bigger animals like bears and wolves eat these animals. Finally, we reach the 7._____ of the food chain. The most dangerous animal of all is here: man.

B Read the passage above and answer the following questions.

_____ 8. Which sentence best expresses the main idea of the article?

  a Animals eat other animals in the food chain.

  b Plants are at the bottom of the food chain.

  c There is no such thing as a food chain.

  d The food chain was created by man.

_____ 9. According to the article, which of the following is considered to be a prey animal?

  a A bear.

  b A wolf.

  c A rabbit.

  d A human.

_____ 10. "All animals must eat to survive." The word "survive" means to _____.

  a dig

  b eat

  c escape

  d remain alive

Unit 16

Listen to the passage and fill in the blanks.

🎧 136 | **An Insect's Body**

There are many kinds of insects. They include ants, bees, 1._____, 2._____, and 3._____. They look different from each other. But they have the same 4._____ in common.

All insects have three main body parts. They are the head, 5._____, and 6._____. The head has the insect's mouth, eyes, and 7._____. An insect uses its antennae to feel and taste things. The thorax is the middle body part. It has three pairs of 8._____. Adult insects have six legs. Some insects have 9._____ on their bodies. The abdomen is the third and final part of the insect.

B **Read the passage above and answer the following questions.**

_____ 10. Which statement best expresses the main idea of this article?
- a Insects have very complicated bodies.
- b All insect bodies are made up of three parts.
- c The thorax is the middle part of an insect's body.
- d Some insects have wings on their body.

_____ 11. According to the article, an insect uses its antennae to _____.
- a fight other insects
- b dig holes
- c find a mate
- d feel and taste things

_____ 12. What does the phrase "in common" mean in the sentence "But they have the same body parts in common"?
- a Different insects live apart from each other.
- b Different insects have things about them that are the same.
- c Different insects will group together to fight other animals.
- d Different insects will share their food with each other.

Unit 17

A Listen to the passage and fill in the blanks.

🎧 137 | **The Phases of the Moon**

The moon takes about 29 days to 1._____ Earth. During this time, the moon seems to change shapes. We call these looks 2._____. The phases change as the moon 3._____ the earth.

The first phase is the new moon. The moon is invisible now. However, it starts to get brighter. It looks like a 4._____. This next phase is called waxing crescent. Waxing means it is getting bigger. Soon, it is at the first 5._____ phase. Half the moon is visible. Then it becomes a 6._____ moon. The entire moon is visible. Now, the moon starts to 7._____. It is beginning to disappear. It goes to the last quarter 8._____. Then it is a waning crescent. Finally, it becomes a new moon again.

B Read the passage above and answer the following questions.

_____ 9. This article focuses on the moon's _____.
- a shape
- b color
- c history
- d importance

_____ 10. Which of the following is the moon's final phase?
- a Waxing crescent.
- b Full moon.
- c Waning crescent.
- d First quarter moon.

_____ 11. "The moon is invisible now." In this sentence, the word "invisible" means that something cannot _____.
- a be measured
- b be seen
- c be heard
- d be stopped

A Listen to the passage and fill in the blanks.

🎧 138 | **The Organs of the Human Body**

Organs are very important parts of the human body. They help do certain body functions. There are many different 1._____. One important organ is the heart. It 2._____ blood all throughout the body. Without a heart, a person cannot live. The brain runs the body's 3._____. It controls both 4._____ and physical activities. People can breathe thanks to their lungs. A person has two lungs. The stomach helps 5._____ food. It 6._____ food down into nutrients so the rest of the body can use it. The 7._____ also helps with digestion. One of the most important organs is the biggest. It's the 8._____. It covers a person's entire body!

B Read the passage above and answer the following questions.

_____ 9. What is closest to the main point the author wants to make in this article?
   a The human body is the most important organ of all.
   b Organs are the smallest part of the human body.
   c The human body has several important organs.
   d Skin is the largest organ in the human body.

_____ 10. Which of the following controls the body's mental and physical activities?
   a The skin.   b The stomach.
   c The heart.   d The brain.

_____ 11. "It breaks food down into nutrients so the rest of the body can use it." What does it mean to "break something down"?
   a To turn something into smaller bits.
   b To make one thing into something else.
   c To release something into the air.
   d To build one thing into something bigger.

Unit 19

A Listen to the passage and fill in the blanks.

🎧 139 | **How a Magnet Works**

Some objects are 1._____ to each other. And some objects 2._____ each other. A 3._____ is an object that can attract or repel other objects. Magnets can 4._____ things like iron or steel without touching them. How does a magnet work? A magnet is a piece of 5._____ metal like iron or nickel. It has two separate 6._____. It has a north-seeking pole, or N pole, and a south-seeking pole, or S pole. This creates a 7._____. So it can attract or repel different metals. If the north pole of a magnet is near the south pole of another one, the two will be attracted. But if two north poles of two magnets are near each other, they will repel each other.

B Read the passage above and answer the following questions.

_____ 8. This article focuses on a(n)_____.
     a experiment   b scientist
     c special kind of metal   d magnetic field on our planet

_____ 9. According to the article, which of the following statements about magnets is TRUE?
     a They are extremely rare.
     b North poles attract south poles.
     c Two magnets will always repel each other.
     d They can be dangerous.

_____ 10. The article mentions that magnets "can attract or repel other objects."
The word with the same meaning as "attract" is _____.
     a complete
     b outline
     c represent
     d draw

A Listen to the passage and fill in the blanks.

🎧 140

The Invention of the Telephone

A long time ago, there were no telephones. But people knew that 1._____ travels by 2._____. So many people tried to invent the telephone. Alexander Graham Bell was one of these people. He wanted to use electricity to 3._____ sound. He thought he could turn sound into electric 4._____. Then it could 5._____ wires. He worked very hard on his project. One day in 1876, he had an accident in his office. He needed his assistant Watson. He said, "Watson, come here. I want you." Watson was in another part of the house. But he 6._____ Bell over the telephone. Finally, Bell was successful. He had invented the telephone!

B Read the passage above and answer the following questions.

_____ 7. What is closest to the main point the author wants to make in the article?
   a Alexander Graham Bell's assistant is the true hero.
   b Alexander Graham Bell discovered sound vibrations.
   c Alexander Graham Bell invented the telephone.
   d Alexander Graham Bell worked in an office.

_____ 8. According to the article, who was Watson?
   a Alexander Graham Bell's father.
   b Alexander Graham Bell's competitor.
   c Alexander Graham Bell's assistant.
   d Alexander Graham Bell's boss.

_____ 9. "He wanted to use electricity to transmit sound." The word with the same meaning as "transmit" is _____.
   a measure
   b leave
   c send
   d destroy

A **Listen to the passage and fill in the blanks.**

🎧 141 | **Number Sentences**

People use sentences when they speak, but they can also use sentences when they do 1._____. How can they do this? It's easy. They use 2._____.

Let's think of a math problem. You have four apples, but then you 3._____ two more. That gives you a 4._____ of six apples. Now, let's make that a number sentence. It would look like this: 4+2=6. You can make number sentences for 5._____, and you can make them for 6._____, too. Your friend has ten pieces of candy, but he eats five pieces. Now he has five pieces left. Let's make a number sentence for that. Here it is: 10-5=5.

B **Read the passage above and answer the following questions.**

_____ 7. Which statement best expresses the main idea of this article?
   ⓐ Number sentences are no longer used.
   ⓑ Number sentences turn math into a sentence.
   ⓒ You shouldn't eat your friend's candy.
   ⓓ Apples are the best way to solve math problems.

_____ 8. Which of the following statements about number sentences is TRUE?
   ⓐ They give steps on how to solve math problems.
   ⓑ They can be used for addition or subtraction.
   ⓒ They don't contain any actual numbers.
   ⓓ They are only used by math experts.

_____ 9. "You can make number sentences for addition, and you can make them for subtraction, too." The word "subtraction" means _____.
   ⓐ taking something away
   ⓑ adding something
   ⓒ leaving something alone
   ⓓ showing something

Unit 22

A Listen to the passage and fill in the blanks.

🎧 142 | **Time Passes**

John wakes up in the morning at seven A.M. School starts at eight 1._____,
so he has one 2._____ to get there. When he arrives at school, it's
seven forty-five. School will begin in fifteen 3._____. School runs
from eight 4._____ three o'clock. That's a total of seven hours. In
the morning, John has class from eight until 5._____, so he has a
total of four hours of class. Then he has lunch from twelve o'clock until a
6._____ to one. After that, from twelve forty-five until three 7._____,
he has more classes. That's a total of two hours and fifteen minutes. Finally,
at three, school finishes, and John can go home.

B Read the passage above and answer the following questions.

_____ 8. Which sentence below best expresses the main idea of this article?
    a John goes to school from 8:00 A.M. to 3:00 P.M.
    b John goes to the best school in town.
    c John is thinking about leaving school at 12:45 P.M.
    d John's favorite class is math.

_____ 9. Which of the following is the best ending for the sentence: "A quarter is _____."
    a a type of animal
    b a replacement
    c something that is late
    d one-fourth of a whole

_____ 10. "School runs from eight until three o'clock." Which of the following uses "run"
    in the same way as this sentence?
    a He wakes up every morning and goes on a 10 km run.
    b John has had a good run of luck at the horse track lately.
    c The sale runs until the end of July.
    d The prisoner escaped from jail and is now on the run.

Unit 23

Listen to the passage and fill in the blanks.

🎧 143 | **Plane Figures and Solid Figures**

Geometry is the study of regular 1._____. We can divide these shapes into two kinds: plane figures and 2._____. There are many kinds of plane figures. Squares, 3._____, triangles, and circles are all plane figures. Plane figures have both length and width. They are 4._____, so you can draw them on a piece of paper. Solid figures are different from plane figures. They have 5._____, width, and height. A box is a solid figure. We call that a 6._____ in geometry. A globe is a solid figure. That's a 7._____. Also, a 8._____ and a 9._____ are two more solid figures.

B **Read the passage above and answer the following questions.**

_____ 10. Another good title for this article is _____.

      a Shapes and Figures

      b The Importance of Shapes

      c Solving the Mysterious Pentagon

      d The Three Points of a Triangle

_____ 11. Which of the following best describes a plane figure?

      a A shape with length, width, and height.

      b A shape made up of squares and triangles.

      c An octagon drawn on a plane.

      d A shape with length and width.

_____ 12. "They are flat surfaces, so you can draw them on a piece of paper." A word with a similar meaning to "flat" is _____.

      a ugly

      b smooth

      c creative

      d fancy

Unit 24

A Listen to the passage and fill in the blanks.

🎧 144 | **Why Do We Multiply?**

Sometimes, you might want to 1._____ many groups of things together. For example, you might have five groups of apples. Each group has two apples. You could add 2 five 2._____ like this: 2 + 2 + 2 + 2 + 2 = 10. But that's too long. Instead, use 3._____. You can write that as a multiplication problem like this: 2×5 = 10. When you 4._____, you add 5._____ of numbers many times. Multiplication is useful because it makes math easier. However, remember a couple of things about it. First, when you multiply any number by 1, the 6._____ is always the same as that number: 5×1 = 5. 100×1 = 100. Also, when you multiply any number by 0, the product is always 0: 2×0 = 0. 100×0 = 0.

B Read the passage above and answer the following questions.

_____ 7. What is closest to the main point the author wants to make?

    a Multiplication is the most difficult of all math skills.

    b Multiplication can make complex addition easier.

    c Multiplying something by 0 will equal 0.

    d Apples should be grouped in twos.

_____ 8. The answer to a multiplication question is called the _____.

    a sum   b difference

    c product   d remainder

_____ 9. "When you multiply, you add equal groups of numbers many times." In this example, the word "equal" means _____.

    a the numbers are very large

    b the numbers are small

    c the numbers are the same

    d the numbers include zero

Unit 25

A Listen to the passage and fill in the blanks.

🎧 145 **Parts of Speech**

There are many words in the English language. We use words to make

1._____. But there are also many types of words. We call these

"2._____," and we make sentences with them. Nouns,

3._____, adjectives, and 4._____ are all parts of speech.

Every sentence needs a 5._____ and a verb. The subject is often a

6._____. Nouns are words that name a person, place, or thing. Look

around your room. Think of the names of everything you see. All those words

are nouns. Verbs 7._____ actions. Think of some activities you do. The

names of those activities are verbs. Sometimes we also use other parts of

speech. Adjectives describe other words like nouns and 8._____. Hot,

cold, white, black, windy, rainy, and sunny are all 9._____.

B Read the passage above and answer the following questions.

_____ 10. Which statement best expresses the main idea of this article?

  [a] Parts of speech are used to describe actions.

  [b] Every word has its own part of speech.

  [c] Sometimes we also use other parts of speech.

  [d] A noun is the most common part of speech.

_____ 11. This article focuses on _____.

  [a] words   [b] sentences   [c] verbs   [d] adjectives

_____ 12. "Every sentence needs a subject and a verb." The word "subject"

  means _____.

  [a] a description of something

  [b] a type of fruit

  [c] an action being performed

  [d] the main person or thing

Unit 26

Listen to the passage and fill in the blanks.

🎧 146 | **Some Common Sayings**

Every language has common 1._____. People use them in various situations. They are hard to 2._____ into other languages. But they 3._____ in their own language. English has many common sayings. One is "Better 4._____ than never." This means it is better to do something late than never to do it. Another is "Two 5._____ are better than one." This means a second person can often help one person doing something. And "An apple a day 6._____ the doctor away" is a common saying. It means that eating apples every day helps keep you healthy. So the person will not get sick and won't have to see a doctor.

B **Read the passage above and answer the following questions.**

_____ 7. Which statement best expresses the main idea of this article?
- [a] English does not have any common sayings.
- [b] Common sayings are difficult to learn.
- [c] Every language has common sayings.
- [d] It's important to eat an apple every day.

_____ 8. The saying "Better late than never" means _____.
- [a] always finish what you start
- [b] never be late for a meeting
- [c] even if you're late, finish it
- [d] finish it before you're late

_____ 9. "English has many common sayings." The word with the opposite meaning of "common" is _____.
- [a] rare
- [b] angry
- [c] complicated
- [d] exciting

Unit 27

A Listen to the passage and fill in the blanks.

🎧 147

Realistic Art and Abstract Art

There are two main kinds of art. They are 1._____ and 2._____. Some artists like realistic art, but others prefer abstract art. Realistic art 3._____ objects as they look in reality. For example, a realistic artist 4._____ a picture of an apple. The picture will look exactly like an apple. Most art in the past was realistic art. Abstract art looks 5._____ than realistic art. Abstract art does not always look exactly like the real thing. For example, an abstract artist paints a picture of an apple. It will not 6._____ an apple. It might just be a red ball. That is abstract art. Nowadays, much art is abstract.

B Read the passage above and answer the following questions.

_____ 7. Which statement best expresses the main idea of this article?
- a All kinds of art are important.
- b There are two main kinds of art.
- c Realistic art is very difficult to paint.
- d Abstract art was invented in Europe.

_____ 8. According to the article, which of the following statements is TRUE?
- a Abstract art was more popular in the past.
- b There is a lot of abstract art now.
- c Realistic artists draw apples that look like red balls.
- d There are no more realistic artists.

_____ 9. The article describes a type of art that is abstract. A word with a similar meaning to "abstract" is _____.
- a expensive
- b natural
- c romantic
- d unreal

Unit 28

A Listen to the passage and fill in the blanks.

🎧 148 | **What Do Architects Do?**

Architects have very important jobs. They 1._____ buildings. Some design tall buildings like 2._____. Others design restaurants, hotels, or banks. And others just design houses. Architects need to have many skills. They must be 3._____. They must be good at 4._____. They must be able to 5._____. They must have a good imagination. And they must work well with the 6._____, too. Architects draw 7._____ for their buildings. Blueprints show how the building will look. They are very detailed. When the blueprints are done, the builders can start working.

B Read the passage above and answer the following questions.

_____ 8. Which sentence best expresses the main idea of this article?
- a Architects are not finding jobs.
- b Architects require many years of school.
- c Architects are people who design buildings.
- d Architects make lots of money.

_____ 9. Which of the following is NOT something that architects design?
- a Skyscrapers.
- b Hotels.
- c Houses.
- d Watches.

_____ 10. "They must have a good imagination." An "imagination" is _____.
- a a person's ability to think up ideas
- b having lots of money in the bank
- c a special tool used to melt metal
- d the muscle between the hand and the elbow

Unit 29

A **Listen to the passage and fill in the blanks.**

🎧 149 | **Different Kinds of Music**

People have different tastes in music. Some like 1._____ music. Others like fast music. Some like to hear 2._____. Others like to hear 3._____. So there are many different kinds of music. Classical music relies upon musical instruments. It has very little singing in it. On the other hand, 4._____ and 5._____ use both instruments and singing. Every country has its own kind of folk music. It's usually fun to listen to. There are also many kinds of modern music. Rock music is one 6._____ genre. So is 7._____. Some people prefer 8._____ or R&B. Overall, there is some kind of music for everyone.

B **Read the passage above and answer the following questions.**

_____ 9. What is another good title for this article?
- a What Is Your Kind of Music?
- b Where Jazz Came From.
- c Why Do People Listen to Music?
- d A Brief History of Music.

_____ 10. According to the article, which of the following is NOT considered to be modern music?
- a Rock music.
- b R&B music.
- c Jazz music.
- d Classical music.

_____ 11. "Rock music is one popular genre." A "genre" is _____.
- a a popular song
- b a musician's skill
- c a certain group of art
- d a large group of musicians

30

A Listen to the passage and fill in the blanks.

🎧 150 | **Different Kinds of Musical Instruments**

Some instruments 1._____ or have common characteristics. We can put many of these instruments into families. There are some different families of musical instruments.

Keyboard instruments have keys to 2._____. The piano, 3._____, and keyboard are in the keyboard family. The violin, viola, and 4._____ have strings. So they are called 5._____. There are two kinds of 6._____: brass and 7._____. Brass instruments include the 8._____, trombone, and tuba. Woodwinds are the 9._____, flute, oboe, and saxophone. Percussion instruments are fun to play. You 10._____ or shake them with your hand or with a 11._____. There are many other kinds of instruments. Apart, they make lots of 12._____. Together, they combine to make beautiful music.

B Read the passage above and answer the following questions.

_____ 13. Which sentence best expresses the main idea of this article?

a Musical instruments can be difficult to master but are worth it.

b There are many types of instruments that can make music.

c You play percussion instruments by hitting them with a stick.

d Sometimes instruments can look alike but sound very different.

_____ 14. Which of the following is NOT mentioned about percussion instruments?

a They are fun to play.   b They can be shaken.

c They can be hit.   d They include the tuba.

_____ 15. The article states, "Some instruments look alike." This means _____.

a they look broken

b they come from the same place

c they look very similar

d they are difficult to find

Answer Key

Unit 01
1 countryside 2 urban 3 millions 4 communities
5 populations 6 rural 7 families 8 b 9 b 10 a

Unit 02
1 expanded 2 immigrants 3 moved to 4 came from
5 made 6 improved 7 powerful 8 a 9 b 10 d

Unit 03
1 jobs 2 categories 3 service 4 deliver 5 cashiers
6 manufacturing 7 professional 8 engineers
9 lawyers 10 learn 11 a 12 c 13 b

Unit 04
1 region 2 geographical 3 hilly 4 mountains
5 Midwest 6 located 7 deserts 8 Rocky 9 forests
10 b 11 a 12 d

Unit 05
1 federal 2 central 3 governor 4 legislature
5 represent 6 laws 7 mayors 8 council 9 c
10 a 11 d

Unit 06
1 came from 2 continents 3 Native 4 tribes 5 nomads
6 buffalo 7 crops 8 hunted 9 b 10 c 11 a

Unit 07
1 settled 2 built 3 empires 4 jungle 5 drawing
6 temples 7 ruled 8 battles 9 defeated 10 a
11 c 12 a

Unit 08
1 Europeans 2 sent out 3 explorers 4 water route
5 Central 6 founded 7 landed in 8 claimed
9 settled in 10 a 11 b 12 a

Unit 09
1 gold 2 colonies 3 settled 4 colonists 5 hunger
6 religious 7 founded 8 d 9 b 10 b

Unit 10
1 settlers 2 colonies 3 ruled 4 free 5 signed
6 declaration 7 fought 8 commanded 9 soldiers
10 Independence 11 b 12 d 13 c

Unit 11
1 nonliving 2 alive 3 plants 4 oxygen 5 nutrients
6 sunlight 7 breathe 8 b 9 d 10 c

Unit 12
1 mammals 2 reptiles 3 birth 4 young 5 feed
6 feathers 7 amphibians 8 lay 9 gills 10 a 11 d
12 d

Unit 13
1 life cycle 2 death 3 born 4 feeds 5 adult 6 hatch
7 tadpoles 8 tails 9 grow 10 lungs 11 a 12 c 13 b

Unit 14
1 seed 2 cones 3 ground 4 pick 5 fall 6 sprout
7 seedlings 8 a 9 d 10 c

Unit 15
1 survive 2 food chain 3 relationship 4 plant eaters
5 prey 6 snakes 7 top 8 a 9 c 10 d

Unit 16
1 butterflies 2 grasshoppers 3 crickets
4 body parts 5 thorax 6 abdomen 7 antennae
8 legs 9 wings 10 b 11 d 12 b

Unit 17
1 orbit 2 phases 3 moves around 4 crescent
5 quarter 6 full 7 wane 8 stage 9 a 10 c 11 b

Unit 18
1 organs 2 pumps 3 nervous system 4 mental
5 digest 6 breaks 7 liver 8 skin 9 c 10 d 11 a

Unit 19
1 attracted 2 repel 3 magnet 4 move 5 magnetized
6 poles 7 magnetic field 8 c 9 b 10 d

Unit 20
1 sound 2 vibrations 3 transmit 4 pulses
5 move through 6 heard 7 c 8 c 9 c

Unit 21
1 math 2 number sentences 3 add 4 total
5 addition 6 subtraction 7 b 8 b 9 a

Unit 22
1 o'clock 2 hour 3 minutes 4 until 5 noon
6 quarter 7 P.M. 8 a 9 d 10 c

Unit 23
1 shapes 2 solid figures 3 rectangles
4 flat surfaces 5 length 6 cube 7 sphere
8 pyramid 9 cone 10 a 11 d 12 b

Unit 24
1 add 2 times 3 multiplication 4 multiply
5 equal groups 6 product 7 b 8 c 9 c

Unit 25
1 sentences 2 parts of speech 3 verbs
4 prepositions 5 subject 6 noun 7 describe
8 pronouns 9 adjectives 10 b 11 a 12 d

Unit 26
1 sayings 2 translate 3 make sense 4 late
5 heads 6 keeps 7 c 8 c 9 a

Unit 27
1 realistic art 2 abstract art 3 shows 4 paints
5 different 6 look like 7 b 8 b 9 d

Unit 28
1 design 2 skyscrapers 3 engineers 4 math
5 draw 6 builders 7 blueprints 8 c 9 d 10 a

Unit 29
1 slow 2 singing 3 musical instruments 4 folk music
5 traditional music 6 popular 7 jazz 8 rap
9 a 10 d 11 c

Unit 30
1 look alike 2 press 3 organ 4 cello 5 string
instruments 6 wind instruments 7 woodwinds
8 trumpet 9 clarinet 10 hit 11 stick 12 sounds
13 b 14 d 15 c

FUN 學美國英語課本：各學科關鍵英單

進入明星學校必備的英文單字

用美國教科書學英文是最道地的學習方式，有越來越多的學校選擇以美國教科書作為教材，用全英語授課（immersion）的方式教學，讓學生把英語當成母語學習。在一些語言學校裡，也掀起了一波「用美國教科書學英文」的風潮。另外，還有越來越多的父母優先考慮讓子女用美國教科書來學習英文，讓孩子將來能夠進入明星學校或國際學校就讀。

為什麼要使用美國教科書呢？TOEFL 等國際英語能力測驗都是以各學科知識為基礎，使用美國教科書不但能大幅提升英文能力，也可以增加數學、社會、科學等方面的知識，因此非常適合用來準備考試。即使不到國外留學，也可以像在美國上課一樣，而這也是使用美國教科書最吸引人的地方。

以多樣化的照片、插圖和例句來熟悉跨科學習中的英文單字

到底該使用何種美國教科書呢？還有如何才能讀懂美國教科書呢？美國各州、各學校的課程都不盡相同，而學生也有選擇教科書的權利，所以單單是教科書的種類就多達數十種。若不小心選擇到程度不適合的教科書，就很容易造成孩子對學英語的興趣大減。

因此，正確的作法應該要先累積字彙和相關知識背景。我國學生的學習能力很強，只需要培養對不熟悉的用語和跨科學習（Cross-Curricular Study）的適應能力。

本系列網羅了在以全英語教授社會、科學、數學、語言、藝術、音樂等學科時，所有會出現的必備英文單字。只要搭配書中真實的照片、插圖和例句，就能夠把這些在美國小學課本中會出現的各學科核心單字記起來，同時還可以熟悉相關的背景知識。

四種使用頻率最高的美國教科書的字彙分析

本系列套書規畫了 6 個階段的字彙學習課程，搜羅了 McGraw Hill、Harcourt、Pearson 和 Core Knowledge 等四大教科書中的主要字彙，並且整理出各科目、各主題的核心單字，然後依照學年分為 Grade 1 到 Grade 6。

本套書的適讀對象為「準備大學學測指考的學生」和「準備參加 TOEFL 等國際英語能力測驗的學生」。對於「準備赴美唸高中的學生」和「想要看懂美國教科書的學生」，本套書亦是最佳的先修教材。

《FUN 學美國英語課本：各學科關鍵英單》系列的結構與特色

1. 本套書中所收錄的英文單字都是美國學生在上課時會學到的字彙和用法。

2. 將美國小學教科書中會出現的各學科核心單字，搭配多樣化照片、插圖和例句，讓讀者更容易熟記。

3. 藉由閱讀教科書式的題目，來強化讀、聽、寫的能力。透過各式各樣的練習與題目，不僅能夠全盤吸收與各主題有關的字彙，也能夠熟悉相關的知識背景。

4. 每一冊的教學大綱（syllabus）皆涵蓋了社會、歷史、地理、科學、數學、語言、美術和音樂等學科，以循序漸進的方式，學習從基礎到高級的各科核心字彙，不僅能夠擴增各科目的字彙量，同時還提升了運用句子的能力。（教學大綱請參考第 8 頁）

5. 可學到社會、科學等的相關背景知識和用語，也有助於準備 TOEFL 等國際英語能力測驗。

6. 對於「英語程度有限，但想看懂美國教科書的學生」來說，本套書是很好的先修教材。

7. 全系列 6 階段共分為 6 冊，可依照個人英語程度，選擇合適的分冊。

   Grade 1 美國小學 1 年級課程　　　**Grade 2** 美國小學 2 年級課程

   Grade 3 美國小學 3 年級課程　　　**Grade 4** 美國小學 4 年級課程

   Grade 5 美國小學 5 年級課程　　　**Grade 6** 美國小學 6 年級課程

8. 書末附有關鍵字彙的中英文索引，方便讀者搜尋與查照（請參考第 141 頁）。

強烈建議下列學生使用本套書：

1. 「準備大學學測指考」的學生

2. 「準備參加以全英語授課的課程，想熟悉美國學生上課時會用到的各科核心字彙」的學生

3. 「對美國小學各科必備英文字彙已相當熟悉，想朝高級單字邁進」美國學校的七年級生

4. 「準備赴美唸高中」的學生

MP3

收錄了本書的「Key Words」、「Power Verbs」、「Word Families」單元中的所有單字和例句，和「Checkup」中 E 大題的文章，以及 Workbook 中 A 大題聽寫練習文章。

How to Use This Book

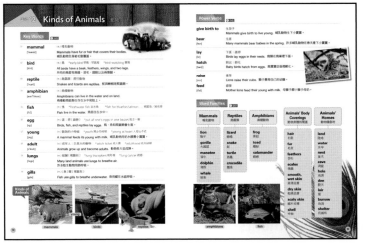

Key Words　熟記和主題有關的 10 個關鍵字彙，同時也記下該字的例句，並且瀏覽相關補充用語。搭配 MP3 反覆聽三遍，一直到熟悉字義和發音為止。

Power Verbs　熟記和主題相關的高頻率核心動詞和動詞片語。片語是用簡單的字來表達複雜的涵義，常在 TOEFL 等國際英語能力測驗中的題目出現，所以要確實地將這些由 2—3 個字所組成的片語記熟。

Word Families　將容易聯想在一起的字彙或表現形式，以獨特的圈組方式來幫助記憶。這些字就像針線一樣，時常在一起出現，因此要熟知這些字的差異和使用方法。

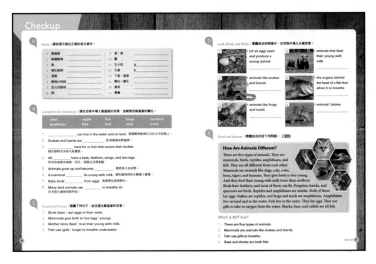

Checkup

Ⓐ **Write**｜練習寫出本書所學到的字彙，一方面能夠熟悉單字的拼法，一方面也能夠幫助記憶。

Ⓑ **Complete the Sentences**｜將本書所學到的字彙和例句，確實背熟。

Ⓒ **Read and Choose**｜透過多樣化的練習，熟悉本書所學到的字彙用法。

Ⓓ **Look, Read, and Write**｜透過照片、插畫和提示，加深對所學到的字彙的印象。

Ⓔ **Read and Answer**｜透過與各單元主題有關的「文章閱讀理解測驗」，來熟悉教科書的出題模式，並培養與各學科相關的背景知識和適應各種考試的能力。

Review Test 1　每 5 個單元結束會有一回總複習測驗，有助於回想起沒有辦法一次就記起來或忘記的單字，並且再次複習。

Table of Contents

Introduction
How to Use This Book

Workbook 聽力閱讀試題本

Syllabus Vol.2

Subject	Topic & Area	Title
Social Studies ● History and Geography	Citizenship Society Economics Geography Government American History American History American History American History American History	Building Citizenship Moving to a New Community Lots of Jobs The Geography of the United States American State and Local Governments Native Americans and Their Culture The Early Americans The Europeans Come to the New World The English Come to America American Independence
Science	A World of Living Things Animals Animals Plants Ecosystems Insects The Solar System The Human Body Motion and Forces Sound	Living and Nonliving Things Kinds of Animals The Life Cycle of an Animal Plants The Food Chain Insects The Solar System The Human Body Motion and Forces Sound
Mathematics	Numbers and Number Sense Time Geometry Computation	Numbers From 1 to 100 Time Solid and Plane Figures Multiplication and Division
Language and Literature	Language Arts Language Arts	Learning About Language Familiar Sayings
Visual Arts	Visual Arts Architecture	Visual Arts Architecture
Music	A World of Music Musical Instruments	Many Kinds of Music Musical Instruments

CHAPTER 1

Social Studies • History and Geography ①

Building Citizenship 建立公民權

● 001

01	**citizenship** [ˈsɪtəzn̩ˌʃɪp]	*(n.)* 公民身分；公民權　　*citizen 公民；市民 Good **citizenship** means being a responsible person. 良好公民意味著成為一個負責之人。
02	**caring** [ˈkɛrɪŋ]	*(n.)* 關懷感受　　*caring (a.) 有愛心的 **Caring** for others is important.　重要的是要關懷他人。
03	**respect** [rɪˈspɛkt]	*(n.)* 尊重；尊敬　　*have/show respect for 尊敬…… We have great **respect** for good citizens.　我們對優良市民十分尊敬。
04	**responsibility** [rɪˌspɑnsəˈbɪlətɪ]	*(n.)* 責任；職責　　*a sense of responsibility 責任感 It is our **responsibility** to help our neighbors. 幫助鄰居是我們的職責。
05	**fairness** [ˈfɛrnɪs]	*(n.)* 公正；公平　　*fair enough 有道理 The government should treat people with **fairness**. 政府應該公平對待每個人。
06	**honesty** [ˈɑnɪstɪ]	*(n.)* 正直；誠實　　*to be honest 坦白說 **Honesty** means telling the truth.　誠實意味說實話。
07	**courage** [ˈkɝɪdʒ]	*(n.)* 勇氣　　*encourage 鼓勵 We need **courage** to do the right thing. 我們需要勇氣去做正確的事。
08	**law** [lɔ]	*(n.)* 法律　　*against the law 違反法律的　　*lawyer 律師 Good citizens should obey the **law**.　良好市民應該遵守法律。
09	**area** [ˈɛrɪə]	*(n.)* 地區；區域　　*residential area 住宅區　　*area code（電話等的）區域號碼 People live in many different **areas**.　人們住在不同區域。
10	**population** [ˌpɑpjəˈleʃən]	*(n.)* 人口　　*dense population 人口稠密 Urban communities have large **populations**.　都市社區擁有眾多人口。

Good Citizens

respect each other

care for their neighbors

treat others with kindness

rural community

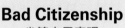

care for	照顧；照料
	Parents **care for** their children. 父母照料自己的孩子。
take care of	照顧；注意
	Parents **take care of** their children. 父母照顧自己的孩子。
treat [trit]	對待
	We should **treat** others with kindness and respect.
	我們應以善意與尊重對待他人。
act	舉止；表現
	We should **act** nicely toward others. 我們應該好好對待他人。
live in	居住
	What kind of community do you **live in**? 你住在什麼樣的社區裡？
be located	座落於
	Where is your community **located**? 你的社區位於哪裡？

urban community

Word Families ⊙ 003

rural community	鄉村社區
	A rural community is in the countryside. 鄉村社區位於鄉間。
urban community	都市社區
	An urban community is in the city. 都市社區位於都市裡。
suburban community	郊區社區
	A suburban community is near a big city. 近郊社區鄰近大城市。

Different Age Groups in a Community
一個社群中的不同年齡層

child 孩童

teenager 青少年

young adult 年輕人

adult 成年人

middle-aged man 中年男性

middle-aged woman 中年女性

senior citizen 老年人

Good Citizenship
良好市民表現

responsibility 責任

respect 尊重

caring 關懷

fairness 公平

honesty 誠實

courage 勇氣

leadership 領導力

loyalty 忠誠

Bad Citizenship
劣等市民表現

lying 說謊

cowardice 懦弱

cheating 欺騙

dishonesty 不正直

responsibility

11

Checkup

A

Write | 請依提示寫出正確的英文單字。

1	尊敬	_____	
2	責任	_____	
3	公平	_____	
4	誠實	_____	
5	勇氣	_____	
6	人口	_____	
7	法律	_____	
8	地區	_____	
9	公民身分；公民權	_____	
10	關懷感受	_____	
11	照顧	t_____	
12	對待	_____	
13	居住	_____	
14	鄉村社區	_____	
15	都市社區	_____	
16	郊區社區	_____	

B

Complete the Sentences | 請在空格中填入最適當的答案，並視情況做適當的變化。

caring	courage	law	honesty	responsibility
citizenship	treat	respect	area	locate

1 It is our _____ to help our neighbors. 幫助鄰居是我們的職責。

2 We need _____ to do the right thing. 我們需要勇氣去做正確的事。

3 We have great _____ for good citizens. 我們對優良市民十分尊敬。

4 Good _____ means being a responsible person.
良好公民意味著成為一個負責之人。

5 _____ for others is important. 重要的是要關懷他人。

6 Where is your community _____? 你的社區位於哪裡？

7 The government should _____ people with fairness.
政府應該公平對待每個人。

8 Good citizens should obey the _____. 良好市民應該遵守法律。

C

Read and Choose | 閱讀下列句子，並且選出最適當的答案。

1 Where is your community (located | lived in)?

2 Urban communities have (small | large) populations.

3 Parents (take | care) for their children.

4 We should (act | treat) others with kindness and respect.

D

Look, Read, and Write | 看圖並且依照提示，在空格中填入正確答案。

 ▶ a community in the city

_____

 ▶ the ability to do something that you know is difficult

_____

 ▶ a community near a big city

_____

 ▶ behavior that is reasonable, right, and just

_____

 ▶ telling the truth

_____

 ▶ the system of rules that people in a country must obey

_____

E

Read and Answer | 閱讀並且回答下列問題。 🔊 004

Kinds of Communities

People live in many different places. Some like big cities. Others like living in the countryside. And others like neither place. They prefer small cities or towns. Big cities are urban communities. Some cities have millions of people. People in big cities live closely together. They often live in apartments. They might use the bus or subway very often. Rural communities are in the countryside. They have small populations. Farmers live in rural areas. People live in houses and often drive cars. Suburban communities are small cities near big ones. Many families live there. But they might work in a big city. They might drive or take buses and subways.

Fill in the blanks.

1   Some people live in small _____ or towns.

2   Big cities might have _____ of people.

3   _____ areas are in the countryside.

4   _____ communities are near big cities.

Key Words
🔊 005

01	**homeland** [ˈhomˌlænd]	*(n.)* 祖國；家鄉 (= motherland) People sometimes leave their **homelands** for new places. 人們有時會離開祖國前往新的地方。
02	**faraway** [ˈfɑrəˈwe]	*(a.)* 遠方的；遙遠的　*faraway times 很久很久以前 Many immigrants move to **faraway** lands. 許多人移民到遙遠的國家。
03	**opportunity** [ˌɑpɚˈtjunətɪ]	*(n.)* 機會　*take the opportunity 藉此機會 Immigrants often look for new **opportunities**. 移民通常會尋覓新的機會。
04	**immigrant** [ˈɪməɡrənt]	*(n.)* 移民；僑民　*illegal immigrant 非法移民 **Immigrants** want to find hope in new places. 移民們希望在新國家找到希望。
05	**improvement** [ɪmˈpruvmənt]	*(n.)* 改善；改進　*a great/significant improvement 大幅改善 Immigrants are seeking **improvement** in their lives. 移民們尋求自己的生活獲得改善。
06	**custom** [ˈkʌstəm]	*(n.)* 社會習俗；個人習慣　*folk custom 民俗　*customs 海關 Every country has different **customs**. 每個國家都有不同的風俗。
07	**culture** [ˈkʌltʃɚ]	*(n.)* 文化　*corporate culture 企業文化　*oriental culture 東方文化 They must learn another **culture** in their new home. 他們必須在新的家園學習另一種文化。
08	**manual labor** [ˈmænjʊəl ˈlebɚ]	*(n.)* 體力勞動 Immigrants often get jobs in **manual labor**. 外來移民通常會從事勞力工作。
09	**low-paying** [ˈloˈpeɪŋ]	*(a.)* 報酬低的；低薪的　*non-paying 無酬的 People with **low-paying** jobs don't make much money. 從事低薪工作的人，無法賺取太多錢。
10	**ethnic** [ˈɛθnɪk]	*(a.)* 種族上的　*ethnic origin/background 種族文化起源／背景 Immigrants sometimes live with people of the same **ethnic** background. 移民們有時和具有同樣種族背景的同胞住在一起。

immigrants

people from different ethnic groups

manual labor

immigrate [ˈɪməˌgret]	移民（外來） They immigrated to the United States from China. 他們從中國移民來美國。
emigrate [ˈɛməˌgret]	移居外國 They emigrated from China to the United States. 他們從中國移居到美國。

move to	搬去 The family moved to a new country. 這家人搬去新的國家。
come from	來自 The family came from Ireland. 這家人來自愛爾蘭。
move from	從……搬來 The family moved from Ireland. 這家人從愛爾蘭搬來。

seek [sik]	尋求；追求 The immigrants are seeking better lives. 移民們追求更好的生活。
look for	尋覓；希望得到 The immigrants are looking for better lives. 移民們希望得到更好的生活。

get used to	習慣於 It is hard to get used to living in another country. 要習慣住在另一個國家十分困難。
improve [ɪmˈpruv]	改善 He moved to another city to improve his life. 他為了改善生活搬到另一個城市。

Word Families 🔊 007

the Statue of Liberty, a symbol of freedom to immigrants to America

Reasons People Immigrate
人們移民的原因

- **new life** 新的生活
- **new chance** 新的機運
- **better opportunity** 更好的機會
- **family** 家庭
- **education** 教育
- **job** 工作

Places Immigrants Often Work
移民者常見的工作地點

- **factory** 工廠
- **farm** 農場
- **supermarket** 超市
- **convenience store** 便利商店
- **restaurant** 餐廳
- **laundromat** 自助洗衣店
- **dry cleaner's** 乾洗店

Checkup

A

Write | 請依提示寫出正確的英文單字。

1 祖國	_____	9 遠方的；遙遠的	_____
2 機會	_____	10 種族的	_____
3 移民 (n.)	_____	11 移民 (v.)	_____
4 改善 (n.)	_____	12 移居外國	_____
5 社會習俗	_____	13 搬去	_____
6 文化	_____	14 來自	_____
7 體力勞動	_____	15 尋求；追求	_____
8 低薪的	_____	16 習慣於	_____

B

Complete the Sentences | 請在空格中填入最適當的答案，並視情況做適當的變化。

low-paying	homeland	opportunity	faraway	culture
move from	custom	improvement	emigrate	ethnic

1 Every country has different _____. 每個國家都有不同的風俗。

2 People sometimes leave their _____ for new places.
人們有時會離開祖國前往新的地方。

3 Many immigrants move to _____ lands. 許多人移民到遙遠的國家。

4 Immigrants often look for new _____. 移民通常會尋覓新的機會。

5 Immigrants are seeking _____ in their lives.
移民們尋求自己的生活獲得改善。

6 People with _____ jobs don't make much money.
從事低薪工作的人，無法賺取太多錢。

7 Immigrants sometimes live with people of the same _____ background.
移民們有時和具有同樣種族背景的同胞住在一起。

8 They must learn another _____ in their new home.
他們必須在新的家園學習另一種文化。

C

Read and Choose | 閱讀下列句子，並且選出最適當的答案。

1 It is hard to (get used to | get to know) living in another country.

2 They (immigrated | looked) to the United States from China.

3 The family (went | came) from Ireland.

4 He (moved | made) to another city to improve his life.

D Look, Read, and Write | 看圖並且依照提示，在空格中填入正確答案。

1 ▶ the country where a person is born

_____

2 ▶ of or relating to a group of people with the same culture and traditions

_____

3 ▶ physical work that does not need a lot of skill

_____

4 ▶ to move to another country

_____

5 ▶ a usual manner of behaving or doing

_____

6 ▶ to become better or to make something better

_____

E Read and Answer | 閱讀並且回答下列問題。 🔊 008

19th Century American Immigration

In 1789, the United States became a country. It was a huge land. And the country expanded and got bigger. But, at that time, few people lived in the U.S.

The country needed immigrants. So, during the nineteenth century, millions of people moved to the U.S. Most of them were from Europe. They also came from Ireland. They came from Germany. They came from Italy, Russia, and other countries. Millions of them came to America. These immigrants worked hard. But they often made little money. Yet they slowly improved their lives. And they helped the U.S. become a great and powerful country.

Fill in the blanks.

1 The United States became a country in _____.

2 Many immigrants came to the U.S. in the _____ century.

3 _____ of immigrants came to America.

4 Immigrants often made _____ money at first.

Lots of Jobs 工作千百種

Key Words ● 009

01	**job** [dʒɑb]	*(n.)* 工作；職業　*apply for a job 求職　*out of a job 失業 A **job** is work that people do.　一份職業指的是人所從事的工作。
02	**work** [wɜk]	*(n.)* 工作；作業；勞動　*work force 勞動力　*work out 想出；制訂出 What kind of **work** would you like to do?　你想要從事什麼樣的工作？
03	**service** [ˋsɜvɪs]	*(n.)* 服務　*at sb.'s service 聽候某人差遣　*service charge 服務費 Some workers earn money by doing **service** jobs. 某些勞工從事服務業賺錢。
04	**employment** [ɪmˋplɔɪmənt]	*(n.)* 職業；工作；受雇　*employee 受雇者　*employer 雇主 Most people look for **employment** after they finish school. 大多數人畢業後開始找工作。
05	**factory** [ˋfæktrɪ]	*(n.)* 工廠　*set up a factory 設立工廠　*factory worker 工廠工人 Workers make products at **factories**.　工人在工廠裡生產產品。
06	**company** [ˋkʌmpənɪ]	*(n.)* 公司　*limited company 股份有限公司　*keep sb. company 陪伴某人 Businessmen and women work at **companies**.　男女實業家在公司工作。
07	**trade** [tred]	*(n.)* 貿易　*trade in sth. 以某物做買賣　*a good trade 好生意 **Trade** is buying and selling products.　貿易是指商品的買賣。
08	**salary** [ˋsælərɪ]	*(n.)* 薪水；薪資　*high/low salary 高／低薪　*salary increase 加薪 Lots of businessmen receive monthly **salaries**.　很多實業家領月薪。
09	**wage** [wedʒ]	*(n.)* 工資；報酬　*living wage 夠維持生活之薪資　*minimum wage 最低薪資 Some workers get paid hourly **wages**.　某些工人拿時薪。
10	**volunteer** [ˏvɑlənˋtɪr]	*(n.)* 志願者；志工　*volunteer to V. / for sth. 志願做某事 A **volunteer** works for free.　志工免費工作。

Different Kinds of Jobs

teacher　firefighter　aerobics instructor　painter　musician　cook　doctor　maid

factory worker

work　工作
He works from nine to six five days a week.
他一週有五天要上班，時間是從早上九點到下午六點。

learn [lɜn]　習得；學習
She is learning new skills at her job.　她從工作中學習到新技術。

earn [ɜn]　賺得
How much money do you earn?　你賺多少錢？

make　賺取
How much money do you make?　你賺多少錢？

pay　支付
They are paid weekly.　他們每週領錢。

get paid　支領
They get paid monthly.　他們每月支領薪水。

spend [spɛnd]　花費
You shouldn't spend your entire salary.　你不應該花掉你所有的薪水。

save　節省
You should save part of your salary.　你應該存下部分薪水。

Word Families ⊙ 011

Service Jobs 服務工作	**Professional Jobs** 專業工作
waiter 男服務生	**doctor** 醫師
waitress 女服務生	**nurse** 護士
cook 廚師	**lawyer** 律師
deliveryman 送貨員	**teacher** 教師
cashier 出納員	**engineer** 工程師
salesperson 售貨員	**designer** 設計師

medical worker

waitress

waiter

shop assistant

cashier

deliveryman

Checkup

A

Write | 請依提示寫出正確的英文單字。

1	職業；工作 _____	9	服務 _____
2	工作；勞動 _____	10	職業；工作；受雇 _____
3	工廠 _____	11	薪水；薪資 _____
4	公司 _____	12	工資；報酬 _____
5	貿易 _____	13	賺得錢 e_____
6	志願者 _____	14	賺取錢 m_____
7	工作 (v.) _____	15	支付 _____
8	學習 _____	16	支領 _____

B

Complete the Sentences | 請在空格中填入最適當的答案，並視情況做適當的變化。

employment	wage	earn	trade	work
salary	job	save	service	pay

1 A _____ is work that people do. 一份職業指的是人所從事的工作。

2 Some workers earn money by doing _____ jobs.
某些勞工從事服務業賺錢。

3 Most people look for _____ after they finish school.
大多數人畢業後開始找工作。

4 What kind of _____ would you like to do? 你想要從事什麼樣的工作？

5 Lots of businessmen receive monthly _____. 很多實業家領月薪。

6 Some workers get paid hourly _____. 某些工人拿時薪。

7 How much money do you _____? 你賺多少錢？

8 You should _____ part of your salary. 你應該存下部分薪水。

C

Read and Choose | 閱讀下列句子，並且選出最適當的答案。

1 He (works | saves) from nine to six five days a week.

2 How much money do you (service | make)?

3 They (get | make) paid monthly.

4 You shouldn't (earn | spend) your entire salary.

Look, Read, and Write | 看圖並且依照提示，在空格中填入正確答案。

1 ► an amount of money that you earn from your job

_____

4 ► buying and selling products

_____

2 ► a job people do to provide service to others

_____

5 ► a place where workers make products

_____

3 ► a person who works for free to help others

_____

6 ► to keep something so that you can use it in the future

_____

E

Read and Answer | 閱讀並且回答下列問題。 012

Different Kinds of Jobs

After people finish school, they often look for jobs. There are many kinds of jobs people do. But there are three main categories of jobs. They are service jobs, manufacturing jobs, and professional jobs. People with service jobs provide services for others. They might deliver the mail or food. They often work in restaurants. And they work in stores as salespeople and cashiers. People with manufacturing jobs make things. They make TVs, computers, cars, and other objects. People with professional jobs often have special training. They are doctors and engineers. They are lawyers and teachers. They might need to attend school to learn their skills.

Answer the questions.

1   When do people often look for jobs?   _____

2   What are the three main categories of jobs?   _____

3   What do people with manufacturing jobs do?   _____

4   What are some professional jobs?   _____

Unit 04 The Geography of the United States

Key Words 🔊 013

01	**geography**	*(n.)* 地理學;地形　*geography lesson 地理課
	[ˈdʒɪˈɑgrəfɪ]	Geography is the study of Earth and the land. 地理學是地球與土地的研究。
02	**geographical**	*(a.)* 地理學的;地理的　*geographical location 地理位置
	[dʒɪəˈgræfɪkḷ]	The United States has many different geographical features. 美國擁有許多不同的地理特徵。
03	**region**	*(n.)* 地區(=area)　*remote region 偏遠地區　*in the region of 大約
	[ˈridʒən]	Arizona is in the Southwest region of the United States. 亞利桑那州位於美國的西南部。
04	**location**	*(n.)* 位置;所在地　*convenient location 交通方便的地點
	[loˈkeʃən]	Do you know the locations of all 50 states? 你知道美國 50 個州的位置嗎?
05	**landform**	*(n.)* 地形　*wetland landform 濕地地形　*natural landform 自然地貌
	[ˈlændˌfɔrm]	Mountains, hills, and valleys are all landforms. 山脈、丘陵與溪谷全都屬於地形。
06	**climate**	*(n.)* 氣候　*a change of climate 換換環境　*continental climate 大陸性氣候
	[ˈklaɪmɪt]	Climate is the kind of weather in a region. 氣候是某個區域的天氣型態。
07	**environment**	*(n.)* 環境;自然環境　*environmental protection 環保
	[ɪnˈvaɪrənmənt]	Each region has a different environment. 每個地區都有不同的自然環境。
08	**physical environment**	*(n.)* 自然環境;物理環境
	[ˈfɪzɪkḷ ɪnˈvaɪrənmənt]	The physical environment is a region's landforms and climate. 物理環境指的是一個地區的地形與氣候。
09	**natural resource**	*(n.)* 自然資源　*renewable resource 可再生資源 *nonrenewable resource 不可再生資源
	[ˈnætʃərəl rɪˈsors]	Coal and oil are two important natural resources. 煤炭與石油是兩種重要的自然資源。
10	**natural feature**	*(n.)* 自然特徵
	[ˈnætʃərəl ˈfitʃɚ]	Some natural features of Hawaii are volcanoes and islands. 夏威夷的部分自然特徵是火山與島嶼。

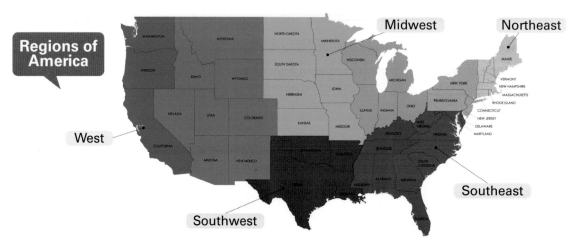

Regions of America

Midwest　Northeast

West

Southwest

Southeast

Power Verbs 🔊 014

form 形成；塑造
What **forms** the physical environment of a region?
是什麼形成某地區的物理環境？

Alaska

make up 構成
What **makes up** the physical environment of a region?
是什麼構成某地區的物理環境？

change 改變
People **change** their physical environment in many ways.
人們在許多方面改變了他們的物理環境。

adapt [ə`dæpt] 使適應
People **adapt** to their physical environment in many ways.
人們在許多方面適應他們的物理環境。

Hawaii

affect [ə`fɛkt] 影響
Location, climate, and natural resources **affect** the people living in an area.
位置、氣候，與自然資源影響居住在當地的人們。

Word Families 🔊 015

West Region （美國）西部
states: California, Washington, Nevada
features: coastal area 海岸地區、deserts 沙漠、mountains 山脈、hot weather 炎熱氣候

Midwest Region （美國）中西部
states: Ohio, Illinois, Michigan, Iowa
features: farming 農業、flat land 平地、lakes and rivers 湖泊與河流、cold weather 寒冷氣候

Southeast Region （美國）東南部
states: Georgia, South Carolina, Alabama, Florida
features: rural areas 鄉村地區、hot weather 炎熱氣候、rainy 多雨、humid 潮濕

Southwest Region （美國）西南部
states: Arizona, New Mexico, Texas
features: canyons (Grand Canyon) 峽谷（大峽谷）、mountains (Rocky Mountains) 山脈（落磯山脈）、deserts 沙漠、very hot weather 極度炎熱氣候

Northeast Region （美國）東北部
states: Maine, Massachusetts, Connecticut, Rhode Island
features: rocky soil 石質土、hills and forests 山丘與森林、cold and snowy weather 寒冷與下雪氣候

Alaska 阿拉斯加
the 49th state in the U.S. 美國第 49 州
very cold weather 嚴寒氣候
Hawaii 夏威夷
the 50th state in the U.S. 美國第 50 州
a group of islands and volcanoes 群島與火山
very hot weather 極度炎熱氣候

Checkup

A

Write | 請依提示寫出正確的英文單字。

1	地理學	_____	9	地理學的；地理的 _____
2	地區	_____	10	物理環境 _____
3	位置	_____	11	形成；塑造 _____
4	地形	_____	12	構成 _____
5	氣候	_____	13	改變 _____
6	環境	_____	14	使適應 _____
7	自然資源	_____	15	影響 _____
8	自然特徵	_____	16	（美國）西南部 _____

B

Complete the Sentences | 請在空格中填入最適當的答案，並視情況做適當的變化。

physical environment	location	geographical	landform
natural resource	climate	natural feature	geography

1 Do you know the _____ of all 50 states? 你知道美國 50 個州的位置嗎？

2 _____ is the study of Earth and the land. 地理學是地球與土地的研究。

3 Mountains, hills, and valleys are all _____. 山脈、丘陵與溪谷全都屬於地形。

4 _____ is the kind of weather in a region. 氣候是某個區域的天氣型態。

5 The _____ _____ is a region's landforms and climate.
物理環境指的是一個地區的地形與氣候。

6 Coal and oil are two important _____ _____.
煤炭與石油是兩種重要的自然資源。

7 Some _____ _____ of Hawaii are volcanoes and islands.
夏威夷的部分自然特徵是火山與島嶼。

8 The United States has many different _____ features.
美國擁有許多不同的地理特徵。

C

Read and Choose | 閱讀下列句子，並且選出最適當的答案。

1 What (makes up | lies in) the physical environment of a region?

2 Location, climate, and natural resources (form | affect) people.

3 People (adapt | change) to their physical environment in many ways.

4 Mountains, hills, and valleys are all (landforms | locations).

Look, Read, and Write | 看圖並且依照提示，在空格中填入正確答案。

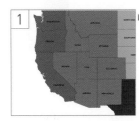 ▸ the region that includes California and Washington

_____

 ▸ the region that includes Ohio, Illinois, and Michigan

_____

 ▸ a state in northwestern North America; the largest state in the U.S.

_____

 ▸ the region that includes Georgia, Alabama, and Florida

_____

 ▸ the region that includes the Grand Canyon

_____

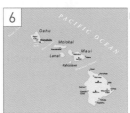 ▸ the 50th state in the U.S. and which lies in Pacific Ocean

_____

E

Read and Answer | 閱讀並且回答下列問題。 ⊙ 016

American Geography

The United States is a huge country with 50 states. Each region in the U.S. has different geographical features. The Northeast is the New England area. It includes Massachusetts and Connecticut. The land there is hilly. The Southeast is another region. It includes Alabama, Tennessee, and Florida. It has some low mountains. There are many rivers and lakes, too. The Midwest is a very flat land. There are miles and miles of farms. Iowa and Illinois are located there. The Southwest is hot. It has some deserts. The Grand Canyon is located there. The Rocky Mountains are also there. The West includes California and Washington. It has both mountains and big forests.

Fill in the blanks.

1 Massachusetts is in the _____ area.

2 The Southeast has some low _____.

3 Iowa and Illinois are in the _____.

4 The _____ Mountains are in the Southwest.

Unit 05 American State and Local Governments

01 governor
[ˈɡʌvənɚ]
(n.) 州長　*prison governor 典獄長
The governor is the leader of a state. 州長是一州的領袖。

02 legislature
[ˈlɛdʒɪsˌletʃɚ]
(n.) 立法機關　*legislator 立法委員
The legislature passes the state's laws. 立法機關通過一州的法律。

03 state capitol
[stet ˈkæpət!]
(n.) 州議會大廈　*Capitol 美國國會大廈
The main government building in each state is called the state capitol.
每一州的主要政府大樓稱為州議會大廈。

04 mayor
[ˈmeɚ]
(n.) 市長；鎮長
People elect the mayor of a city. 人民選出一市的市長。

05 city council
[ˈsɪtɪ ˈkaʊns!]
(n.) 市議會　*city councilor 市議員
The city council helps run the city. 市議會協助管理都市。

06 county
[ˈkaʊntɪ]
(n.) 郡；縣　*county councilor 郡政務委員
A county is a large area with many cities in it.
一郡是包含許多都市的廣大區域。

07 town
[taʊn]
(n.) 鎮　*go to town 進城　*downtown 城市商業區
A town is a small area with no local government.
一個城鎮是沒有地方政府的小型區域。

08 local
[ˈlok!]
(a.) 本地的；地方性的　*local culture 地方文化　*local time 當地時間
City and state governments are local governments.
市政府與州政府屬於地方政府。

09 federal
[ˈfɛdərəl]
(a.) 聯邦的；聯邦政府的　*federal system 聯邦制　*federal court 聯邦法院
The federal government is the central government of the U.S.
聯邦政府是美國的中央政府。

10 national
[ˈnæʃən!]
(a.) 全國性的　*national affairs 國家大事　*national strike 全國性罷工
The federal government takes care of national and international issues.
聯邦政府負責管理全國性與國際性事務。

State Capitols

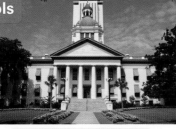

Florida State Capitol

New Jersey State House

New York State Capitol

govern
['gʌvən]

統治；管理
The governor **governs** his or her state.　州長治理他（她）的州。

represent
[ˌrɛprɪˈzɛnt]

代表
State representatives **represent** the people in their areas.
州議員代表他們區域的人民。

support
[səˈport]

擁護；支持
The city council **supports** the mayor.　市議會擁護市長。

protect
[prəˈtɛkt]

保護
The National Guard helps **protect** a state's citizens.
國民警衛隊幫助保護州民。

guard
[gɑrd]

保衛；守護
The National Guard helps **guard** a state's citizens.
國民警衛隊幫助保衛州民。

maintain
[menˈten]

維持
The police **maintain** law and order.　警方維持法律與治安。

Word Families　⊙ 019

Types of Governments 政府的種類	**Duties of Local Governments** 地方政府的職責
federal government　聯邦政府 state government　州政府 county government　縣政府 city government　市政府	police　警方 fire station　消防局 local court　地方法院 road maintenance　道路維修

the Capitol Building in Washington, D.C.

Checkup

A

Write | 請依提示寫出正確的英文單字。

1	州長	_____	9	聯邦（政府）的	_____
2	市長	_____	10	全國性的	_____
3	立法機關	_____	11	統治；管理	_____
4	州議會大廈	_____	12	代表	_____
5	市議會	_____	13	擁護；支持	_____
6	郡	_____	14	保護	_____
7	鎮	_____	15	維持	_____
8	本地的	_____	16	地方政府	_____

B

Complete the Sentences | 請在空格中填入最適當的答案，並視情況做適當的變化。

legislature	local	county	govern	represent
city council	state	federal	national	mayor

1 The _____ passes the state's laws. 立法機關通過一州的法律。

2 People elect the _____ of a city. 人民選出一市的市長。

3 City and state governments are _____ governments.
市政府與州政府屬於地方政府。

4 The _____ government is the central government of the U.S.
聯邦政府是美國的中央政府。

5 State representatives _____ the people in their areas.
州議員代表他們區域的人民。

6 A _____ is a large area with many cities in it.
一郡是包含許多都市的廣大區域。

7 The federal government takes care of _____ and international issues.
聯邦政府負責管理全國性與國際性事務。

8 The _____ _____ helps run the city. 市議會協助管理都市。

C

Read and Choose | 閱讀下列句子，並且選出最適當的答案。

1 The city council (supports | maintains) the mayor.

2 The governor (elects | governs) his or her state.

3 The National Guard helps (protect | rule) a state's citizens.

4 The police (govern | maintain) law and order.

Look, Read, and Write | 看圖並且依照提示，在空格中填入正確答案。

1  ▸ a small area with no local government

_____

4  ▸ a station housing fire equipment and firemen

_____

2  ▸ the leader of a state

_____

5  ▸ city and state governments

_____

3  ▸ the main government building in each state

_____

6  ▸ to act or speak officially for someone or something

_____

E

Read and Answer | 閱讀並且回答下列問題。 ● 020

State and Local Governments

The federal government in the U.S. is very important. It is the central government of the U.S. But every state has its own government, too. And cities have governments also. Every state has a governor. A governor is like the president. The governor is the most powerful person in the state. And every state has a legislature. There are many members in these legislatures. They represent small sections of their states. They pass the bills that become laws in the states. Cities have governments, too. Most cities have mayors. Some have city managers though. A city manager is like a mayor. And the city council is like a legislature. But it usually has just a few members.

Answer the questions.

1 What is the central government called? _____

2 Who is the most powerful person in a state? _____

3 Who passes bills? _____

4 What is a city manager like? _____

Review Test 1

A

Write | 請依提示寫出正確的英文單字。

1	職責	11	鄉村社區
2	平等	12	都市社區
3	祖國；家鄉	13	移民 (v.)
4	移民 (n.)	14	種族上的
5	志工	15	賺得錢 e
6	工作	16	薪水；薪資
7	地理學	17	物理環境
8	自然資源	18	地形
9	州長	19	聯邦（政府）的
10	立法機關	20	地方政府

B

Choose the Correct Word | 請選出與鋪底字意思相近的答案。

1 What makes up the physical environment of a region?

    a. lies in   b. forms   c. changes

2 The National Guard helps protect a state's citizens.

    a. rule   b. guard   c. improve

3 How much money do you earn?

    a. pay   b. save   c. make

4 The immigrants are seeking better lives.

    a. looking for   b. moving to   c. leaving

C

Complete the Sentences | 請在空格中填入最適當的答案，並視情況做適當的變化。

improvement	courage	geographical	service

1 We need _____ to do the right thing. 我們需要勇氣去做正確的事。

2 Immigrants are seeking _____ in their lives.
移民們尋求自己的生活獲得改善。

3 Some workers earn money by doing _____ jobs. 某些勞工從事服務業賺錢。

4 The United States has many different _____ features.
美國擁有許多不同的地理特徵。

CHAPTER 2

Social Studies ● History and Geography ②

Unit 06 Native Americans and Their Culture

Key Words ⊙ 021

01 tribe
[traɪb]

(n.) 部落；種族　*Indian tribes 印第安部落　*tribal culture 部落文化

There were many different **tribes** in the Americas.
美洲有許多不同的部落。

02 nomad
[ˋnomæd]

(n.) 游牧民　*Arab nomads 阿拉伯游牧民族

Nomads traveled from place to place to find fields for their animals.
游牧民族從一地遷徙到另一地，替他們的牲畜尋找牧地。

03 wilderness
[ˋwɪldənɪs]

(n.) 荒野；荒漠　*to be in the wilderness 在野外　*wildlife 野生生物

A lot of tribes lived in the **wilderness**.　許多部落居住在荒漠中。

04 tepee
[ˋtipi]

(n.) 印第安帳篷（圓錐形帳篷）

Some Native Americans lived in **tepees**.　部分印第安人住在圓錐形帳篷。

05 canoe
[kəˋnu]

(n.) 獨木舟　*kayak 輕量運動型獨木舟，船身有包覆　*paddle 槳；用槳划（船）

Some tribes used **canoes** to travel on water.
某些部落利用獨木舟在水上行動。

06 bow
[bo]

(n.) 弓　*bow [baʊ] (v.) (n.) 鞠躬；欠身　*bow to sb. 對某人鞠躬

A **bow** and arrow is a kind of weapon.　弓與箭屬於一類武器。

07 buffalo
[ˋbʌfḷ͵o]

(n.) 水牛；北美野牛　*water buffalo 水牛

The **buffalo** was an important animal to Native Americans.
水牛對印地安人是十分重要的牲畜。

08 totem pole
[ˋtotəm pol]

(n.) 圖騰柱

totem pole

Totem poles were large carved pieces of wood.
圖騰柱是大型的雕刻柱。

09 spirit
[ˋspɪrɪt]

(n.) 靈魂　*in spirit 精神上　*Holy Spirit 聖靈

Many Native Americans believed in ancient **spirits**.
許多印地安人相信古老靈魂。

10 worship
[ˋwɝʃɪp]

(n.) 崇拜；信奉　*nature worship 自然崇拜　*worship the Gods 信奉神明

Ancestor **worship** was common for many tribes.
祖先崇拜在許多部落經常見到。

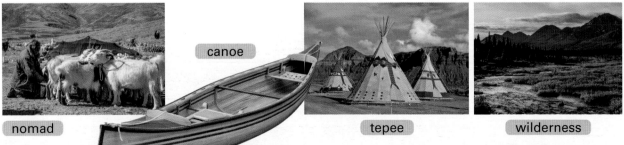

canoe

nomad

tepee

wilderness

wander
[ˈwɑndɚ]
徘徊
Early Native Americans wandered the land. 早期的印地安人徘徊於這片土地。

roam
[rom]
漫遊
Early Native Americans roamed the land. 早期的印地安人漫遊於這片土地。

hunt
[hʌnt]
狩獵　*hunter 獵人
Many tribes hunted buffalo, deer, and other animals.
許多部落獵取水牛、鹿與其他動物。

shoot
[ʃut]
發射；射箭　*shooter 射手
They could shoot arrows very far. 他們可以射出很遠的箭。

believe in
信仰
That tribe believes in ancestor worship. 那個部落信仰祖先崇拜。

worship
[ˈwɝʃɪp]
崇拜；信奉
Some tribes worshipped the spirits of mountains and rivers.
某些部落信奉山神與河神。

worship

Word Families 🔘 023

Native American Tribes
印地安部落

Cherokee 郤洛奇族	**Sioux** 蘇族
Apache 阿帕契族	**Comanche** 卡曼其族
Creek 克里克族	**Seminole** 塞米諾族

Native American Skills
印地安技術

hunting 狩獵

fishing 捕魚

trapping 設陷阱捕捉動物

tracking 追蹤動物足跡

Sioux war dance

buffalo hunting

Checkup

A Write | 請依提示寫出正確的英文單字。

1	部落	_____	9	印地安（圓錐形）帳篷	_____
2	游牧民	_____	10	圖騰柱	_____
3	荒漠	_____	11	靈魂	_____
4	獨木舟	_____	12	祖先崇拜	_____
5	弓	_____	13	徘徊	_____
6	箭	_____	14	漫遊	_____
7	水牛	_____	15	發射；射箭	_____
8	狩獵	_____	16	信仰	_____

B Complete the Sentences | 請在空格中填入最適當的答案，並視情況做適當的變化。

roam	wilderness	canoe	buffalo	ancestor worship
tepee	spirit	wander	tribe	bow and arrow

1 There were many different _____ in the Americas. 美洲有許多不同的部落。

2 A lot of tribes lived in the _____. 許多部落居住在荒漠中。

3 The _____ was an important animal to Native Americans.
水牛對印第安人是十分重要的牲畜。

4 Some Native Americans lived in _____. 部分印地安人住在圓錐形帳篷。

5 _____ _____ was common for many tribes.
祖先崇拜在許多部落經常見到。

6 Some tribes used _____ to travel on water.
某些部落利用獨木舟在水上行動。

7 A _____ _____ _____ is a kind of weapon. 弓與箭屬於一類武器。

8 Many Native Americans believed in ancient _____.
許多印地安人相信古老靈魂。

C

Read and Choose | 閱讀下列句子，並且選出最適當的答案。

1 Early Native Americans (nomad | roamed) the land.

2 Many tribes (believed | lived) in ancestor worship.

3 They could (hunt | shoot) arrows very far.

4 Many tribes (wandered | hunted) buffalo, deer, and other animals.

D Look, Read, and Write | 看圖並且依照提示，在空格中填入正確答案。

1 ▶ large carved pieces of wood
_____

2 ▶ people who travel from place to place to find fields for their animals
_____

3 ▶ a round tent used by some Native Americans
_____

4 ▶ to eject or impel by sudden release of tension
_____

E Read and Answer | 閱讀並且回答下列問題。 🔊 024

How Native American Tribes Came to America

The first people to America came from Asia. They crossed a land bridge, a narrow strip of land that connected Russia and Alaska. It was just ice that connected the continents across the sea. Then, they traveled down into the land from North to South America. They became Native Americans. In the area that became the United States, there were a large number of tribes. Some were very powerful. Others were not. All of the tribes lived off the land. Some were nomads. They followed herds of buffalo all year long. Others lived in small groups or villages. They knew how to farm. They grew various crops. And they also hunted and fished.

What is NOT true?

1 People first went to Asia from America.

2 Asia and America were once connected.

3 There were many different Native American tribes.

4 Many Native Americans were nomads.

Key Words 🔊 025

01 ancestor
[`ænsɛstɚ]
(n.) 祖先
The ancestors of Native Americans are from Asia.
印第安人的祖先來自亞洲。

02 land bridge
[lænd brɪdʒ]
(n.) 陸橋　　*cross a land bridge 跨越陸橋
A land bridge connected Asia and North America.
一座陸橋連結亞洲與北美。

03 crop
[krɑp]
(n.) 作物（通常作複數 crops）　　*rotation of crops 輪作　　*main crops 主要作物
Early Americans grew crops such as corn and beans.
早期印第安人種植如玉米和豆子等作物。

04 rainforest
[ren `fɔrɪst]
(n.) 熱帶雨林　　*tropical rainforest 熱帶雨林　　*dense rainforest 濃密雨林
The Amazon Rainforest is in South America. 亞馬遜雨林位於南美。

05 temple
[`tɛmpḷ]
(n.) 寺廟；神殿　　*Buddhist temple 佛寺
Early Americans built temples for their gods.
早期美國人替神明建造殿堂。

06 canal
[kə`næl]
(n.) 運河　　*Panama Canal 巴拿馬運河
The Aztecs built canals to connect islands.
阿茲提克人興建運河來連接島嶼。

07 legend
[`lɛdʒənd]
(n.) 傳說；傳奇故事　　*legend has it that . . . 傳說……
　　　　　　　　　　　　　*a living legend 當代傳奇人物
Legends tell stories about gods and heroes.
傳說敘述神明與英雄的故事。

08 ancient
[`enʃənt]
(a.) 古代的；古老的　　*ancient times 古代　　*ancient Rome 古羅馬
Ancient people worshiped animal gods. 古代人崇拜動物神。

09 nature gods
[`netʃɚ gɑdz]
(n.) 自然神
The Mayans worshiped nature gods such as the gods of the wind and the rain. 馬雅人崇拜如風神和雨神等自然神。

10 empire
[`ɛmpaɪr]
(n.) 帝國　　*Inca empire 印加帝國
The Mayans had a great empire in Central America.
馬雅人在中美洲建立了一個強大的帝國。

Three Great American Empires

Maya

Inca

Aztec

follow
['fɑlo]
追逐;追趕
Some Asians **followed** animals over a land bridge to North America.
某些亞洲人橫跨陸橋追逐動物到北美。

chase
[tʃes]
追捕
Some Asians **chased** animals over a land bridge to North America.
某些亞洲人橫跨陸橋到北美追捕動物。

build
建立
The ancient Mayans **built** great cities. 古代馬雅人建立了強大的城市。

construct
[kən'strʌkt]
興建
The ancient Mayans **constructed** great cities. 古代馬雅人興建了強大的城市。

carve
[kɑrv]
雕刻
People used to **carve** letters into stones. 從前人們經常將字母刻在石頭上。

cut
雕;挖;切割
People used to **cut** letters into stones. 從前人們經常在石頭上刻挖出字母。

conquer
['kɑŋkɚ]
戰勝;征服
The Aztecs **conquered** many people around them.
阿茲提克人征服鄰近的許多種族。

defeat
[dɪ'fit]
擊敗
The Aztecs **defeated** many people around them.
阿茲提克人擊敗鄰近的許多種族。

Maya Empire 馬雅帝國
The Mayans built a great city in the rainforests of Central America.
馬雅人在中美洲的熱帶雨林建立了一座偉大的城市。

Aztec Empire 阿茲提克帝國
The Aztecs built a great city on some islands in a lake.
阿茲提克人在湖邊幾座島嶼上建立了一座偉大的城市。

Inca Empire 印加帝國
The Incas built their cities in the Andes Mountains.
印加人在安地斯山脈建立了他們的城市。

Early American Empires
早期的美洲帝國

Gods
神

wind god 風神
sun god 太陽神
rain god 雨神
war god 戰神

Crops
作物

corn 玉米　　**rice** 米
wheat 小麥　**beans** 豆子
potatoes 馬鈴薯

Checkup

A

Write | 請依提示寫出正確的英文單字。

1	祖先	_____	9	古代的；古老的 _____
2	雨林	_____	10	自然神 _____
3	寺廟；神殿	_____	11	追逐；追趕 _____
4	運河	_____	12	建立 b _____
5	傳說	_____	13	切割 _____
6	帝國	_____	14	雕刻 _____
7	作物	_____	15	戰勝；征服 _____
8	陸橋	_____	16	擊敗 _____

B

Complete the Sentences | 請在空格中填入最適當的答案，並視情況做適當的變化。

empire	ancient	land bridge	conquer	crop
legend	ancestor	carve	defeat	canal

1 The _____ of Native Americans are from Asia. 印地安人的祖先來自亞洲。

2 Early Americans grew _____ such as corn and beans.
早期印地安人種植如玉米和豆子等作物。

3 A _____ _____ connected Asia and North America.
一座陸橋連結亞洲與北美。

4 The Aztecs built _____ to connect islands. 阿茲提克人興建運河來連接島嶼。

5 _____ tell stories about gods and heroes. 傳說敘述神明與英雄的故事。

6 _____ people worshiped animal gods. 古代人崇拜動物神。

7 The Mayans had a great _____ in Central America.
馬雅人在中美洲建立了一個強大的帝國。

8 People used to _____ letters into stones. 從前人們習慣將字母刻在石頭上。

C

Read and Choose | 請選出與鋪底字意思相近的答案。

1 Some Asians followed animals over a land bridge to North America.

   a. challenged   b. chased   c. conquered

2 The Aztecs conquered many people around them.

   a. constructed   b. connected   c. defeated

3 The ancient Mayans built great cities.

   a. worshiped   b. constructed   c. had

Look, Read, and Write I 看圖並且依照提示，在空格中填入正確答案。

1  ▶ the early American empire built on some islands in a lake

_____

4  ▶ a forest in a tropical region where it rains a lot

_____

2  ▶ the early American empire built in the Andes Mountains

_____

5  ▶ a waterway that connects two bodies of water

_____

3  ▶ the early American empire built in a rainforest

_____

6  ▶ a connecting strip of land between two continents

_____

E

Read and Answer I 閱讀並且回答下列問題。 028

Three Great American Empires

The first Americans from Asia settled in North and South America. As they learned to farm and made their homes, they built towns and cities. Some of these people made great empires. The first were the Mayans. They lived in Central America. They lived in the jungle. But they had a great empire. They were very advanced. The Mayans knew how to write by drawing pictures. They were also good at math. They built many amazing temples and other buildings. The Incas lived in South America. They ruled much land there. And they built cities high in the Andes Mountains. The Aztecs lived in North America. Their capital was in modern-day Mexico. They were very warlike. They fought many battles. And they often defeated their enemies.

Answer the questions.

1 Where did the first Americans come from? _____

2 Where in Central America did the Mayans live? _____

3 How did the Mayans write? _____

4 Where did the Aztecs live? _____

Key Words 🔊 029

01	**European** [ˌjʊrəˈpiən]	*(n.)* 歐洲人　　*European Union 歐盟　　*Indo-European Languages 印歐語系 Europeans were interested in trade with China and India. 歐洲人對和中國與印度進行貿易很感興趣。
02	**spice** [spaɪs]	*(n.)* 香料；調味品　　*spice sth. with . . . 增添某物於…… People in Europe wanted spices from India and China. 歐洲當地的人需要來自印度與中國的香料。
03	**explorer** [ɪkˈsplorɚ]	*(n.)* 探險家；探勘者　　*explore 探險；探勘 Spain sent explorers across the Atlantic Ocean. 西班牙派遣探勘者橫渡大西洋。
04	**water route** [ˈwɔtɚ rut]	*(n.)* 水路　　*trade route 商隊路線　　*railway route 鐵道線 Explorers from Europe wanted to find a water route to Asia. 來自歐洲的探險家希望找到通往亞洲的水路。
05	**adventure** [ədˈvɛntʃɚ]	*(n.)* 冒險　　*adventure story 冒險故事　　*space adventure 太空探險 Sailing across the Atlantic Ocean was an adventure. 航行橫渡大西洋是一個冒險。
06	**claim** [klem]	*(v.)* 要求；聲稱　　*claim (that) . . . 聲稱……　　*claim for damages 索賠 When Columbus landed on the island, he claimed the land for Spain. 當哥倫布抵達陸地時，他宣稱這塊土地是屬於西班牙的。
07	**attack** [əˈtæk]	*(v.)* 攻擊　　*under attack 遭到攻擊　　*heart attack 心臟病發 The Spanish who first arrived in Florida attacked the natives. 西班牙人初次到達佛羅里達時，攻擊了當地的原住民。
08	**conqueror** [ˈkaŋkərɚ]	*(n.)* 征服者　　*conquer 攻克；戰勝 Hernando Cortéz was a Spanish conqueror. 赫爾南‧科爾特斯是一位西班牙的征服者。
09	**warrior** [ˈwɔrɪɚ]	*(n.)* 戰士；勇士 Aztec warriors fought against the Spanish. 阿茲提克的戰士們對抗西班牙。
10	**difference** [ˈdɪfərəns]	*(n.)* 差別；差異　　*make a/no difference 有／無影響或關係 *tell the difference 區分 The differences between the Native Americans and the explorers caused fights. 印地安人與外來探險家之間的差異造成了戰爭。

Hernando Cortéz

the Spanish attacking Native Americans

Christopher Columbus

set sail　出航
The explorers **set sail** for America.　探險家出航至美國。

depart [dɪˋpɑrt]　啟程
The explorers **departed** for America.　探險家啟程前往美國。

send out　派出
Why did some countries **send out** explorers?　為何某些國家派出探險家？

arrive in　到達
The Spanish explorers **arrived in** Florida.　西班牙探險家到達佛羅里達州。

land in　抵達；登陸
The Spanish explorers **landed in** Florida.　西班牙探險家抵達佛羅里達州。

create [krɪˋet]　建造；創造
The French **created** settlements in Canada.　法國人在加拿大建造了殖民地。

build　興建
The French **built** a city in Quebec, Canada.　法國人在加拿大的魁北克興建了一座城市。

Word Families ⊙ 031

explore　探險
The Spanish **explored** much of the New World.　西班牙探勘了大半個新世界。

explorer　探險家
The Spanish **explorers** traveled around much of the New World.
西班牙探險家遊遍了大半個新世界。

conquer　征服；戰勝
The Europeans **conquered** many Native American tribes.
歐洲人征服了許多印地安部落。

conqueror　征服者
The European **conquerors** defeated many Native American tribes.
歐洲征服者擊敗了許多印地安部落。

Weapons
武器

sword 劍　　**gun** 槍

cannon 大砲　**spear** 長矛

bow and arrow 弓與箭

Reasons to Visit the New World
拜訪新世界的原因

gold 黃金　　**silver** 銀

spices 香料　**slaves** 奴隸

to spread Christianity 傳播基督教

Checkup

Write | 請依提示寫出正確的英文單字。

1	歐洲人	_____	9	要求；聲稱	_____
2	香料	_____	10	差別；差異	_____
3	探險家	_____	11	出航	_____
4	水路	_____	12	派出	_____
5	冒險	_____	13	抵達；登陸	_____
6	攻擊	_____	14	探險	_____
7	征服者	_____	15	征服；戰勝	_____
8	戰士	_____	16	武器	_____

B

Complete the Sentences | 請在空格中填入最適當的答案，並視情況做適當的變化。

European	explore	adventure	weapon	spice
attack	difference	claim	conquer	difference

1 People in Europe wanted _____ from India and China.
歐洲當地的人需要來自印度與中國的香料。

2 _____ were interested in trade with China and India.
歐洲人對和中國與印度進行貿易很感興趣。

3 Sailing across the Atlantic Ocean was an _____.
航行橫渡大西洋是一個冒險。

4 The Spanish _____ much of the New World.
西班牙探險家遊遍了大半個新世界。

5 The Spanish who first arrived in Florida _____ the natives.
西班牙人初次到達佛羅里達時，攻擊了當地的原住民。

6 The Europeans _____ many Native American tribes.
歐洲人征服了許多印地安部落。

7 When Columbus landed on the island, he _____ the land for Spain.
當哥倫布抵達陸地時，他宣稱這塊土地是屬於西班牙的。

8 The _____ between the Native Americans and the explorers caused
fights. 印地安人與外來探險家之間的差異造成了戰爭。

C

Read and Choose | 請選出與鋪底字意思相近的答案。

1 The explorers set sail for America.
a. sent out   b. departed   c. settled

2 The Spanish explorers landed in Florida.
a. arrived   b. discovered   c. sailed

3 The French built settlements in Canada.
a. settled   b. claimed   c. created

Look, Read, and Write | 看圖並且依照提示，在空格中填入正確答案。

1
▸ to use violence to hurt something or someone

_____

4
▸ a person who travels looking for new lands and discoveries

_____

2
▸ a way to get somewhere by water

_____

5
▸ a fighter or soldier, especially a very brave and experienced one

_____

3
▸ a powder or seed taken from plants such as pepper and ginger

_____

6
▸ someone who has taken control of land or people by force

_____

E

Read and Answer | 閱讀並且回答下列問題。　 032

The Europeans Come to the Americas

After Christopher Columbus, many Europeans sailed to America. Portugal, Spain, France, and England sent out explorers to find a water route to Asia. Spanish explorers went to present-day Florida. They went to Mexico and other places in Central America. And they went to South America, too. The Portuguese mostly went to South America. They founded colonies in Brazil. The French soon followed. They landed in present-day Canada. The French claimed very large areas of land in Canada and settled in there. The English went to present-day Virginia.

Hernando Cortéz
John Smith
Juan Ponce De León

Which is NOT true?

1　European explorers wanted to find a water route to Asia.

2　The Spanish explored Central America.

3　The French founded colonies in Brazil.

4　The English settled parts of Virginia.

Key Words 🔊 033

01	**cross** [krɔs]	(v.) 越過；渡過　*crossing 交叉；十字路口　*cross swords 交鋒；爭論
		In 1607, people from England **crossed** the Atlantic and arrived in Jamestown. 1607 年，來自英格蘭的人民橫渡大西洋到達了美國的詹姆士鎮。
02	**colony** [ˋkɑlənɪ]	(n.) 殖民地；聚居地　*British colony 英國的殖民地　*a colony of 一群
		They lived in places called **colonies**. 他們住在稱作殖民地的地方。
03	**settlement** [ˋsɛtḷmənt]	(n.) 殖民地；新拓居地　*settle in 適應於新環境　*settle down 安頓下來
		Jamestown was the first English **settlement** in Virginia. 詹姆士鎮是維吉尼亞州的第一個英國殖民地。
04	**settler** [ˋsɛtlɚ]	(n.) 移居者　*settle 使定居；移民於
		Many English **settlers** died of hunger and disease. 許多英國移居者死於飢餓與疾病。
05	**independence** [ˏɪndɪˋpɛndəns]	(n.) 獨立　*achieve/gain/win independence from . . . 從……獲得獨立
		People came to America to get **independence**. 人們為了獲得獨立而來到美國。
06	**religious** [rɪˋlɪdʒəs]	(a.) 宗教的　*religious belief 宗教信仰　*religious freedom 宗教自由
		In 1620, the pilgrims came to North America looking for **religious** freedom. 1620 年，清教徒來到北美尋求宗教自由。
07	**plantation** [plænˋteʃən]	(n.) 農園；大農場　*tea/cotton plantation 茶／棉花園
		Plantations are very large farms. 農園是大型的農場。
08	**tax** [tæks]	(n.) 稅　*pay tax on sth. 為某物繳稅　*heavily taxed 課以重稅的
		Colonists had to pay **taxes** on many items. 殖民地居民需要繳納許多項目的稅金。
09	**port** [port]	(n.) 港口　*fishing port 漁港　*come into port 進港
		Boston was an early American **port** city. 波士頓是早期美國的港口城市。
10	**slave** [slev]	(n.) 奴隸　*slavery 奴隸身分　*slave driver 管理奴隸者；苛刻的老闆
		Many Africans were forced to work as **slaves** on plantations. 許多非洲人被迫在農園從事奴隸的工作。

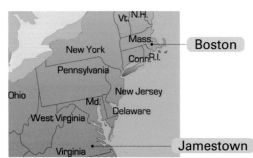
Boston
Jamestown

English settlers

slaves on plantation

start 開始
The settlers wanted to **start** new lives. 移居者想要開始新生活。

begin 展開
The settlers wanted to **begin** new lives. 移居者想要展開新生活。

found [faʊnd] 建立
It was difficult to **found** a colony. 建立殖民地很困難。

settle [ˈsɛtl] 定居
The first English settlers **settled** in Virginia. 第一批英國移居者定居於維吉尼亞州。

plant [plænt] 種植
The settlers **planted** many different crops. 移居者種植許多不同的作物。

pay 付（錢）
The colonists had to **pay** taxes to England. 殖民地居民必須向英國繳納稅金。

Word Families ● 035

colony 殖民地
The English founded a colony at Jamestown. 英國人在詹姆士鎮建立了殖民地。

colonist 殖民地開拓者
Many English colonists lived in Jamestown. 許多英國的拓殖者居住在詹姆士鎮。

colonize 開拓為殖民地
The English colonized the land around Jamestown.
英國人拓殖詹姆士鎮附近的土地。

settlement 新拓居地；殖民地
The Puritans had a settlement in Boston. 清教徒在波士頓拓居了一處殖民地。

settler 移居者；殖民者
The Puritan settlers lived in Boston. 清教徒移居者居住於波士頓。

settle 定居；殖民於
The Puritans settled the land around Boston. 清教徒定居於波士頓附近。

Early English Settlements
早期英國移居地

Jamestown 詹姆士鎮	Plymouth 普利茅斯
Boston 波士頓	Providence 普洛威頓斯
Roanoke 羅阿諾克	

Taxes
稅金

sugar tax 糖稅
tea tax 茶稅
stamp tax 印花稅
paper tax 紙稅

Mayflower in Plymouth Harbor

Checkup

A Write | 請依提示寫出正確的英文單字。

1 越過；渡過 _____	9 移居者 _____
2 殖民地；聚居地 _____	10 奴隸 _____
3 新拓居地 _____	11 建立 _____
4 港口城市 _____	12 定居 _____
5 獨立 _____	13 種植 _____
6 宗教的 _____	14 付（錢） _____
7 農園 _____	15 殖民地開拓者 _____
8 稅 _____	16 開拓為殖民地 _____

B Complete the Sentences | 請在空格中填入最適當的答案，並視情況做適當的變化。

independence	colony	religious	settler	cross
port city	found	colonize	plant	slave

1 In 1607, people from England _____ the Atlantic and arrived in Jamestown.
1607 年，來自英格蘭的人民橫渡大西洋到達了美國的詹姆士鎮。

2 People came to America to get _____.
人們為了獲得獨立而來到美國。

3 Many English _____ died of hunger and disease.
許多英國移居者死於飢餓與疾病。

4 They lived in places called _____. 他們住在稱作殖民地的地方。

5 The pilgrims came to North America looking for _____ freedom.
清教徒來到北美尋求宗教自由。

6 Boston was an early American _____ _____. 波士頓是早期美國的港口城市。

7 The English _____ the land around Jamestown.
英國人拓殖詹姆士鎮附近的土地。

8 Many Africans were forced to work as _____ on plantations.
許多非洲人被迫在農園從事奴隸的工作。

C Read and Choose | 閱讀下列句子，並且選出最適當的答案。

1 The first English settlers (settled | colonized) in Virginia.

2 The English (founded | settled) a colony at Jamestown.

3 The colonists had to (get | pay) taxes to England.

4 The Puritans had a (port city | settlement) in Boston.

Look, Read, and Write | 看圖並且依照提示，在空格中填入正確答案。

1
▶ an area of water where ships stop, with buildings around it

_____

4
▶ someone who is owned by another person and works for him

_____

2
▶ a place that is ruled by a country that is far away

_____

5
▶ freedom from control by another country

_____

3
▶ very large farms

_____

6
▶ the money you have to pay the government

_____

E

Read and Answer | 閱讀並且回答下列問題。 ○ 036

The English in America

The Spanish came to the New World for gold. But the English had another reason to go there. They wanted colonies. The English settled in North America. They started many colonies. Two were Virginia and Massachusetts. The first English colony was Jamestown. It was in Virginia. Life was very hard for the colonists. Many died of hunger and disease. But more and more people came from England. Many of them wanted new lives in America. They came for religious freedom. That was why the Pilgrims and Puritans came. They founded colonies near Boston. They lived in Massachusetts.

Fill in the blanks.

1   The Spanish were looking for _____ in the New World.

2   The English started colonies in _____ and Massachusetts.

3   The first English colony was _____.

4   The Puritans were looking for religious _____ in America.

Key Words
🔊 037

| 01 | **revolution**
[ˌrɛvəˈluʃən] | (n.) 革命;大變革　*stir up revolution 煽動革命
The American **Revolution** began in 1775.
美國革命於 1775 年展開。 |

| 02 | **declaration**
[ˌdɛkləˈreʃən] | (n.) 宣布;宣言　*declaration of war 宣戰　*customs declaration 報關單
The **Declaration** of Independence was signed on July 4, 1776.
《獨立宣言》於 1776 年 7 月 4 日簽訂。 |

| 03 | **rule**
[rul] | (v.) 統治　*under the rule of . . . 在……的統治下
*rules and regulations 規章制度
The colonies were **ruled** by the king in faraway England.
殖民地由遙遠的英國國王統治。 |

| 04 | **equality**
[iˈkwɑlətɪ] | (n.) 平等;相等　*racial equality 種族平等
Americans wanted **equality** with England.　美國人民希望能和英國平等。 |

| 05 | **right**
[raɪt] | (n.) 權利　*human rights 人權　*have a/the right to do sth. 有權做某事
The Americans demanded their **rights** from England.
美國人民向英國要求他們的權利。 |

| 06 | **signer**
[ˈsaɪnɚ] | (n.) 簽名者;簽訂人　*sign (v.) 簽名;簽訂　*signature (n.) 簽名
John Hancock was the first **signer** of the Declaration of Independence.
約翰・漢考克是第一位在《獨立宣言》上簽名的人。 |

| 07 | **soldier**
[ˈsoldʒɚ] | (n.) 士兵;軍人　*military service 兵役
American **soldiers** fought British **soldiers**. 美國士兵對抗英國士兵。 |

| 08 | **battle**
[ˈbætl̩] | (n.) 戰役;戰鬥　*a losing battle 不可能獲勝的爭鬥　*battlefield 戰場
There were many **battles** in the Revolutionary War.
獨立戰爭包括許多戰役。 |

| 09 | **war**
[wɔr] | (n.) 戰爭　*at war 處於交戰狀態　*prepare for war 備戰
The Americans won the Revolutionary **War**. 美國人贏得了獨立戰爭。 |

| 10 | **commander**
[kəˈmændɚ] | (n.) 指揮官;司令官
George Washington was the **commander** of the American soldiers.
喬治・華盛頓是美國士兵的指揮官。 |

The Declaration of Independence

John Hancock's signature

Revolutionary War

British surrender

Power Verbs 🔊 038

sign
[saɪn]
簽訂
56 leaders **signed** the Declaration of Independence.
56 位領袖簽訂《獨立宣言》。

fight
打仗
The Americans **fought** the English. 美國人和英國人打仗。

battle
[ˋbætl̩]
與……作戰
The Americans **battled** the English. 美國人和英國人作戰。

command
[kəˋmænd]
命令;指揮　　*commander 指揮官
George Washington **commanded** the American soldiers.
喬治‧華盛頓指揮美國士兵。

lead
[lid]
領導;率領　　*leader 領導者
George Washington **led** the American soldiers. 喬治‧華盛頓率領美國士兵。

Word Families 🔊 039

symbol
象徵
The Liberty Bell is a **symbol** of freedom. 自由鐘是自由的象徵。

sign
記號
The Liberty Bell is a **sign** of freedom. 自由鐘是自由的記號。

freedom
自由;獨立自主
The colonists wanted **freedom** from England.
殖民地開拓者希望從英國得到自由。

liberty
自由權
The colonists wanted **liberty** from England.
殖民地居民希望從英國得到自由權利。

The Liberty Bell
in Philadelphia, Pennsylvania

Famous Early Americans 美國早期著名領袖

Benjamin Franklin
班傑明‧富蘭克林 (1706~1790)

George Washington
喬治‧華盛頓 (1732~1799)

Thomas Paine
湯瑪斯‧潘恩 (1737-1809)

John Adams
約翰‧亞當斯 (1735-1826)

Thomas Jefferson
湯瑪斯‧傑弗遜 (1743-1826)

Checkup

A

Write | 請依提示寫出正確的英文單字。

1	革命	_____	9	戰爭	_____
2	宣言	_____	10	指揮官；司令官	_____
3	統治	_____	11	記號	_____
4	平等	_____	12	打仗	_____
5	權利	_____	13	命令；指揮	_____
6	簽訂人	_____	14	領導；率領	_____
7	士兵	_____	15	自由	_____
8	與⋯⋯作戰	_____	16	自由權	_____

B

Complete the Sentences | 請在空格中填入最適當的答案，並視情況做適當的變化。

equality	declaration	soldier	war	sign
right	revolution	rule	signer	battle

1 The American _____ began in 1775. 美國革命於 1775 年展開。

2 Americans wanted _____ with England. 美國人民希望能和英國平等。

3 The colonies were _____ by the king in faraway England.
殖民地由遙遠的英國國王統治。

4 The Americans demanded their _____ from England.
美國人民向英國要求他們的權利。

5 The _____ of Independence was signed on July 4, 1776.
《獨立宣言》於 1776 年 7 月 4 日簽訂。

6 56 leaders _____ the Declaration of Independence. 56 位領袖簽訂《獨立宣言》。

7 John Hancock was the first _____ of the Declaration of Independence.
約翰・漢考克是第一位在《獨立宣言》上簽名的人。

8 There were many _____ in the Revolutionary War. 獨立戰爭包括許多戰役。

C

Read and Choose | 請選出與鋪底字意思相近的答案。

1 George Washington commanded the American soldiers.
   a. signed   b. led   c. fought

2 American soldiers fought British soldiers.
   a. battled   b. won   c. ruled

3 The colonists wanted freedom from England.
   a. symbol   b. sign   c. liberty

D

Look, Read, and Write | 看圖並且依照提示，在空格中填入正確答案。

 1 ▸ a person who is in an army

_____

 3 ▸ a person who commands an army

_____

 2 ▸ an important document that made the colonies become free

_____

_____

 4 ▸ the War of American Independence

_____

E

Read and Answer | 閱讀並且回答下列問題。 🔊 040

The Colonies Become Free

After the first English settlers arrived in Jamestown, more and more people moved from Europe to America. They lived in places called colonies. As the years passed, there were 13 colonies. These colonies were

ruled by the king of England. But many colonies did not want to be ruled by England. They wanted to be free. On July 4, 1776, many leaders in the colonies signed the Declaration of Independence. In the declaration, they wrote that Americans wanted to be free and start their own country. The colonies fought a war with England. The war lasted for many years. George Washington commanded the American soldiers and led them to victory. After the war, the colonies became a country. The country was called the United States of America. Today, American celebrates Independence Day on July 4.

What is true? Write T(true) or F(false).

1 There were 13 English colonies in America. _____

2 The colonies wanted the English to rule them. _____

3 George Washington was the English leader. _____

4 American Independence Day is July 4. _____

Review Test 2

A

Write | 請依提示寫出正確的英文單字。

1	部落	_____	11	靈魂	_____
2	游牧民	_____	12	崇拜；信奉	_____
3	帝國	_____	13	古代的；古老的	_____
4	祖先	_____	14	征服；戰勝	_____
5	探險家	_____	15	要求；聲稱	_____
6	水路	_____	16	出航	_____
7	殖民地	_____	17	移居者	_____
8	新拓居地	_____	18	殖民地開拓者	_____
9	革命	_____	19	戰役；戰鬥	_____
10	宣言	_____	20	自由；獨立自主	_____

B

Choose the Correct Word | 請選出與鋪底字意思相近的答案。

1 The Aztecs conquered many people around them.

   a. constructed　　　　　b. connected　　　　　c. defeated

2 The ancient Mayans built great cities.

   a. worshiped　　　　　b. constructed　　　　　c. had

3 The explorers set sail for America.

   a. sent out　　　　　b. departed　　　　　c. settled

4 The Spanish explorers landed in Florida.

   a. arrived　　　　　b. discovered　　　　　c. sailed

C

Complete the Sentences | 請在空格中填入最適當的答案，並視情況做適當的變化。

conquer	sign	tribe	colonize

1 Ancestor worship was common for many _____. 祖先崇拜在許多部落經常見到。

2 The Europeans _____ many Native American tribes.
歐洲征服者征服了許多印地安部落。

3 The English _____ the land around Jamestown.
英國人拓殖詹姆士鎮附近的土地。

4 56 leaders _____ the Declaration of Independence. 56 位領袖簽訂《獨立宣言》。

52

CHAPTER 3

Science ①

Living and Nonliving Things
生物與非生物

01	**living** [ˈlɪvɪŋ]	(a.) 活的；活著的　*living (n.) 生計　*living language 現行語言 All animals and plants are living things. 所有的動植物都是生物。
02	**nonliving** [nɑnˈlɪvɪŋ]	(a.) 非活著的；非生物的　*nonliving resource 非生物資源 Rocks, glass, and water are nonliving things. 岩石、玻璃與水都是非生物。
03	**oxygen** [ˈɑksədʒən]	(n.)〔化〕氧；氧氣　*lack of oxygen 缺氧　*give out oxygen 釋放氧氣 Animals and plants need oxygen to survive. 動物與植物需要氧氣才能存活。
04	**nutrient** [ˈnjutrɪənt]	(n.) 營養物；滋養物　*nutrition 營養 Nutrients let plants and animals grow. 營養物讓植物與動物得以生長。
05	**shelter** [ˈʃɛltɚ]	(n.) 庇護所；遮蔽　*shelter from 躲避　*give sb. a shelter 提供某人庇護 Animals need shelter to keep them safe. 動物需要庇護所來保持安全。
06	**growth** [groθ]	(n.) 成長；增長　*growth factor 生長因子　*economic growth 經濟發展 The growth of some animals happens quickly. 有些動物的成長非常快速。
07	**alive** [əˈlaɪv]	(a.) 活著的　*to be captured alive 被活捉　*come alive 活躍起來 Living things need food, water, and oxygen to stay alive. 生物需要食物、水與氧氣來維持生命。
08	**need** [nid]	(v.) 需要　*in need of 需要　*meet one's need 滿足某人的需要 Animals need space to move around. 動物需要空間四處活動。
09	**room** [rum]	(n.) 空間；場所　*there's room for sb./sth. 有某人／某物的位置 Plants need room to grow bigger. 植物需要空間茁壯。
10	**alike** [əˈlaɪk]	(a.) 相像的；相似　*look alike 外貌相似　*young and old alike 老少咸宜 How are animals and plants alike? 動物與植物哪裡相似？

living things

nonliving things

alive

dead

survive 活下來
[sə`vaɪv]
Animals always try to **survive**. 動物總會想辦法活下去。

stay alive 生存
Animals always try to **stay alive**. 動物總會想辦法生存。

stay healthy 保持健康
Animals need many things to **stay healthy**. 動物需要許多條件保持健康。

grow bigger 茁壯
Animals and plants **grow bigger** and change. 動植物茁壯成長並改變。

breathe 呼吸
[brið]
Some animals **breathe** with lungs. 某些動物用肺呼吸。

Word Families 🔘 043

Things That Animals Need to Survive 動物賴以維生的條件

food and water 食物與水

space and shelter 空間與庇護

oxygen from the air or water 空氣或水中的氧氣

space to move around 能活動的空間

Things That Plants Need to Grow 植物茁壯生長的條件

water, sunlight, and oxygen 水、日光與氧氣

nutrients from the soil 土壤中的養分

room to grow bigger 足夠的生長空間

Differences between Living Things and Nonliving Things 生物與非生物的相異處

Living Things 生物
　Living things need food, water, and oxygen. 生物需要食物、水與氧氣。
　Living things need shelter. 生物需要庇護所。
　Living things make new living things. 生物製造出新的生物。

Nonliving Things 非生物
　Nonliving things do not need food, water, and oxygen. 非生物不需要食物、水與氧氣。
　Nonliving things do not need shelter. 非生物不需要庇護所。
　Nonliving things cannot make new things. 非生物無法製造出新的事物。

Checkup

A

Write | 請依提示寫出正確的英文單字。

1	活著的	_____	9	活動	_____
2	非生物的	_____	10	空間；場所	_____
3	氧氣	_____	11	空間	_____
4	營養素	_____	12	活下去	_____
5	庇護所	_____	13	生存	_____
6	成長	_____	14	保持健康	_____
7	需要	_____	15	茁壯	_____
8	相像的	_____	16	呼吸	_____

B

Complete the Sentences | 請在空格中填入最適當的答案，並視情況做適當的變化。

alike	shelter	water	oxygen	grow bigger
alive	growth	need	nutrient	living thing

1 How are animals and plants _____? 動物與植物哪裡相似？

2 All animals and plants are _____ _____. 所有的動植物都是生物。

3 _____ let plants and animals grow. 營養物讓植物與動物得以生長。

4 The _____ of some animals happens quickly. 有些動物的成長非常快速。

5 Living things need food, water, and oxygen to stay _____.
生物需要食物、水與氧氣來維持生命。

6 Animals _____ space to move around. 動物需要空間四處活動。

7 Animals need _____ to keep them safe. 動物需要庇護所來保持安全。

8 Animals and plants _____ _____ and change. 動植物茁壯成長並改變。

C

Read and Choose | 閱讀下列句子，並且選出最適當的答案。

1 Rocks, glass, and water are (living | nonliving) things.

2 Animals always try to (change | survive).

3 Animals and plants need (water | oxygen) to breathe.

4 Some animals (breathe | need) with lungs.

Look, Read, and Write ┃ 看圖並且依照提示，在空格中填入正確答案。

1  ▶ all animals and plants that are alive

_____

2  ▶ to take air into your lungs and let it out again

_____

3  ▶ a safe place to live

_____

4  ▶ space to move around or to grow bigger

_____

5  ▶ a substance in food that plants and animals need to live and grow

_____

6  ▶ similar in some way

_____

E

Read and Answer ┃ 閱讀並且回答下列問題。 044

Living Things vs. Nonliving Things

Everything on Earth is either living or nonliving. A living thing is alive. A nonliving thing is not alive. Both animals and plants are living things. Rocks, air, and water are nonliving things. There are many kinds of animals and plants. But they are similar in some ways. All of them need oxygen to survive. They also need food and water. When they eat and drink, they get nutrients. Nutrients provide energy for them. Most plants and animals need sunlight, too. Living things also can make new living things like themselves. Nonliving things are not alive. They cannot move. They cannot breathe. They cannot make new things like themselves.

Fill in the blanks.

1 Everything on Earth is either _____ or nonliving.

2 _____ and plants are living things.

3 Living things need oxygen, food, and _____ to survive.

4 Nonliving things cannot _____ new things like themselves.

Key Words ● 045

01	**mammal** [ˈmæml̩]	*(n.)* 哺乳動物 **Mammals** have fur or hair that covers their bodies. 哺乳動物全身被毛髮覆蓋。
02	**bird** [bɝd]	*(n.)* 鳥　*early bird 早鳥；早起者　*bird-watching 賞鳥 All **birds** have a beak, feathers, wings, and two legs. 所有的鳥都有鳥喙、羽毛、翅膀以及兩隻腳。
03	**reptile** [ˈrɛptl̩]	*(n.)* 爬蟲類；爬行動物 Snakes and lizards are **reptiles**.　蛇與蜥蜴是爬蟲類。
04	**amphibian** [æmˈfɪbɪən]	*(n.)* 兩棲動物 **Amphibians** can live in the water and on land. 兩棲動物能夠生存在水中和陸上。
05	**fish** [fɪʃ]	*(n.)* 魚　*freshwater fish 淡水魚　*fish for bluefish/salmon . . . 捕藍魚／鮭魚等 **Fish** live in the water.　魚居住在水中。
06	**egg** [ɛg]	*(n.)* 蛋；卵（細胞）　*put all one's eggs in one basket 孤注一擲 Birds, fish, and reptiles lay **eggs**.　鳥、魚和爬蟲類會生蛋。
07	**young** [jʌŋ]	*(n.)* 動物的小時候　*youth 青少年時期　*young at heart 人老心不老 A mammal feeds its **young** with milk.　哺乳動物用奶水餵養小寶寶。
08	**adult** [əˈdʌlt]	*(n.)* 成年人；已長大的動物　*adult ticket 成人票　*adulthood 成年時期 Animals grow up and become **adults**.　動物長大並成熟。
09	**lungs** [lʌŋz]	*(n.)* 肺臟（複數形）　*lung transplant 肺移植　*lung cancer 肺癌 Many land animals use **lungs** to breathe air. 許多陸生動物用肺呼吸。
10	**gills** [gɪls]	*(n.)*（魚）鰓（複數形） Fish use **gills** to breathe underwater.　魚用鰓在水底呼吸。

Kinds of Animals

young

mammals　　　birds　　　reptiles

give birth to 生孩子
Mammals give birth to live young. 哺乳動物生下小寶寶。

bear 生產
[bɛr]
Many mammals bear babies in the spring. 許多哺乳動物在春天產下小寶寶。

lay 下蛋；產卵
[le]
Birds lay eggs in their nests. 鳥類在鳥巢裡下蛋。

hatch 孵出；孵化
[hætʃ]
Baby birds hatch from eggs. 鳥寶寶從蛋裡孵化。

raise 養育
[rez]
Lions raise their cubs. 獅子養育自己的幼獅。

feed 餵養
[fid]
Mother lions feed their young with milk. 母獅子餵小獅子母奶。

Word Families 🔊 047

Mammals 哺乳動物	**Reptiles** 爬蟲類	**Amphibians** 兩棲動物	**Animals' Body Coverings** 動物身體的覆蓋	**Animals' Homes** 動物棲息地
lion 獅子	**lizard** 蜥蜴	**frog** 青蛙	**hair** 毛髮	**land** 陸地
gorilla 大猩猩	**snake** 蛇	**toad** 蟾蜍	**fur** 毛皮	**water** 水中
manatee 海牛	**turtle** 烏龜	**salamander** 蠑螈	**feathers** 羽毛	**nest** 巢穴
dolphin 海豚	**crocodile** 鱷魚		**scales** 魚鱗	**cave** 洞窟
whale 鯨魚			**smooth, wet skin** 濕滑皮膚	**hole** 地洞
			dry skin 乾燥皮膚	**den** 獸穴
			scaly skin 鱗片皮膚	**lair** 窩
			shell 甲殼	**burrow** 地洞
				shelter 庇護所

amphibians

fish

Checkup

A Write l 請依提示寫出正確的英文單字。

1	爬蟲類	_____	9 蛋；卵	_____
2	兩棲動物	_____	10 鰓	_____
3	魚	_____	11 生小孩	g_____
4	哺乳動物	_____	12 生產	b_____
5	鳥類	_____	13 下蛋；產卵	_____
6	動物小時候	_____	14 孵出；孵化	_____
7	長大的動物	_____	15 養育	_____
8	肺	_____	16 餵養	_____

B Complete the Sentences l 請在空格中填入最適當的答案，並視情況做適當的變化。

adult	reptile	fish	lungs	mammal
amphibian	feed	bird	raise	hatch

1 _____ can live in the water and on land. 兩棲動物能夠生存在水中和陸上。

2 Snakes and lizards are _____. 蛇與蜥蜴是爬蟲類。

3 _____ have fur or hair that covers their bodies.
哺乳動物全身被毛髮覆蓋。

4 All _____ have a beak, feathers, wings, and two legs.
所有的鳥都有鳥喙、羽毛、翅膀以及兩隻腳。

5 Animals grow up and become _____. 動物長大並成熟。

6 A mammal _____ its young with milk. 哺乳動物用奶水餵養小寶寶。

7 Baby birds _____ from eggs. 鳥寶寶從蛋裡孵化。

8 Many land animals use _____ to breathe air.
許多陸生動物用肺呼吸。

C

Read and Choose l 閱讀下列句子，並且選出最適當的答案。

1 Birds (bear | lay) eggs in their nests.

2 Mammals give birth to live (egg | young).

3 Mother lions (feed | live) their young with milk.

4 Fish use (gills | lungs) to breathe underwater.

D

Look, Read, and Write | 看圖並且依照提示，在空格中填入正確答案。

► (of an egg) open and produce a young animal

_____

► animals like snakes and lizards

_____

► animals like frogs and toads

_____

► animals that feed their young with milk

_____

► the organs behind the head of a fish that allow it to breathe

_____

► animals' babies

_____

E

Read and Answer | 閱讀並且回答下列問題。　⊙ 048

How Are Animals Different?

There are five types of animals. They are mammals, birds, reptiles, amphibians, and fish. They are all different from each other. Mammals are animals like dogs, cats, cows, lions, tigers, and humans. They give birth to live young. And they feed their young with milk from their mothers. Birds have feathers, and most of them can fly. Penguins, hawks, and sparrows are birds. Reptiles and amphibians are similar. Both of them lay eggs. Snakes are reptiles, and frogs and toads are amphibians. Amphibians live on land and in the water. Fish live in the water. They lay eggs. They use gills to take in oxygen from the water. Sharks, bass, and catfish are all fish.

Which is NOT true?

1　There are five types of animals.

2　Mammals are animals like snakes and lizards.

3　Fish use gills to breathe.

4　Bass and sharks are both fish.

The Life Cycle of an Animal 動物的生命週期

Key Words 🔊 049

01 life cycle
[laɪf `saɪkl]

(n.) 生命週期　*life span 壽命

Every animal has a **life cycle**. 所有動物都擁有生命週期。

02 stage
[stedʒ]

(n.) 階段；時期　*at an early stage 在早期　*go/be on stage 登臺演出

Animals go through four **stages** during their life cycles.
動物在生命週期中會歷經四個階段。

03 birth
[bɜθ]

(n.) 出生　*give birth to 生產　*by birth 血統上；天生

An animal's life begins with its **birth**. 動物的生命始於出生。

04 growth and change
[groθ ænd tʃendʒ]

(n.) 生長與變化

The **growth and change** of butterflies are unique.
蝴蝶的生長與變化很特殊。

05 reproduction
[,riprə`dʌkʃən]

(n.) 繁育；生殖　*sexual/asexual reproduction 有性／無性生殖

Reproduction lets animals have babies. 繁殖使動物擁有自己的寶寶。

06 death
[dɛθ]

(n.) 死亡　*put sb. to death 處死某人　*starve/freeze to death 餓死／凍死

An animal's life ends with its **death**. 動物的生命由死亡完結。

07 maturity
[mə`tjʊrətɪ]

(n.) 成熟　*reach maturity 成熟　*at full maturity 處於完全成熟狀態

When an animal reaches **maturity**, it can reproduce.
當動物長至成熟，便有能力繁殖。

08 go through
[go θru]

(v.) 歷經；經過　*go through with 堅持完成　*go through a list 仔細檢查清單

Most insects **go through** big changes as they grow.
大多數的昆蟲在成長階段會經歷巨大變化。

09 hibernate
[`haɪbɚ,net]

(v.) 冬眠　*go into hibernation 進入冬眠
*emerge from hibernation 自冬眠中甦醒

Most bears **hibernate** in winter. 多數的熊會在冬天冬眠。

10 tadpole
[`tæd,pol]

(n.) 蝌蚪

A baby frog is called a **tadpole**. 青蛙小時候稱為蝌蚪。

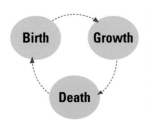

life cycle

reproduction

mate

hibernate

🔘 050

be born	出生 Many animals **are born** in the spring. 許多動物在春天出生。
grow up	成長 After about 14 weeks, a tadpole **grows up** and loses its tail. 14 週之後，蝌蚪成長並失去尾巴。
grow older	長大 Animals get bigger as they **grow older**. 動物會隨著年齡成長而長大。
mate [met]	交配；配對 When animals **mate**, they can reproduce. 當動物交配，牠們能夠繁殖。
reproduce [ˌriprəˈdjus]	繁殖；生殖 Animals **reproduce** by having babies. 動物產下幼兒得以繁殖。
fertilize [ˈfɝtḷˌaɪz]	受精 A male frog **fertilizes** eggs. 雄蛙使卵受精。

Word Families 🔘 051

Animals' Life Cycles
動物的生命週期

Frog 青蛙
egg 卵→ tadpole 蝌蚪→ grow legs 長出腳→ adult frog 成蛙

Cat 貓
newborn kitten 新生小貓→ young cat 幼貓→ adult cat 成貓

Butterfly 蝴蝶
egg 卵→ caterpillar 毛毛蟲→ pupa 蛹→ adult butterfly 成蝶

Animals' Babies
動物的小寶寶

cub 幼獸（熊、獅、虎、狼等）

kitten 小貓

tadpole 蝌蚪

caterpillar 毛毛蟲

chick 小雞

puppy 小狗

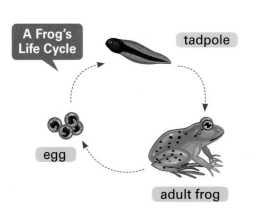

A Frog's Life Cycle

tadpole

egg

adult frog

A Dog's Life Cycle

newborn puppy

young dog

adult dog

Checkup

A

Write | 請依提示寫出正確的英文單字。

1	生命週期	_____	9	生長與變化	_____
2	階段	_____	10	歷經；經過	_____
3	出生 (n.)	_____	11	出生 (v.)	_____
4	繁殖 (n.)	_____	12	成長	_____ u
5	死亡	_____	13	長大	_____ o
6	成熟	_____	14	交配；配對	_____
7	蝌蚪	_____	15	繁殖；生殖 (v.)	_____
8	冬眠	_____	16	受精	_____

B

Complete the Sentences | 請在空格中填入最適當的答案，並視情況做適當的變化。

reproduce	life cycle	growth	maturity	hibernate
reproduction	go through	grow up	stage	death

1 Animals go through four _____ during their life cycles.
動物在生命週期中會歷經四個階段。

2 Every animal has a _____ _____. 所有動物都擁有生命週期。

3 _____ lets animals have babies. 繁殖使動物擁有自己的寶寶。

4 The _____ and change of butterflies are unique.
蝴蝶的生長與變化很特殊。

5 Most bears _____ in winter. 多數的熊會在冬天冬眠。

6 When an animal reaches _____, it can reproduce.
當動物長至成熟，便有能力繁殖。

7 Most insects _____ _____ big changes as they grow.
大多數的昆蟲在成長階段會經歷巨大變化。

8 After about 14 weeks, a tadpole _____ _____ and loses its tail.
14 週之後，蝌蚪成長並失去尾巴。

C

Read and Choose | 閱讀下列句子，並且選出最適當的答案。

1 Animals (produce | reproduce) by having babies.

2 Many animals are (born | slept) in the spring.

3 When animals (go through | mate), they can reproduce.

4 An animal's life begins with its (birth | death).

D

Look, Read, and Write | 看圖並且依照提示，在空格中填入正確答案。

1  ▸ a young bear, lion, fox, wolf, or other wild animal

_____

4 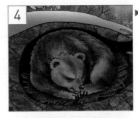 ▸ to sleep all the time during the winter

_____

2  ▸ the act or process of having babies

_____

5  ▸ a young dog

_____

3  ▸ a baby frog

_____

6  ▸ a small worm that becomes a butterfly later on

_____

E

Read and Answer | 閱讀並且回答下列問題。　🔊 052

The Life Cycles of Cats and Frogs

Every animal has a life cycle. This is the period from birth to death.

Cats are mammals, so they are born alive. Baby cats are called kittens. A mother cat takes care of her kittens for many weeks. The mother cat feeds her kittens with milk from her body. As the kittens get bigger, they become more independent. After about one year, they become adult cats, and they can take care of themselves.

Frogs have different life cycles. Frogs are born in eggs. When they hatch, they are called tadpoles. Tadpoles have long tails and no legs. They use gills to breathe in the water. Soon, they grow legs and start to use lungs to breathe. Later, they can leave the water. When this happens, they become adult frogs.

Answer the questions.

1   What is a baby cat called?　_____

2   How long does it take for kittens to become adults?　_____

3   How are frogs born?　_____

4   When do frogs leave the water?　_____

Key Words 🔊 053

| 01 | **seed** | (n.) 種子　*go to seed 結籽 |
| | [sid] | A plant's life cycle begins with a seed. 植物的生命週期從種子開始。 |

| 02 | **pollen** | (n.) 花粉 |
| | [ˈpɑlən] | Pollen helps a plant make seeds. 花粉幫助植物發展種子。 |

| 03 | **sprout** | (n.) 新芽；嫩枝　*Brussels sprout 球芽甘藍　*sprout shoots 發芽 |
| | [spraʊt] | A sprout is a small plant that has just come above ground. 新芽是剛從土裡冒出的幼小植物。 |

04	**fruit**	(n.) 水果　*bear fruit 結果；取得成果
	[frut]	*the fruits of one's hard labor 辛勤的成果
		Every plant bears some kind of fruit. 每種植物都會結出某類果實。

| 05 | **trunk** | (n.) 樹幹　*trunk 汽車行李廂；旅行大皮箱　*trunks 男用運動短褲 |
| | [trʌŋk] | A trunk is the main stem of a tree. 樹幹是一棵樹的主幹。 |

| 06 | **petal** | (n.) 花瓣 |
| | [ˈpɛtl] | Most roses have red petals. 多數玫瑰擁有紅色花瓣。 |

| 07 | **energy** | (n.) 能量　*have the energy to do sth. 有精力做某事　*save energy 節約能源 |
| | [ˈɛnədʒɪ] | Plants need energy to survive. 植物需要能量維生。 |

| 08 | **warmth** | (n.) 溫暖　*the warmth of one's greeting/welcome 某人的熱烈歡迎 |
| | [wɔrmθ] | The warmth of the sun helps give plants energy. 太陽的溫暖幫助提供植物能量。 |

| 09 | **store** | (v.) 儲存　*in store 儲藏　*store away 保管；收好 |
| | [stor] | A cactus stores water in its thick stem. 仙人掌將水儲存在肥厚的莖裡。 |

10	**hold**	(v.) 抓住；支撐　*hold a conference 舉行會議
	[hold]	*hold it / hold a moment 等一下
		Roots hold a plant in the ground. 根部支撐在地面上的植物。

A Rose's Life Cycle

petal

seed　　sprout　　bud　　flower　　withered flower

pollinate
[ˈpɑləˌnet]

給……授花粉

Honeybees help pollinate many flowers and vegetables.
蜜蜂幫助傳遞許多花朵與植物的花粉。

germinate
[ˈdʒɜməˌnet]

生長；發芽

Many plants germinate in the spring. 許多植物在春天發芽。

sprout
[spraʊt]

發芽；抽條

The plant is sprouting. 這棵植物正在發芽。

shoot up

急速生長

The plant is shooting up. 這棵植物正快速生長。

mature
[məˈtjʊr]

變成熟；使長成

Many fruits mature in summer or fall. 許多水果在夏天或秋天長成。

ripen
[ˈraɪpən]

使成熟；變鮮美

Many fruits ripen in summer or fall. 許多水果在夏天或秋天成熟。

anchor
[ˈæŋkɚ]

固定

Roots anchor a plant to the ground. 根部幫助植物在地面固定。

absorb
[əbˈsɔrb]

吸收

Plant leaves absorb sunlight and use it to make food.
植物的葉子吸收太陽光並製造養分。

bush	灌木叢	A bush is a plant with many woody stems. 一株灌木指的是有許多岔枝叢生的植物。
shrub	灌木；矮樹	A shrub is a plant with many woody stems. 一株矮樹是指有許多岔枝叢生的植物。

sprout	新芽；嫩枝	A sprout is a small plant that has just come above ground. 新芽是剛冒出土的幼小植物。
bud	葉芽；花蕾	A bud is a part of a plant that will become a leaf or a flower. 葉芽是植物中會長成葉子或花朵的某部分。

Kinds of Plants
不同種類的植物

maple tree 楓樹　　**fern** 蕨類

oak tree 橡樹　　**pine tree** 松樹

spruce tree 雲杉木　　**cactus** 仙人掌

corn 玉米　　**bean** 豆子

Kinds of Leaves
不同種類的葉子

broad leaf 闊葉

needle leaf 針葉

Checkup

A

Write | 請依提示寫出正確的英文單字。

1	種子	_____	9	樹幹	_____
2	花粉	_____	10	儲存	_____
3	新芽	_____	11	抓住；支撐	_____
4	水果	_____	12	生長；發芽	_____
5	花瓣	_____	13	給……授花粉	_____
6	能量	_____	14	變成熟；使長成	_____
7	溫暖	_____	15	灌木；矮樹	_____
8	吸收	_____	16	固定	_____

B

Complete the Sentences | 請在空格中填入最適當的答案，並視情況做適當的變化。

hold	ripen	germinate	warmth	pollen
store	seed	pollinate	petal	fruit

1   A plant's life cycle begins with a _____. 植物的生命週期從種子開始。

2   Every plant bears some kind of _____. 每種植物都會結出某類果實。

3   Most roses have red _____. 多數玫瑰擁有紅色花瓣。

4   _____ helps a plant make seeds. 花粉幫助植物發展種子。

5   The _____ of the sun helps give plants energy.
太陽的溫暖幫助提供植物能量。

6   A cactus _____ water in its thick stem. 仙人掌將水儲存在肥厚的莖裡。

7   Roots _____ a plant in the ground. 根部支撐在地面上的植物。

8   Honeybees help _____ many flowers and vegetables.
蜜蜂幫助傳遞許多花朵與植物的花粉。

C

Read and Choose | 閱讀下列句子，並且選出最適當的答案。

1   Many plants (germinate | mature) in the spring.

2   A (bush | bud) is a plant with many woody stems.

3   Many fruits (anchor | mature) in summer or fall.

4   Plant leaves (pollinate | absorb) sunlight and use it to make food.

D Look, Read, and Write | 看圖並且依照提示，在空格中填入正確答案。

 1 ▸ the main stem of a tree

_____

 4 ▸ the colored part of a flower

_____

 2 ▸ a fine powder produced by flowers

_____

 5 ▸ a small part that grows on a plant and develops into a flower

_____

 3 ▸ a small hard object produced by a plant that can grow into a new plant

_____

 6 ▸ a plant with many woody stems

_____

E Read and Answer | 閱讀並且回答下列問題。 🔊 056

The Life Cycle of a Pine Tree

pine trees

Every plant, like pine trees, has its own life cycle. A pine tree's life cycle begins with a seed. Adult pine trees have pine cones. Inside the pine cones are tiny seeds. Every year, many pine cones fall to the ground. Some of them stay near the pine tree, but, other times, animals pick them up and move them. The wind and rain might move them, too. Sometimes, the seeds fall out of the pine cones and get buried in the ground. They often start to sprout. These are called seedlings. These seedlings get bigger and bigger. After many years, they become adult pine trees. Then they too have pine cones with seeds. So a new life cycle begins again.

pine cones

Fill in the blanks.

1 Pine trees have pine _____.

2 Pine cones fall to the _____ every year.

3 When a buried seed sprouts, it is called a _____.

4 Seedlings will later become _____ pine trees.

The Food Chain 食物鏈

01	**food chain** [fud tʃen]	*(n.)* 食物鏈 The food chain starts with sunlight and plants. 食物鏈的開端是太陽和植物。
02	**food web** [fud wɛb]	*(n.)* 食物網 A food web connects the animals on the food chain. 食物網將食物鏈上的動物彼此連結。
03	**energy pyramid** [ˈɛnədʒɪ ˈpɪrəmɪd]	*(n.)* 能量塔　*food pyramid 飲食金字塔 An energy pyramid shows where each animal gets its energy from. 能量塔顯示每一種動物獲得能量的出處。
04	**plant eater** [plænt ˈitɚ]	*(n.)* 草食動物 Plant eaters only eat food like fruits and vegetables. 草食動物只吃如水果和植物等食物。
05	**meat eater** [mit ˈitɚ]	*(n.)* 肉食動物 Meat eaters eat other animals. 肉食動物以其他動物為食物。
06	**prey** [pre]	*(n.)* 被獵捕的動物；獵物　*fall prey to sth./sb. 被某物／某人捕食 　　　　　　　　　　　　　　*prey on sth. 捕食某物 Prey are animals that get hunted. 獵物是指被獵捕的動物。
07	**ecosystem** [ˈɛko͵sɪstəm]	*(n.)* 生態系統　*ecology 生態學　*marine ecosystem 海洋生態系統 Ecosystems are made up of living and nonliving things. 生態系統由生物和非生物組成。
08	**relationship** [rɪˈleʃən͵ʃɪp]	*(n.)* 關係；親屬關係　*relation 關係；關聯　*customer relationship 客戶關係 Let's learn about relationships among living things. 讓我們學習生物間的關係。
09	**depend on** [dɪˈpɛnd ɑn]	*(v.)* 依賴；依靠　*that/it depends 看情況 Plants and animals depend on one another for food. 植物與動物靠依賴彼此為食物來維生。
10	**make up** [mek ʌp]	*(v.)* 構成；組合　*be made up of . . . 由……組成 　　　　　　　　　*make up sth. with . . . 用……補償某物 What makes up a food chain? 食物鏈由什麼組成？

plant eaters

meat eaters

prey

adapt [ə`dæpt]	使適應 Animals must **adapt** to their environment. 動物必須適應牠們的環境。
be linked to	連接到 Zebras and lions are **linked to** each other on the food chain. 斑馬和獅子在食物鏈中互相連接。
be connected to	與⋯⋯連結 Zebras and lions are **connected to** each other on the food chain. 斑馬和獅子在食物鏈中互相連結。
decay [dɪ`ke]	腐爛 A dead animal's body **decays**. 動物的死屍腐爛。
decompose [͵dikəm`poz]	分解 A dead animal's body **decomposes**. 動物的死屍分解。

Word Families 🔊 059

Food Chain Examples
食物鏈範例

Grass grows. 長草

↓

A grasshopper eats the grass.
蚱蜢吃草

↓

A frog eats the grasshopper.
青蛙吃蚱蜢

↓

A snake eats the frog.
蛇吃青蛙

↓

A hawk eats the snake.
老鷹吃蛇

Energy Pyramid
能量塔

Animals
that are not hunted
by other animals
不被其他動物獵捕的動物

Animals
that eat other animals
以其他動物為食的動物

Animals that eat plants
以植物為食的動物

Plants
植物

Checkup

A

Write I 請依提示寫出正確的英文單字。

1	食物鏈	_____	9	依賴；依靠	_____
2	食物網	_____	10	構成；組合	_____
3	能量塔	_____	11	使適應	_____
4	草食動物	_____	12	連接到	be l _____
5	肉食動物	_____	13	與……連結	be c _____
6	被捕食的動物	_____	14	腐爛	_____
7	生態系統	_____	15	分解	_____
8	關係	_____	16	被獵捕	_____

B

Complete the Sentences I 請在空格中填入最適當的答案，並視情況做適當的變化。

food chain	food web	depend on	meat	plant
ecosystem	make up	relationship	prey	energy pyramid

1 The _____ _____ starts with sunlight and plants.
食物鏈的開端是太陽和植物。

2 _____ eaters only eat food like fruits and vegetables.
草食動物只吃如水果和植物等食物。

3 _____ are made up of living and nonliving things.
生態系統由生物和非生物組成。

4 A _____ _____ connects the animals on the food chain.
食物網將食物鏈上的動物彼此連結。

5 _____ are animals that get hunted. 獵物是指被獵捕的動物。

6 Plants and animals _____ _____ one another for food.
植物與動物靠依賴彼此為食物來維生。

7 What _____ _____ a food chain? 食物鏈由什麼組成？

8 Let's learn about _____ among living things. 讓我們學習生物間的關係。

C

Read and Choose I 閱讀下列句子，並且選出最適當的答案。

1 Animals must (adapt | decay) to their environment.

2 Zebras and lions are (hunted | linked) to each other on the food chain.

3 A dead animal's body (decomposes | connects).

4 (Plant | Meat) eaters eat other animals.

Look, Read, and Write | 看圖並且依照提示，在空格中填入正確答案。

 1 ▶ all the living things in a particular area and the way they affect each other

_____

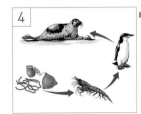 4 ▶ It shows the relationship of animals that depend on one another for food.

_____

 2 ▶ animals that eat other animals

_____

 5 ▶ to be gradually destroyed by natural processes

_____

 3 ▶ animals that get hunted

_____

 6 ▶ It shows where each animal gets its energy from.

_____

E

Read and Answer | 閱讀並且回答下列問題。　🔊 060

The Food Chain

All animals must eat to survive. Some eat plants. Some eat animals. And others eat both plants and animals. The food chain shows the relationship of each animal to the others. At the bottom of the food chain are the plant eaters. They are often prey animals. They are usually small animals like squirrels and rabbits. Sometimes they are bigger animals like deer. Animals higher on the food chain eat these animals. They might be owls, snakes, and raccoons. Then, bigger animals like bears and wolves eat these animals. Finally, we reach the top of the food chain. The most dangerous animal of all is here: man.

Fill in the blanks.

1 Some animals eat both _____ and animals.

2 Plant eaters are at the _____ of the food chain.

3 Squirrels and rabbits are _____ animals.

4 The most dangerous animal is _____ .

Review Test 3

A

Write | 請依提示寫出正確的英文單字。

1	活著的		11	呼吸
2	非生物		12	相像的；相似
3	兩棲動物		13	爬蟲類
4	哺乳動物		14	餵養
5	生命週期		15	成熟 (n.)
6	繁殖 (n.)		16	歷經；經過
7	種子		17	發芽；生長
8	花粉		18	給……授花粉
9	食物鏈		19	依賴；依靠
10	食物網		20	被獵捕

B

Choose the Correct Word | 請選出與鋪底字意思相近的答案。

1 Animals always try to stay alive.
   a. stay healthy   b. grow bigger   c. survive

2 Mammals give birth to live young.
   a. bear   b. raise   c. lay

3 A bush is a plant with many woody stems.
   a. sprout   b. shrub   c. bud

4 A dead animal's body decomposes.
   a. decays   b. germinates   c. adapts

C

Complete the Sentences | 請在空格中填入最適當的答案，並視情況做適當的變化。

stage	absorb	lungs	living thing

1 All animals and plants are _____ _____. 所有的動植物都是生物。

2 Many land animals use _____ to breathe air. 許多陸生動物用肺呼吸。

3 Animals go through four _____ during their life cycles.
   動物在生命週期中會歷經四個階段。

4 Plant leaves _____ sunlight and use it to make food.
   植物的葉子吸收太陽光並製造養分。

CHAPTER 4

Science ②

Key Words 🔊 061

01	**insect** [ˈɪnsɛkt]	(n.) 昆蟲　　*insect repellent 驅蟲藥 Crickets, grasshoppers, and ants are all **insects**. 蟋蟀、蚱蜢和螞蟻都屬於昆蟲。
02	**head** [hɛd]	(n.) 頭部　　*nod one's head 點頭　　*head for 向……走去 The **head** is one of an insect's three main body parts. 頭部是昆蟲身體主要三部分的其中之一。
03	**thorax** [ˈθoræks]	(n.) 胸部；胸甲 The **thorax** is the middle part of an insect's body. 胸甲是昆蟲身體的中間部分。
04	**abdomen** [ˈæbdəmən]	(n.) 腹部　　*pain in one's abdomen 腹痛　　*upper/lower abdomen 上／下腹 The **abdomen** is the rear part of an insect's body.　腹部是昆蟲身體的後部。
05	**leg** [lɛg]	(n.) 腳　　*one-legged 獨腳的　　*leggings 內搭褲 Every insect has six **legs**.　每種昆蟲都有六隻腳。
06	**antenna** [ænˈtɛnə]	(n.) 觸角　　*television antenna 電視天線 Insects use their **antennae** to feel and taste things. 昆蟲使用觸角來感覺與辨別事物的味道。
07	**exoskeleton** [ˌɛksoˈskɛlətn̩]	(n.) 外骨骼；外甲　　*skeleton 骨骼 An **exoskeleton** is the hard outer body of an insect. 外骨骼是昆蟲身體外部的一層硬殼。
08	**caterpillar** [ˈkætəˌpɪlə]	(n.) 毛毛蟲 A **caterpillar** hatches from an egg.　毛毛蟲從卵裡孵化出來。
09	**pupa** [ˈpjupə]	(n.) 蛹 When a caterpillar matures, it becomes a **pupa**.　毛毛蟲成熟時，會形成蛹。
10	**metamorphosis** [ˌmɛtəˈmɔfəsɪs]	(n.)〔生〕變態　　*metamorphoses【複數形】 　　　　　　　　　　*metamorphosis from A to B 從 A 到 B 的蛻變 A **metamorphosis** is a big change in body form. 變態指的是身體形態的巨大變化。

various insects

Metamorphosis

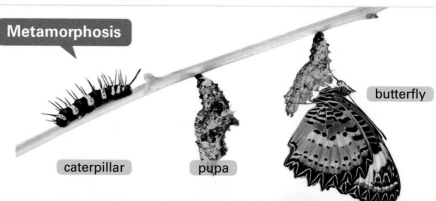

caterpillar　　　pupa　　　butterfly

larva

red palm weevil

change	變化	A caterpillar **changes** into a butterfly. 毛毛蟲變成一隻蝴蝶。
undergo [ˌʌndəˈgo]	經受；忍受	Most insects **undergo** a metamorphosis during their lives. 大部分的昆蟲在一生中需經受一次變態。
go through	經歷	Most insects **go through** a metamorphosis during their lives. 大部分的昆蟲在一生中需經歷一次變態。
gather [ˈgæðə]	採集；收集	Some ants **gather** food for other ants. 部分螞蟻替其他螞蟻收集食物。
cooperate [koˈɑpəˌret]	合作	Ants live in groups and **cooperate** with each other. 螞蟻成群生活並互相合作。

Word Families 063

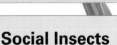

ladybug

caterpillar	毛毛蟲	A caterpillar is a baby insect before it changes into a butterfly. 毛毛蟲在變成蝴蝶前是幼蟲。
larva	幼體	A caterpillar is a larva before it changes into a butterfly. 毛毛蟲是在轉化為蝴蝶前的幼體。

The Three Parts of Insects
昆蟲的三個部分

six legs 六隻腳

three main body sections
(head, thorax, and abdomen)
身體主要三節（頭部、胸部、腹部）

a hard exoskeleton 堅硬的外骨骼

abdomen

head

thorax

leg

antenna

Kinds of Insects
昆蟲的種類

ant 螞蟻

cricket 蟋蟀

grasshopper 蚱蜢

bee 蜂；蜜蜂

caterpillar 毛毛蟲

butterfly 蝴蝶

moth 蛾

Social Insects
群居昆蟲

ant 螞蟻

honeybee 蜜蜂

Checkup

A

Write | 請依提示寫出正確的英文單字。

1	昆蟲	_____	9	蛹	_____
2	頭部	_____	10	變態	_____
3	胸部；胸甲	_____	11	變化	_____
4	腹部	_____	12	經受；忍受	_____
5	腳	_____	13	經歷	_____
6	觸角	_____	14	採集；收集	_____
7	外甲	_____	15	合作	_____
8	毛毛蟲	_____	16	幼體	_____

B

Complete the Sentences | 請在空格中填入最適當的答案，並視情況做適當的變化。

caterpillar	abdomen	exoskeleton	larva	leg
insect	antennae	metamorphosis	thorax	head

1 The _____ is one of an insect's three main body parts.
頭部是昆蟲身體主要三部分的其中之一。

2 Crickets, grasshoppers, and ants are all _____. 蟋蟀、蚱蜢和螞蟻都屬於昆蟲。

3 Insects use their _____ to feel and taste things.
昆蟲使用觸角來感覺與辨別事物的味道。

4 The _____ is the middle part of an insect's body. 胸甲是昆蟲身體的中間部分。

5 The _____ is the rear part of an insect's body. 腹部是昆蟲身體的後部。

6 A _____ hatches from an egg. 毛毛蟲從卵裡孵化出來。

7 A _____ is a big change in body form.
變態指的是身體形態的巨大變化。

8 A caterpillar is a _____ before it changes into a butterfly.
毛毛蟲是在轉化為蝴蝶前的幼體。

Read and Choose | 閱讀下列句子，並且選出最適當的答案。

1 A (grasshopper | caterpillar) changes into a butterfly.

2 Most insects (change | undergo) a metamorphosis during their lives.

3 Ants live in groups and (cooperate | gather) with each other.

4 When a caterpillar matures, it becomes a (larva | pupa).

Look, Read, and Write | 看圖並且依照提示，在空格中填入正確答案。

 ▸ animals like ants and grasshoppers

_____

 ▸ the hard outer body of an insect

_____

 ▸ an insect in its inactive form between larva and adult

_____

 ▸ a major change in the physical form of an insect or animal

_____

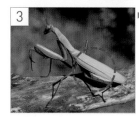 ▸ the rear part of an insect's body

_____

 ▸ two long, thin things on an insect's head that it uses to feel things

_____

E

Read and Answer | 閱讀並且回答下列問題。　🔊 064

An Insect's Body

There are many kinds of insects. They include ants, bees, butterflies, grasshoppers, and crickets. They look different from each other. But they have the same body parts in common.

All insects have three main body parts. They are the head, thorax, and abdomen. The head has the insect's mouth, eyes, and antennae. An insect uses its antennae to feel and taste things. The thorax is the middle body part. It has three pairs of legs. Adult insects have six legs. Some insects have wings on their bodies. The abdomen is the third and final part of the insect.

I have three body parts.

Which is NOT true?

1　Crickets and grasshoppers are insects.

2　All insects have a head, thorax, and abdomen.

3　An insect's antennae are on its thorax.

4　Adult insects have six legs.

The Solar System 太陽系

01	**solar system** [`solə `sɪstəm]	*(n.)* 太陽系 The **solar system** is made of the sun and the objects that move around it. 太陽系由太陽和其他環繞著太陽的物體所構成。
02	**planet** [`plænɪt]	*(n.)* 行星　*minor planet 小行星 There are eight **planets** in the solar system, and Earth is one of them. 太陽系有八大行星，地球就是其中之一。
03	**star** [stɑr]	*(n.)* 星；天體　*North Star 北極星　*five-star hotel 五星級飯店 A **star** is a big ball of hot gas.　星星是一團熾熱的氣體。
04	**satellite** [`sætḷ͵aɪt]	*(n.)* 衛星；人造衛星　*satellite navigation 衛星導航 The moon is Earth's **satellite**.　月亮是地球的衛星。
05	**constellation** [͵kɑnstə`leʃən]	*(n.)* 星座 A **constellation** is a group of stars that forms a pattern in the sky. 星座是天空中一群形成圖像的星星。
06	**rotation** [ro`teʃən]	*(n.)* 旋轉；運轉　*in rotation 輪流地；循環地　*crop rotation【農】輪作 Earth's **rotation** causes day and night.　地球運轉導致白天與夜晚的產生。
07	**orbit** [`ɔrbɪt]	*(n.)* 天體等的運行軌道　*go into orbit 進入軌道 *make an orbit round sth. = orbit around sth. 繞某物運行 Earth's **orbit** around the sun takes one year. 地球繞行太陽的軌道需要花一年。
08	**phase** [fez]	*(n.)* (月)相　*phase 階段 (early phase 早期) The moon has several different **phases**.　月球有許多不同的月相。
09	**cause** [kɔz]	*(v.)* 引起；導致　*have (no) cause to do sth. (沒)有理由做某事 *cause sb. to do sth. 使某人做某事 What **causes** day and night?　是什麼造成了白天與夜晚？
10	**repeat** [rɪ`pit]	*(v.)* 重複　*repeat oneself 重複　*repeat sth. to sb. 將某事告訴某人 The seasons **repeat** in the same pattern each year. 每年的季節都以同樣模式重複。

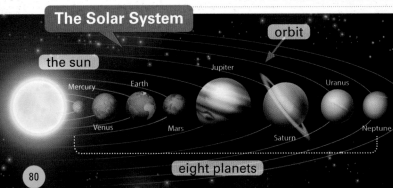

The Solar System

orbit

the sun

Mercury　Earth　Jupiter　Uranus

Venus　Mars　Saturn　Neptune

eight planets

satellite

rotate	運轉；旋轉
['rotet]	It takes 24 hours for Earth to rotate one time. 地球運轉一次需要 24 小時。
spin around	旋轉
	It takes 24 hours for Earth to spin around one time. 地球旋轉一次需要 24 小時。

revolve	自轉；公轉
[rɪ'vɑlv]	Earth revolves around the sun. 地球繞著太陽公轉。
move around	圍繞……轉動
	Earth moves around the sun. 地球圍繞著太陽轉動。

cover	覆蓋；遮蓋
['kʌvɚ]	The moon sometimes covers the sun. 月球有時候會遮蓋太陽。
hide	遮掩掉
	The moon sometimes hides the sun. 月球有時候會遮掩住太陽。

Constellations
星座

The Phases of the Moon
月球的不同月相

- **new moon** 新月
- **first quarter moon** 上弦月
- **full moon** 滿月
- **last quarter moon** 下弦月
- **crescent moon** 眉月

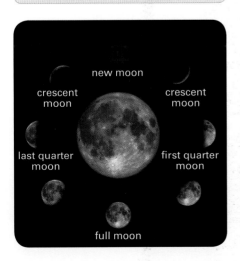

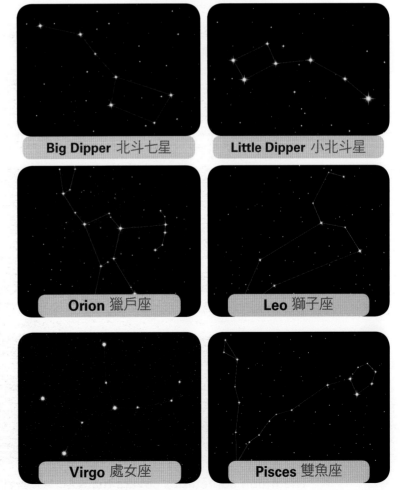

Big Dipper 北斗七星

Little Dipper 小北斗星

Orion 獵戶座

Leo 獅子座

Virgo 處女座

Pisces 雙魚座

Checkup

A

Write | 請依提示寫出正確的英文單字。

1	太陽系	_____	9	引起；導致	_____
2	行星	_____	10	重複	_____
3	星星	_____	11	運轉；旋轉 (v.)	r_____
4	（人造）衛星	_____	12	旋轉	s_____
5	星座	_____	13	自轉；公轉	_____
6	運轉；旋轉 (n.)	_____	14	圍繞……轉動	_____
7	天體的運行軌道	_____	15	覆蓋；遮蓋	_____
8	（月）相	_____	16	遮掩掉	_____

B

Complete the Sentences | 請在空格中填入最適當的答案，並視情況做適當的變化。

cause	rotation	planet	phase	constellation
season	satellite	orbit	star	solar system

1 The _____ _____ is made of the sun and the objects that move around it. 太陽系由太陽和其他環繞著太陽的物體所構成。

2 Earth's _____ around the sun takes one year. 地球繞行太陽的軌道需要花一年。

3 Earth's _____ causes day and night. 地球運轉導致白天與夜晚的產生。

4 There are eight _____ in the solar system, and Earth is one of them.
太陽系有八大行星，地球就是其中之一。

5 The moon is Earth's _____. 月亮是地球的衛星。

6 The _____ repeat in the same pattern each year.
每年的季節都以同樣模式重複。

7 A _____ is a group of stars that forms a pattern in the sky.
星座是天空中一群形成圖像的星星。

8 The moon has several different _____. 月球有許多不同的月相。

C

Read and Choose | 請選出與鋪底字意思相近的答案。

1 It takes 24 hours for Earth to rotate one time.

   a. revolve   b. spin around   c. orbit

2 Earth moves around the sun.

   a. revolves   b. repeats   c. rotates

3 The moon sometimes covers the sun.

   a. changes   b. hides   c. causes

D

Look, Read, and Write | 看圖並且依照提示，在空格中填入正確答案。

▶ an object that moves around a much larger planet

_____

▶ a group of stars that forms a pattern in the sky

_____

▶ the moon's change as it moves around Earth

_____

▶ the time when the moon appears as a bright circle

_____

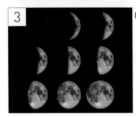
▶ the objects that move around the sun

_____

▶ the path a planet takes as it moves around the sun

_____

E

Read and Answer | 閱讀並且回答下列問題。　068

The Phases of the Moon

The moon takes about 29 days to orbit Earth. During this time, the moon seems to change shapes. We call these looks phases. The phases change as the moon moves around the earth.

The first phase is the new moon. The moon is invisible now. However, it starts to get brighter. It looks like a crescent. This next phase is called waxing crescent. Waxing means it is getting bigger. Soon, it is at the first quarter phase. Half the moon is visible. Then it becomes a full moon. The entire moon is visible. Now, the moon starts to wane. It is beginning to disappear. It goes to the last quarter stage. Then it is a waning crescent. Finally, it becomes a new moon again.

Which is NOT true?

1   The moon orbits Earth in 19 days.
2   The moon has different phases.
3   The moon is not visible during the new moon phase.
4   The full moon is completely visible.

Unit 18 The Human Body 人體奇觀

Key Words

🔊 069

| 01 | **cell** | (n.) 細胞　　*cell membrane 細胞膜 |
| | [sɛl] | The human body is made up of **cells**. 人體由細胞所組成。 |

| 02 | **tissue** | *(n.)*（動植物的）組織　　*tissue paper 衛生紙 |
| | [ˋtɪʃʊ] | **Tissues** are groups of similar cells. 組織指的是一群相似的細胞。 |

| 03 | **skin** | (n.) 皮；皮膚　　*skin-deep 膚淺的　　*skin and bone 極瘦 |
| | [skɪn] | The **skin** covers the outside of the body. 皮膚包覆身體的外部。 |

| 04 | **organ** | (n.) 器官　　*vital organ 重要器官　　*organ donation 器官捐贈 |
| | [ˋɔrgən] | The heart, brain, and liver are important **organs**.
心臟、腦，和肝臟屬於重要器官。 |

| 05 | **skeletal system** | *(n.)* 骨骼系統 |
| | [ˋskɛlətəl ˋsɪstəm] | Bones like the skull and spine form your **skeletal system**.
頭蓋骨與脊椎之類的骨頭形成骨骼系統。 |

| 06 | **muscular system** | (n.) 肌肉系統　　*muscular dystrophy【醫】肌肉萎縮症 |
| | [ˋmʌskjələ ˋsɪstəm] | The muscles in your body form the **muscular system**.
身體中的肌肉形成肌肉系統。 |

| 07 | **circulatory system** | (n.) 循環系統　　*have good/bad circulation 血液循環良好／不好 |
| | [ˋsɝkjələ͵torɪ ˋsɪstəm] | The **circulatory system** moves blood throughout the body.
循環系統幫助血液流過全身。 |

| 08 | **digestive system** | (n.) 消化系統　　*indigestion = digestive disorder 消化不良 |
| | [dəˋdʒɛstɪv ˋsɪstəm] | The stomach is part of the **digestive system**. 胃是消化系統的一部分。 |

| 09 | **nervous system** | (n.) 神經系統　　*be nervous about sth. 對某事感到緊張
*nervous tension 神經緊張 |
| | [ˋnɝvəs ˋsɪstəm] | The brain controls the body's **nervous system**. 大腦控制身體的神經系統。 |

| 10 | **respiratory system** | (n.) 呼吸系統　　*severe acute respiratory syndrome (SARS)
嚴重急性呼吸道症候群 |
| | [rɪˋspaɪrə͵torɪ ˋsɪstəm] | Your mouth, nose, and lungs are parts of your **respiratory system**.
你的嘴、鼻子與肺部都是呼吸系統的一部分。 |

Human Body System

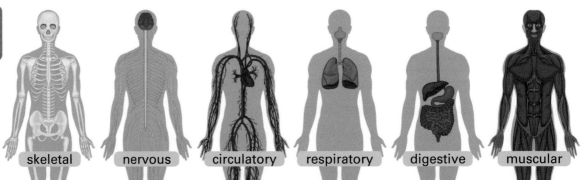

skeletal　　nervous　　circulatory　　respiratory　　digestive　　muscular

pump
[pʌmp]
收縮輸送
The heart is always busy **pumping** blood. 心臟一直不停地收縮輸送血液。

chew
[tʃu]
咀嚼
Teeth help a person **chew** food. 牙齒幫助人咀嚼食物。

swallow
[ˈswɑlo]
吞嚥
The tongue lets a person **swallow** food. 舌頭讓人可以吞下食物。

digest
[daɪˈdʒɛst]
消化
The stomach begins to **digest** food. 胃開始消化食物。

strengthen
[ˈstrɛŋθən]
增強
Calcium can **strengthen** bones. 鈣能夠增強骨頭。

make strong
強化
Calcium can **make** bones **strong**. 鈣能使骨頭強化。

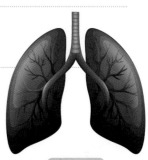

lungs

vitamin
維他命
Vitamins are very important nutrients. 維他命是非常重要的營養素。

mineral
礦物質
Minerals are very important nutrients. 礦物質是非常重要的營養素。

Organs
器官

heart 心臟
brain 腦
liver 肝臟
kidneys 腎臟
spleen 脾臟
stomach 胃
pancreas 胰臟
lungs 肺
small intestines 小腸
large intestines 大腸
appendix 盲腸；闌尾

Your Skeletal System
骨骼系統

skull
頭蓋骨
spine (backbone)
脊椎（脊骨）
arm bones
上臂骨
hip bones
臀骨；髖骨
leg bones
小腿骨

Your Muscular System
肌肉系統

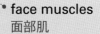
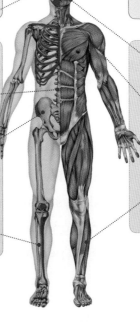

face muscles
面部肌
neck muscles
頸肌
arm muscles
上臂肌
leg muscles
小腿肌

Checkup

A

Write | 請依提示寫出正確的英文單字。

1	細胞	_____	9	神經系統	_____
2	組織	_____	10	呼吸系統	_____
3	皮膚	_____	11	收縮輸送	_____
4	器官	_____	12	咀嚼	_____
5	骨骼系統	_____	13	吞嚥	_____
6	肌肉系統	_____	14	消化	_____
7	循環系統	_____	15	增強	_____
8	消化系統	_____	16	強化	_____

B

Complete the Sentences | 請在空格中填入最適當的答案，並視情況做適當的變化。

tissue	spine	stomach	skeletal	digestive
circulatory	skin	nervous	cell	organ

1 The human body is made up of _____. 人體由細胞所組成。

2 The _____ covers the outside of the body. 皮膚包覆身體的外部。

3 _____ are groups of similar cells. 組織指的是一群相似的細胞。

4 The heart, brain, and liver are important _____.
心臟、腦，和肝臟屬於重要器官。

5 The brain controls the body's _____ system. 大腦控制身體的神經系統。

6 The stomach is part of the _____ system. 胃是消化系統的一部分。

7 The _____ system moves blood throughout the body.
循環系統幫助血液流過全身。

8 Bones like the skull and spine form your _____ system.
頭蓋骨與脊椎之類的骨頭形成骨骼系統。

C

Read and Choose | 閱讀下列句子，並且選出最適當的答案。

1 Calcium can (swallow | strengthen) bones.

2 The heart is always busy (pumping | digesting) blood.

3 Teeth help a person (make | chew) food.

4 The tongue lets a person (swallow | pump) food.

Look, Read, and Write ｜ 看圖並且依照提示，在空格中填入正確答案。

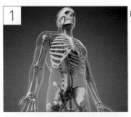 ▶ the system of bones like the skull and spine

_____

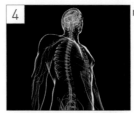 ▶ the system that carries messages to and from your brain

_____

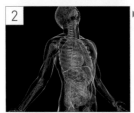 ▶ the system that moves your blood around your body

_____

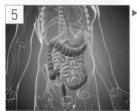 ▶ the system that breaks your food down

_____

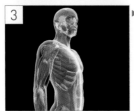 ▶ the system that is made up of your muscles

_____

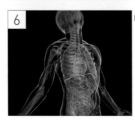 ▶ the system that is made up of your mouth, nose, and lungs

_____

E

Read and Answer ｜ 閱讀並且回答下列問題。　🔘 072

The Organs of the Human Body

Organs are very important parts of the human body. They help do certain body functions. There are many different organs. One important organ is the heart. It pumps blood all throughout the body. Without a heart, a person cannot live. The brain runs the body's nervous system. It controls both mental and physical activities. People can breathe thanks to their lungs. A person has two lungs. The stomach helps digest food. It breaks food down into nutrients so the rest of the body can use it. The liver also helps with digestion. One of the most important organs is the biggest. It's the skin. It covers a person's entire body!

Fill in the blanks.

1　There are many different _____ in the body.

2　The _____ pumps blood throughout the body.

3　People have _____ lungs.

4　The biggest organ is the _____ .

Motion and Forces 運動與力量

Key Words 🔊 073

01	**motion** [`moʃən]	*(n.)*（物體的）移動；動作　　*motionless 不動的；靜止的　　*slow-motion 慢動作的 **Motion** is movement. 物體的移動稱為運動。
02	**speed** [spid]	*(n.)* 速度　　*speeding 超速行車　　*speed up 加速 **Speed** is how fast objects move. 速度指的是物體移動的程度。
03	**force** [fors]	*(n.)*〔物〕力；力的強度　　*force sb. to do sth. 強迫某人做某事　　*air force 空軍 It takes **force** for objects to move. 物體需要力量才能移動。
04	**gravity** [`grævətɪ]	*(n.)* 地心引力　　*center of gravity 重心　　*law of gravity 萬有引力定律 **Gravity** is the force that pulls things toward Earth. 地心引力是將物體拉向地球的力。
05	**friction** [`frɪkʃən]	*(n.)* 摩擦；摩擦力　　*friction between …… 之間的摩擦　　*trade friction 貿易摩擦 **Friction** often occurs when two things rub against each other. 當兩個物體互相摩擦通常會產生摩擦力。
06	**magnet** [`mægnɪt]	*(n.)* 磁鐵　　*permanent magnet 永久磁鐵 A **magnet** pulls metals like iron and steel. 磁鐵吸引如鋼鐵類的金屬。
07	**attraction** [ə`trækʃən]	*(n.)* 吸引力　　*magnetic attraction 磁力　　*tourist attraction 觀光勝地 There is an **attraction** between a magnet and metals. 磁鐵與金屬間存在著吸引力。
08	**pole** [pol]	*(n.)* 極；磁極　　*North/South Pole 北／南極　　*magnetic pole 磁極 All magnets have two **poles** called the North pole and the South pole. 所有的磁鐵都有兩個磁極，稱作北極與南極。
09	**magnetic field** [mæg`nɛtɪk fild]	*(n.)* 磁場 Magnets attract iron when it is inside a **magnetic field**. 當鐵進入磁場裡，就會受到磁鐵的吸引。
10	**compass** [`kʌmpəs]	*(n.)* 羅盤；指南針　　*magnetic compass 磁羅盤　　*pocket compass 袖珍羅盤 A **compass** always points to the north. 指南針總是指向北方。

motion and speed

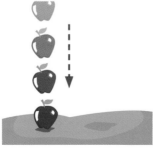
the law of gravity

gravity-free state

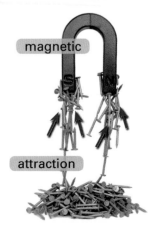
magnetic

attraction

move	移動 What makes things **move**?　是什麼使事物移動？
pull	牽引 Opposite poles **pull** each other.　相反兩極互相牽引。
attract [əˋtrækt]	吸引 Opposite poles **attract** each other.　相反兩極互相吸引。
push away	推開 The same poles on different magnets **push** each other **away**. 兩個磁鐵的同極會互相推擠。
repel [rɪˋpɛl]	排斥 The same poles on different magnets **repel** each other. 兩個磁鐵的同極會互相排斥。

Word Families 🔊 075

Magnets
磁鐵

bar magnet
條狀磁鐵

round magnet
圓形磁鐵

horseshoe magnet
馬蹄型磁鐵

Poles
兩極

N pole 北極

S pole 南極

magnetic pole 磁極

magnetic field 磁場

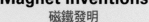
magnetic pole

magnetic field

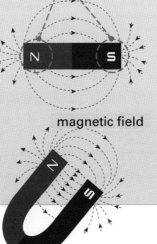

Magnet Inventions
磁鐵發明

can opener
開罐器

magnet kit
磁鐵工具箱

refrigerator magnet
冰箱用磁鐵

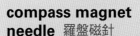

compass magnet needle 羅盤磁針

Checkup

A

Write ｜ 請依提示寫出正確的英文單字。

1	動作	_____	9	磁極	_____
2	速度	_____	10	磁場	_____
3	力（量）	_____	11	羅盤；指南針	_____
4	地心引力	_____	12	移動	_____
5	摩擦力	_____	13	吸引	a_____
6	磁鐵	_____	14	牽引	p_____
7	吸引力	_____	15	排斥	_____
8	（兩）極	_____	16	推開	_____

B

Complete the Sentences ｜ 請在空格中填入最適當的答案，並視情況做適當的變化。

motion	friction	magnetic field	compass	pole
speed	attraction	magnet	gravity	force

1　It takes _____ for objects to move.　物體需要力量才能移動。

2　_____ is movement.　物體的移動稱為運動。

3　_____ is the force that pulls things toward Earth.
地心引力是將物體拉向地球的力。

4　_____ often occurs when two things rub against each other.
當兩個物體互相摩擦通常會產生摩擦力。

5　All magnets have two _____ called the North pole and the South pole.
所有的磁鐵都有兩個磁極，稱作北極與南極。

6　A _____ pulls metals like iron and steel.　磁鐵吸引如鋼鐵類的金屬。

7　There is an _____ between a magnet and metals.
磁鐵與金屬間存在著吸引力。

8　Magnets attract iron when it is inside a _____ _____.
當鐵進入磁場裡，就會受到磁鐵的吸引。

C

Read and Choose ｜ 閱讀下列句子，並且選出最適當的答案。

1　Opposite poles (pull | push) each other.

2　The same poles on different magnets (pull | push) each other away.

3　A magnet (repels | attracts) metals like iron and steel.

4　A compass always points to the (south | north).

Look, Read, and Write | 看圖並且依照提示，在空格中填入正確答案。

 ▸ an object that can pull things made of iron or steel

_____

 ▸ the force that pulls things toward Earth

_____

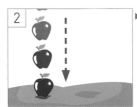 ▸ the lines of force surrounding a magnetic material

_____

 ▸ It means how fast objects move.

_____

 ▸ It always points north.

_____

 ▸ the act of rubbing one thing against another

 E

Read and Answer | 閱讀並且回答下列問題。 076

How a Magnet Works

Some objects are attracted to each other. And some objects repel each other. A magnet is an object that can attract or repel other objects. Magnets can move things like iron or steel without touching them. How does a magnet work? A magnet is a piece of magnetized metal like iron or nickel. It has two separate poles. It has a north-seeking pole, or N pole, and a south-seeking pole, or S pole. This creates a magnetic field. So it can attract or repel different metals. If the north pole of a magnet is near the south pole of another one, the two will be attracted. But if two north poles of two magnets are near each other, they will repel each other.

Answer the questions.

1   What can magnets move without touching them? _____

2   What is a magnet made of?   _____

3   What are a magnet's two poles?   _____

4   If two north poles of two magnets are near, what will happen?

_____

Unit 20 Sound 聲音

Key Words 🔘 077

01	**sound** [saʊnd]	*(n.)*〔物〕聲；聲音　*soundtrack 聲帶；電影配樂　*save and sound 安然無恙 Sound travels through the air. 聲音經由空氣傳遞。
02	**noise** [nɔɪz]	*(n.)* 噪音　*make/produce a noise 發出聲音　*white noise 白噪音 Noise is sound that is unpleasant to the ears. 噪音是指不悅耳的聲音。
03	**vibration** [vaɪˋbreʃən]	*(n.)* 顫動；振動　*seismic vibration 地震振動 Sound is caused by vibrations. 聲音由振動而產生。
04	**tone** [ton]	*(n.)* 聲調　*in a/an . . . tone 以……的口吻 　　　*set the tone for sth. 為某事物定基調 Changing the tone alters the quality of a sound. 改變聲調就是改變聲音的質。
05	**sound wave** [saʊnd wev]	*(n.)* 聲波 Sound waves travel very fast. 聲波的傳遞十分快速。
06	**frequency** [ˋfrikwənsɪ]	*(n.)*〔物〕頻率　*high/low frequency 高／低頻率 　　　　*with increasing frequency 越來越頻繁地 Some sound frequencies are too high for humans to hear. 某些音頻過高，以致於人類無法聽見。
07	**loudness** [ˋlaʊdnɪs]	*(n.)* 響度；音量　*loud 響亮的；大聲的 The loudness of a sound is how loud or soft it is. 聲音的響度指的是大小聲。
08	**pitch** [pɪtʃ]	*(n.)* 音高　*rise in pitch 提高聲調 A whistle makes a sound with a high pitch. 口哨發出高音的聲響。
09	**speed of sound** [spid ɑv saʊnd]	*(n.)* 音速 Some planes can fly faster than the speed of sound. 某些飛機可以比音速移動得更快。
10	**noise pollution** [nɔɪz pəˋluʃən]	*(n.)* 噪音汙染 Noise pollution is very loud and sounds bad to people. 噪音汙染是對人類有害的吵雜聲音。

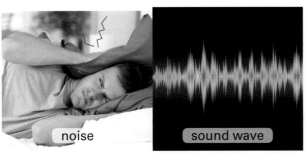
noise

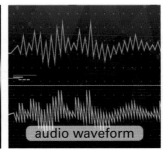
sound wave

audio waveform

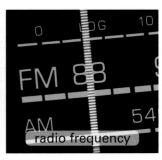
radio frequency

vibrate [ˈvaɪbret]	振動 Objects make sounds when they **vibrate**. 物體振動時會發出聲響。
hear	聽見 Humans can **hear** many different sounds. 人類可以聽見許多不同的聲響。
listen to	聽；收聽 Some people like to **listen to** music. 某些人喜歡聽音樂。
make sound	發出聲響 Dolphins **make sounds** to find things underwater. 海豚藉由發出聲音來偵測海底事物。
travel through	穿過 Sound can also **travel through** solids and liquids. 聲音還可以穿過固體與液體。
move through	穿透 Sound can also **move through** solids and liquids. 聲音還可以穿透固體與液體。

Word Families 🔘 079

What does sound travel through?
聲音可以穿過哪些事物？

gases, such as air
氣體，如空氣

liquids, such as water
液體，如水

solids, such as wood and glass
固體，如木頭與玻璃

Noise Pollution
噪音汙染

airplane 飛機

construction work 建築工程

car 汽車

truck 卡車

bus 公車

train 火車

loud music
吵雜音樂

a string telephone,
sound travels through solids

Checkup

A

Write | 請依提示寫出正確的英文單字。

1	聲音	_____	9	音速	_____
2	噪音	_____	10	噪音汙染	_____
3	振動；顫動 (n.)	_____	11	振動 (v.)	_____
4	聲調	_____	12	聽見	_____
5	聲波	_____	13	聽；收聽	_____
6	頻率	_____	14	發出聲響	_____
7	響度；音量	_____	15	穿過	t_____
8	音高	_____	16	穿透	m_____

B

Complete the Sentences | 請在空格中填入最適當的答案，並視情況做適當的變化。

tone	sound	vibration	pollution	vibrate
pitch	speed	sound wave	loudness	frequency

1 _____ travels through the air. 聲音經由空氣傳遞。

2 Sound is caused by _____. 聲音由振動而產生。

3 Some sound _____ are too high for humans to hear.
某些音頻過高，以致於人類無法聽見。

4 Changing the _____ alters the quality of a sound.
改變聲調就是改變聲音的質。

5 A whistle makes a sound with a high _____. 口哨發出高音的聲響。

6 Some planes can fly faster than the _____ of sound.
某些飛機可以比音速移動得更快。

7 The _____ of a sound is how loud or soft it is.
聲音的響度指的是大小聲。

8 _____ _____ travel very fast. 聲波的傳遞十分快速。

C

Read and Choose | 閱讀下列句子，並且選出最適當的答案。

1 Objects make sounds when they (vibrate | travel).

2 Sound can (cause | travel) through solids and liquids.

3 Humans can (hear | move) many different sounds.

4 A whistle makes a sound with a high (loudness | pitch).

D

Look, Read, and Write | 看圖並且依照提示，在空格中填入正確答案。

► a sound that is unpleasant to hear

_____

► Sound can travel through the air, liquids, and

_____

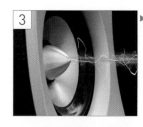
► It is about how loud or soft a sound is.

_____

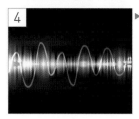
► a wave that transmits sound

_____

E

Read and Answer | 閱讀並且回答下列問題。 ⊙ 080

The Invention of the Telephone

A long time ago, there were no telephones. But people knew that sound travels by vibrations. So many people tried to invent the telephone. Alexander Graham Bell was one of these people. He wanted to use electricity to transmit sound.

He thought he could turn sound into electric pulses. Then it could move through wires. He worked very hard on his project. One day in 1876, he had an accident in his office. He needed his assistant Watson. He said, "Watson, come here. I want you." Watson was in another part of the house. But he heard Bell over the telephone. Finally, Bell was successful. He had invented the telephone!

Fill in the blanks.

1 Alexander Graham Bell wanted to invent the _____.

2 Bell wanted to use _____ to transmit sound.

3 In _____, Bell made the first telephone.

4 Bell called his assistant _____ on the telephone.

Review Test 4

A

Write | 請依提示寫出正確的英文單字。

1	胸部；胸甲 _____	11	變態 _____
2	腹部 _____	12	經受；忍受 _____
3	星座 _____	13	旋轉；運轉 (v.) r_____
4	旋轉；運轉 (n.) _____	14	自轉；公轉 _____
5	器官 _____	15	骨骼系統 _____
6	循環系統 _____	16	呼吸系統 _____
7	移動；動作 _____	17	磁極 _____
8	摩擦 _____	18	磁場 _____
9	顫動；振動 (n.) _____	19	振動 _____
10	頻率 _____	20	穿過 t_____

B

Choose the Correct Word | 請選出與鋪底字意思相近的答案。

1 Most insects undergo a metamorphosis during their lives.

   a. go through   b. cooperate   c. change

2 It takes 24 hours for Earth to rotate one time.

   a. revolve   b. spin around   c. orbit

3 Earth moves around the sun.

   a. revolves   b. repeats   c. rotates

4 Opposite poles pull each other.

   a. repel   b. move   c. attract

C

Complete the Sentences | 請在空格中填入最適當的答案，並視情況做適當的變化。

gravity	cell	planet	caterpillar

1 A _____ hatches from an egg. 毛毛蟲從卵裡孵化出來。

2 There are eight _____ in the solar system, and Earth is one of them.
太陽系有八大行星，地球就是其中之一。

3 The human body is made up of _____. 人體由細胞所組成。

4 _____ is the force that pulls things toward Earth.
地心引力是將物體拉向地球的力。

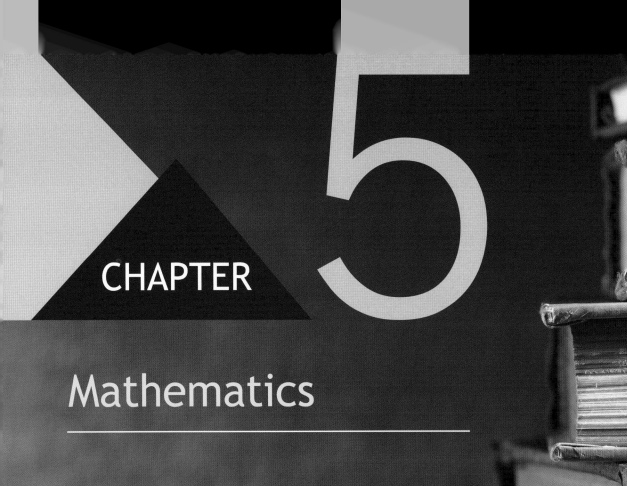

CHAPTER 5

Mathematics

Key Words 🔘 081

01	**number sentence**	*(n.)* 數字方程式
	[ˋnʌmbɚ ˋsɛntəns]	4+5=9 is an example of a **number sentence**. 4+5=9 是一個數字方程式。

02	**addend**	*(n.)*〔數〕加數
	[əˋdɛnd]	4 and 5 are the **addends** in the above number sentence. 4 和 5 是以上數字方程式（4+5=9）的加數。

03	**even number**	*(n.)* 偶數
	[ˋivən ˋnʌmbɚ]	2, 4, 6, 8, and 10 are **even numbers**. 2, 4, 6, 8 和 10 都是偶數。

04	**odd number**	*(n.)* 奇數
	[ɑd ˋnʌmbɚ]	1, 3, 5, 7, and 9 are **odd numbers**. 1, 3, 5, 7 和 9 都是奇數。

05	**equation**	*(n.)* 方程式；等式　*chemical equation 化學方程式
	[ɪˋkweʃən]	*simple/quadratic equation 一次／二次方程式 Can you write this math **equation**? 你可以寫出這道數學方程式嗎？

06	**number line**	*(n.)* 數線
	[ˋnʌmbɚ laɪn]	A **number line** shows the numbers in order. 數線表現數字的順序。

07	**estimate**	*(n.)* 估計；估計數　*at a rough estimate 粗估
	[ˋɛstə‚met]	Circle the better **estimate**. 圈出較好的估計值。

08	**missing number**	*(n.)* 缺少的數字
	[ˋmɪsɪŋ ˋnʌmbɚ]	Find the **missing numbers** in the puzzle. 找出謎題裡缺少的數字。

09	**fraction**	*(n.)* 小部分；〔數〕分數
	[ˋfrækʃən]	A **fraction** represents a portion of a whole. 一個部分代表整體中的幾分之幾。

10	**three-digit**	*(a.)* 三位數的
	[θriˋdɪdʒɪt]	We call numbers like 100 and 250 **three-digit** numbers. 我們稱 100 和 250 這種數字為三位數。

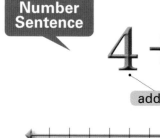
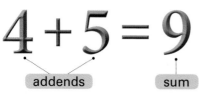

Number Sentence

4 + 5 = 9

addends　　sum

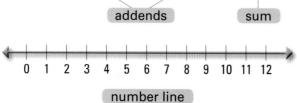

number line

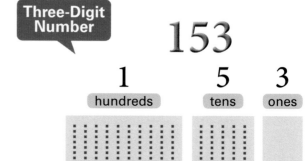

Three-Digit Number

153

1 hundreds　5 tens　3 ones

skip-count　跳位計數
Skip-count by fives. 5, 10, 15.　以 5 為單位來跳位計數，會得到 5、10、15。

estimate　估算；估計
[ˈɛstəˌmet]
Estimate the number of balls in the box.　估算箱子裡面的球數。

double　加倍
If you double 5, you get 10.　如果你將 5 增加一倍，會得到 10。

halve　減半
[hæv]
If you halve 6, you get 3.　如果你將 6 減半，會得到 3。

round　四捨五入
Round the number to the nearest ten.　將這個數字四捨五入。

round to　四捨五入為
56 rounds to 60. 34 rounds to 30.　56 四捨五入為 60，34 四捨五入為 30。

Word Families 🔊 083

ones　一倍
20 ones are the same as 2 tens.　20 個 1 等於 2 個 10。

tens　十倍
2 tens mean 20.　2 個 10 等於 20。

hundreds　百倍
20 tens mean 2 hundreds.　20 個 10 等於 200。

tally mark　劃記號
Make a tally mark for each choice.　替每一個選項劃記號。

tally table　劃記表
What does one tally mark stand for in a tally table?
每一個記號在劃記表上代表什麼？

tally mark

Tally Table

What are your favorite fruits?
（你最喜歡的水果是什麼？）

Name	Tally	Total
Orange	̶卌̶ I	6
Apple	̶卌̶ IIII	9
Banana	IIII	4

Fractions 分數

one half	$\frac{1}{2}$	one third	$\frac{1}{3}$
one fourth	$\frac{1}{4}$	one fifth	$\frac{1}{5}$
one sixth	$\frac{1}{6}$	one seventh	$\frac{1}{7}$
one eighth	$\frac{1}{8}$	one ninth	$\frac{1}{9}$
one tenth	$\frac{1}{10}$	three tenths	$\frac{3}{10}$
two ninths	$\frac{2}{9}$	four fifths	$\frac{4}{5}$

Checkup

A Write | 請依提示寫出正確的英文單字。

1	數字方程式	_____	9	缺少的數字	_____
2	加數	_____	10	三位數的	_____
3	偶數	_____	11	跳位計數	_____
4	奇數	_____	12	估算；估計 (v.)	_____
5	方程式	_____	13	加倍	_____
6	數線	_____	14	減半	_____
7	估計 (n.)	_____	15	四捨五入	_____
8	分數	_____	16	劃記	_____

B Complete the Sentences | 請在空格中填入最適當的答案，並視情況做適當的變化。

number sentence	tally mark	halve	round	fraction
three-digit	equation	tens	addend	estimate

1 4+5=9 is an example of a _____ _____. 4+5=9 是一個數字方程式。

2 Circle the better _____. 圈出較好的估計值。

3 Can you write this math _____? 你可以寫出這道數學方程式嗎？

4 4 and 5 are the _____ in the number sentence 4+5=9.
4 和 5 是數字方程式 4+5=9 的加數。

5 Make a _____ _____ for each choice. 替每一個選項劃記號。

6 56 _____ to 60. 56 四捨五入為整數 60。

7 We call numbers like 100 and 250 _____ numbers.
我們稱 100 和 250 這種數字為三位數。

8 20 ones are the same as 2 _____. 20 個 1 等於 2 個 10。

C Read and Choose | 閱讀下列句子，並且選出最適當的答案。

1 (Estimate | Skip-count) the number of balls in the box.

2 If you (halve | double) 5, you get 10.

3 If you (halve | double) 6, you get 3.

4 (Round | Around) the number to the nearest ten.

100

Look, Read, and Write | 看圖並且依照提示，在空格中填入正確答案。

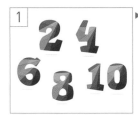
▸ numbers like 2, 4, 6, 8, and 10
_____

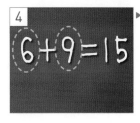
▸ 6 and 9 in the number sentence 6+9=15
_____

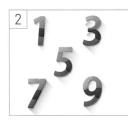
▸ numbers like 1, 3, 5, 7, and 9
_____

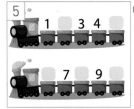
▸ the number that is missing
_____

▸ divide something into two equal parts
_____

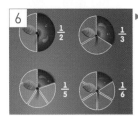
▸ a portion of a whole
_____

Read and Answer | 閱讀並且回答下列問題。 ⦿ 084

Number Sentences

People use sentences when they speak, but they can also use sentences when they do math. How can they do this? It's easy. They use number sentences.

Let's think of a math problem. You have four apples, but then you add two more. That gives you a total of six apples. Now, let's make that a number sentence. It would look like this: 4+2=6. You can make number sentences for addition, and you can make them for subtraction, too. Your friend has ten pieces of candy, but he eats five pieces. Now he has five pieces left. Let's make a number sentence for that. Here it is: 10-5=5.

Fill in the blanks.

1   People use _____ when they speak.

2   People use _____ _____ when they do math.

3   1+3=4 is a _____ sentence.

4   You can make number sentences for _____ and subtraction.

Key Words 🔊 085

| 01 | **time** [taɪm] | (n.) 時間　*in time 及時　*take one's time (to do sth.)（做某事）不著急 |
| | | People can tell **time** with a calendar or a clock.
人們可以用日曆或時鐘知道時間。 |

| 02 | **calendar** [ˋkæləndɚ] | (n.) 日曆　*solar/lunar calendar 陽／陰曆 |
| | | A **calendar** shows time in days, weeks, and months.
日曆用日、週和月的方式表現時間。 |

| 03 | **day** [de] | (n.) 日子；一天　*daybreak 黎明；破曉　*day by day 一天天 |
| | | There are 365 **days** in 1 year.　一年有 365 天。 |

| 04 | **week** [wik] | (n.) 星期　*weekday 平日；工作日　*weekend 週末 |
| | | There are about 4 **weeks** in 1 month.　一個月大約有 4 週。 |

| 05 | **month** [mʌnθ] | (n.) 月分　*next/last month 下個／上個月 |
| | | There are 12 **months** in 1 year.　一年有 12 個月。 |

| 06 | **year** [jɪr] | (n.) 年　*years to come 未來的日子　*all year round 一年到頭 |
| | | There are about 52 weeks in 1 **year**.　一年大約有 52 週。 |

| 07 | **timeline** [ˋtaɪmˋlaɪn] | (n.) 時間軸 |
| | | A **timeline** shows the dates when some events happened.
時間軸顯示某事件發生的日期。 |

| 08 | **second** [ˋsɛkənd] | (n.) 秒　*second hand 秒針　*in a second 馬上 |
| | | There are 60 **seconds** in 1 minute.　一分鐘有 60 秒。 |

| 09 | **minute** [ˋmɪnɪt] | (n.) 分鐘　*any minute 隨時　*the last minute 最後一刻 |
| | | There are 60 **minutes** in 1 hour.　一個小時有 60 分鐘。 |

| 10 | **hour** [aʊr] | (n.) 小時　*hourglass 沙漏　*rush hour 尖峰時刻 |
| | | There are 24 **hours** in 1 day.　一天有 24 個小時。 |

Calendar

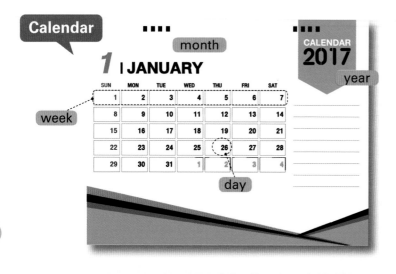

measure
[ˈmɛʒɚ]

測量；計量
We can **measure** time with a calendar or a clock.
我們可以用日曆或時鐘來計量時間。

calculate
[ˈkælkjəˌlet]

計算
We can **calculate** time with a calendar or a clock.
我們可以用日曆或時鐘來計算時間。

pass　　　　推移；流逝　　A day **passes** in 24 hours. 一天 24 小時流逝。
go by　　　（時間）過去　A day **goes by** in 24 hours. 一天 24 小時就過去了。

Word Families　● 087

noon	中午；正午	Noon is 12:00 in the day. 中午是白天十二點。
midnight	午夜；半夜十二點鐘	Midnight is 12:00 at night. 午夜是晚上十二點。
A.M.	午前；上午	A.M. is from midnight until noon. 午前是從午夜到中午。
P.M.	午後；下午	P.M. is from noon until midnight. 午後是從中午到午夜。
half hour	半個鐘頭	There are 30 minutes in a half hour. 半個鐘頭是 30 分鐘。
quarter hour	1/4 個鐘頭；15 分鐘	There are 15 minutes in a quarter hour. 1/4 個鐘頭是 15 分鐘。

Telling Time　報時

`1:00`	It is one o'clock. 現在是一點。
`1:10`	It is one ten. 現在是一點 10 分。 It is ten minutes after 1. 現在是一點又 10 分鐘。
`2:15`	It is two fifteen. 現在是兩點 15 分。 It is fifteen minutes after 2. 現在是兩點又 15 分。 It is a quarter after 2. 現在是兩點又 15 分。
`4:30`	It is four thirty. 現在是四點半。 It is thirty minutes after 4. 現在是四點又 30 分。 It is half past 4. 現在是四點又 30 分。
`5:45`	It is five forty-five. 現在是五點 45 分。 It is forty-five minutes after 5. 現在是五點又 45 分。 It is fifteen minutes before 6. 再 15 分就六點。 It is a quarter to 6. 再 15 分就六點。

Checkup

A

Write | 請依提示寫出正確的英文單字。

1	時間	_____	9	小時	_____
2	日曆	_____	10	測量；計量	_____
3	星期	_____	11	計算	_____
4	月分	_____	12	推移；流逝	_____
5	年	_____	13	（時間）過去	_____
6	時間軸	_____	14	中午；正午	_____
7	秒	_____	15	午夜；半夜十二點鐘	_____
8	分鐘	_____	16	1/4 個鐘頭；15 分鐘	_____

B

Complete the Sentences | 請在空格中填入最適當的答案，並視情況做適當的變化。

calendar	time	timeline	noon	month
calculate	week	second	year	minute

1 People can tell _____ with a calendar or a clock.
   人們可以用日曆或時鐘知道時間。

2 A _____ shows time in days, weeks, and months.
   日曆用日、週和月的方式表現時間。

3 There are 12 _____ in 1 year. 一年有 12 個月。

4 There are about 4 _____ in 1 month. 一個月大約有 4 週。

5 There are about 52 weeks in 1 _____. 一年大約有 52 週。

6 There are 60 _____ in 1 minute. 一分鐘有 60 秒。

7 There are 60 _____ in 1 hour. 一個小時有 60 分鐘。

8 A _____ shows the dates when some events happened.
   時間軸顯示某事件發生的日期。

C

Read and Choose | 閱讀下列句子，並且選出最適當的答案。

1 We can (measure | pass) time with a calendar or a clock.

2 There are 15 minutes in a (half | quarter) hour.

3 There are 30 minutes in a (half | quarter) hour.

4 P.M. is from noon until (night | midnight).

D

Look, Read, and Write | 看圖並且依照提示，在空格中填入正確答案。

Write the time in two ways.

▶ 1) It is _____ _____.
2) It is _____ minutes after ____.

▶ 1) It is _____
_____.
2) It is ____ _____ to ____.

▶ 1) It is _____ _____.
2) It is _____ minutes after ____.

▶ 1) It is _____ minutes before ____.
2) It is _____ to ____.

▶ 1) It is _____ _____.
2) It is _____ past ____.

▶ 1) It is _____ minutes before _____.
2) It is _____ to _____.

E

Read and Answer | 閱讀並且回答下列問題。 🔘 088

Time Passes

John wakes up in the morning at seven A.M. School starts at eight o'clock, so he has one hour to get there. When he arrives at school, it's seven forty-five. School will begin in fifteen minutes. School runs from eight until three o'clock. That's a total of seven hours. In the morning, John has class from eight until noon, so he has a total of four hours of class. Then he has lunch from twelve o'clock until a quarter to one. After that, from twelve forty-five until three P.M., he has more classes. That's a total of two hours and fifteen minutes. Finally, at three, school finishes, and John can go home.

It's time to go home.

Answer the questions.

1 What time does John's school start? _____

2 How many hours of class does John have in the morning? _____

3 When does lunch finish? _____

4 What time does John's school finish? _____

Solid Figures and Plane Figures
立體圖形與平面圖形

Key Words 🔊 089

01 geometry
[dʒɪˈɑmətrɪ]
(n.) 幾何學
We study shapes and figures in **geometry**.
我們在幾何學學到形狀與圖形。

02 figure
[ˈfɪgjɚ]
(n.) 圖形　*figure out 算出；想出　*six-figure 六位數的
A **figure** is a regular shape in geometry. 圖形在幾何學裡是一個規則的形狀。

03 solid figure
[ˈsɑlɪd ˈfɪgjɚ]
(n.) 立體圖形
Spheres, cubes, and pyramids are some **solid figures**.
球體、立方體和三角體是幾種立體圖形。

04 plane figure
[plen ˈfɪgjɚ]
(n.) 平面圖形
A square, triangle, and rhombus are some **plane figures**.
四方形、三角形和菱形是幾種平面圖形。

05 flat surface
[flæt ˈsɝfɪs]
(n.) 平面
A cube has a **flat surface**. 立方體有一個平面。

06 curved surface
[kɝvd ˈsɝfɪs]
(n.) 曲面
A sphere has a **curved surface**. 球體有一個曲面。

07 congruent
[ˈkɑŋgruənt]
(a.) 〔數〕全等的　*be congruent with . . . 與……一致
　　　　　　　　　　*congruent triangles 全等三角形
Two figures with the same size and shape are **congruent**.
兩個擁有同樣大小與形狀的圖形是全等的。

08 line of symmetry
[laɪn ɑv ˈsɪmɪtrɪ]
(n.) 對稱軸
A **line of symmetry** divides a figure into two congruent figures.
對稱軸將一個圖形分成兩個全等形。

09 perimeter
[pəˈrɪmətɚ]
(n.) 〔數〕周長
You get the **perimeter** when you add up the length of each side of a figure. 把圖形的每邊相加會得到周長。

10 area
[ˈɛrɪə]
(n.) 面積　*an area of . . . ……的面積　*disaster area 災區
Find the **area** of the figure. 找出此圖形的面積。

Plane Figures

triangle　square　rectangle　rhombus　pentagon　hexagon

Solid Figures

sphere　cone　cube　cylinder　pyramid　rectangular prism

cross out	刪掉;劃掉 **Cross out** the figures that do not have the same shape. 劃掉不是同樣形狀的圖形。
circle ['sɝkḷ]	圈選;圈出 **Circle** the figures that have 4 faces. 圈出擁有四個面的圖形。
slide [slaɪd]	滑動 Solid figures with a flat surface **slide**. 有平面的立體圖形會滑動。
roll	滾動 Solid figures with a curved surface **roll**. 有曲面的立體圖形會滾動。
connect [kə'nɛkt]	連接;連結 **Connect** the two points by drawing a line. 兩個點間畫上一條線來連接。
find	得到 Add the length of each side to **find** the perimeter. 把每邊的邊長相加便能得到周長。

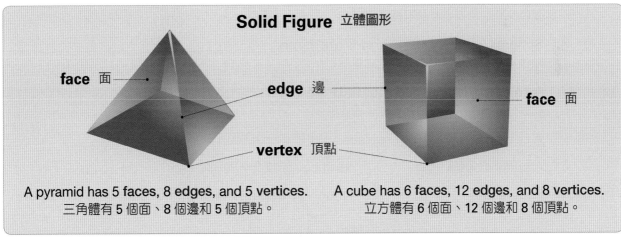

Solid Figure 立體圖形

face 面 — edge 邊 — face 面 — vertex 頂點

A pyramid has 5 faces, 8 edges, and 5 vertices.
三角體有 5 個面、8 個邊和 5 個頂點。

A cube has 6 faces, 12 edges, and 8 vertices.
立方體有 6 個面、12 個邊和 8 個頂點。

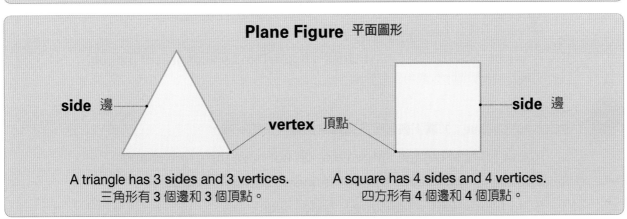

Plane Figure 平面圖形

side 邊 — vertex 頂點 — side 邊

A triangle has 3 sides and 3 vertices.
三角形有 3 個邊和 3 個頂點。

A square has 4 sides and 4 vertices.
四方形有 4 個邊和 4 個頂點。

Checkup

Write | 請依提示寫出正確的英文單字。

1	幾何學	_____	9	對稱軸	_____
2	圖形	_____	10	〔數〕周長	_____
3	立體圖形	_____	11	刪掉；劃掉	_____
4	平面圖形	_____	12	滑動	_____
5	曲面	_____	13	滾動	_____
6	平面	_____	14	面	_____
7	〔數〕全等的	_____	15	邊	_____
8	面積	_____	16	頂點	_____

B

Complete the Sentences | 請在空格中填入最適當的答案，並視情況做適當的變化。

solid figure	geometry	curved	vertex	perimeter
plane figure	congruent	flat	edge	symmetry

1 We study shapes and figures in _____.
我們在幾何學學到形狀與圖形。

2 Spheres, cubes, and pyramids are some _____ _____.
球體、立方體和三角體是幾種立體圖形。

3 A square, triangle, and rhombus are some _____ _____.
四方形、三角形和菱形是幾種平面圖形。

4 A cube has a _____ surface. 立方體有一個平面。

5 A sphere has a _____ surface. 球體有一個曲面。

6 You get the _____ when you add up the length of each side of a figure.
把圖形的每邊相加會得到周長。

7 Two figures with the same size and shape are _____.
兩個擁有同樣大小與形狀的圖形是全等的。

8 A line of _____ divides a figure into two congruent figures.
對稱軸將一個圖形分成兩個全等形。

C

Read and Choose | 閱讀下列句子，並且選出最適當的答案。

1 (Cross | Circle) out the figures that do not have the same shape.

2 Add the length of each side to (connect | find) the perimeter.

3 Solid figures with a flat surface (role | slide).

4 Solid figures with a curved surface (roll | slide).

Look, Read, and Write | 看圖並且依照提示，在空格中填入正確答案。

What am I? Choose the number and write the name.

1 ▶ I'm a plane figure. I have 3 sides and 3 vertices.

_____

4 ▶ I'm a solid figure. I have a circular base that rises to a point.

_____

2 ▶ I'm a plane figure. I have 4 sides and 4 vertices.

_____

5 ▶ I'm a solid figure. I have 6 faces, 12 edges, and 8 vertices.

_____

3 ▶ I'm a plane figure. I have 6 sides and 6 vertices.

_____

6 ▶ I'm a solid figure with a curved surface. I do not have any edges.

_____

E

Read and Answer | 閱讀並且回答下列問題。　🔊 092

Plane Figures and Solid Figures

Geometry is the study of regular shapes. We can divide these shapes into two kinds: plane figures and solid figures. There are many kinds of plane figures. Squares, rectangles, triangles, and circles are all plane figures. Plane figures have both length and width. They are flat surfaces, so you can draw them on a piece of paper. Solid figures are different from plane figures. They have length, width, and height. A box is a solid figure. We call that a cube in geometry. A globe is a solid figure. That's a sphere. Also, a pyramid and a cone are two more solid figures.

Which is NOT true?

1 Geometry is the study of regular shapes.

2 There are two kinds of shapes.

3 A square is a plane figure.

4 A circle is a solid figure.

Key Words 🔊 093

01	**multiplication** [ˌmʌltəplə`keʃən]	*(n.)*〔數〕乘法;乘法運算　*do multiplication 做乘法 *multiply by 乘以 **Multiplication** is a quick way of adding the same number over and over again. 乘法是重複將一樣數字相加的快速方法。
02	**times** [taɪmz]	*(prep.)*〔數〕乘 Two **times** one is two. (2×1=2) 2 乘以 1 等於 2。
03	**equal group** [`ikwəl grup]	*(n.)* 等組 2×3 means that there are 3 **equal groups** of 2. (2+2+2) 2 乘 3 意味著有 3 個 2 的等組。
04	**factor** [`fæktə]	*(n.)* 因數　*(highest) common factor（最大）公因數 The numbers that are being multiplied are the **factors**. 被乘之數就是因數。
05	**product** [`prɑdəkt]	*(n.)*〔數〕（乘）積 The answer to a multiplication problem is the **product**. 乘法問題的答案是乘積。
06	**multiplication table** [ˌmʌltəplə`keʃən `tebl̩]	*(n.)* 乘法表 **Multiplication tables** help us to learn multiplication quickly. 乘法表幫助我們快速學習乘法。
07	**division** [də`vɪʒən]	*(n.)*〔數〕除（法）　*do division 做除法 **Division** separates a number into equal groups. 除法將一個數字平均分割。
08	**divisor** [də`vaɪzə]	*(n.)*〔數〕除數　*(greatest) common divisor（最大）公因數 The **divisor** is the number doing the dividing. 除數是用來進行分割的數字。
09	**dividend** [`dɪvəˌdɛnd]	*(n.)*〔數〕被除數 The **dividend** is the number being divided. 被除數是被用來分割的數字。
10	**quotient** [`kwoʃənt]	*(n.)*〔數〕商（數）　*intelligence quotient (IQ) 智商 *emotional quotient (EQ) 情感商數;情商 The **quotient** is the answer to a division problem. 商數是除法問題的答案。

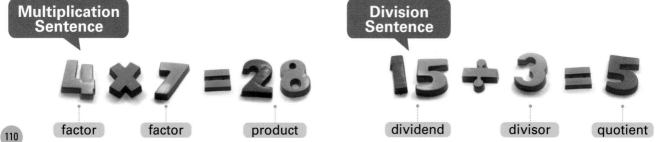

Multiplication Sentence　　　　**Division Sentence**

4 × 7 = 28　　　15 ÷ 3 = 5

factor　factor　product　　dividend　divisor　quotient

multiply
[ˈmʌltəplaɪ]

使相乘

Can you **multiply** 2 times 10? 你能將 2 乘以 10 嗎？

divide
[dəˈvaɪd]

劃分；分成

When you **divide** 10 apples into 5 equal groups, there are 2 in each group.
當你將 10 顆蘋果劃分成 5 組，每一組會得到 2 顆。

divide by

除以

Let's **divide** 10 **by** 5. 把 10 除以 5。

divide into

除以

Let's **divide** 10 **into** 5. 把 10 除以 5。

Word Families ◉ 095

Multiplication Table for 2
2 的乘法表

2 × 1 = 2　Two times one is two.
2 乘以 1 得到 2

2 × 2 = 4　Two times two is four.
2 乘以 2 得到 4

2 × 3 = 6　Two times three is six.
2 乘以 3 得到 6

2 × 4 = 8　Two times four is eight.
2 乘以 4 得到 8

2 × 5 = 10　Two times five is ten.
2 乘以 5 得到 10

2 × 6 = 12　Two times six is twelve.
2 乘以 6 得到 12

2 × 7 = 14　Two times seven is fourteen.
2 乘以 7 得到 14

2 × 8 = 16　Two times eight is sixteen.
2 乘以 8 得到 16

2 × 9 = 18　Two times nine is eighteen.
2 乘以 9 得到 18

2 × 10 = 20　Two times ten is twenty.
2 乘以 10 得到 20

Division Table for 2
2 的除法表

0 ÷ 2 = 0　Zero divided by two is zero.
0 除以 2 得到 0

2 ÷ 2 = 1　Two divided by two is one.
2 除以 2 得到 1

4 ÷ 2 = 2　Four divided by two is two.
4 除以 2 得到 2

6 ÷ 2 = 3　Six divided by two is three.
6 除以 2 得到 3

8 ÷ 2 = 4　Eight divided by two is four.
8 除以 2 得到 4

10 ÷ 2 = 5　Ten divided by two is five.
10 除以 2 得到 5

12 ÷ 2 = 6　Twelve divided by two is six.
12 除以 2 得到 6

14 ÷ 2 = 7　Fourteen divided by two is seven.
14 除以 2 得到 7

16 ÷ 2 = 8　Sixteen divided by two is eight.
16 除以 2 得到 8

18 ÷ 2 = 9　Eighteen divided by two is nine.
18 除以 2 得到 9

Checkup

A

Write | 請依提示寫出正確的英文單字。

1 〔數〕乘法	_____	8 〔數〕商（數）	_____
2 使相乘	m_____	9 〔數〕乘	t_____
3 因數	_____	10 等組	_____
4 〔數〕（乘）積	_____	11 〔數〕除數	_____
5 乘法表	_____	12 〔數〕被除數	_____
6 〔數〕除（法）	_____	13 除以	_____ b
7 劃分；分成	_____	14 除以	_____ i

B

Complete the Sentences | 請在空格中填入最適當的答案，並視情況做適當的變化。

multiply	equal group	factor	division	product
quotient	multiplication	times	multiplication table	

1　_____ is a quick way of adding the same number over and over again.　乘法是重複將一樣數字相加的快速方法。

2　2×3 means that there are 3 _____ _____ of 2.
2 乘 3 意味著有三個 2 的等組。

3　The answer to a multiplication problem is the _____.
乘法問題的答案是乘積。

4　The _____ is the answer to a division problem.　商數是除法問題的答案。

5　The numbers that are being multiplied are the _____.
被乘之數就是因數。

6　Two _____ one is two. (2×1=2)　2 乘以 1 等於 2。

7　_____ separates a number into equal groups.
除法將一個數字平均分割。

8　_____ _____ help us to learn multiplication quickly.
乘法表幫助我們快速學習乘法。

C

Read and Choose | 閱讀下列句子，並且選出最適當的答案。

1　Can you (divide｜multiply) 2 times 10?

2　When you (divide｜multiply) 10 apples into 5 equal groups, there are 2 in each group.

3　Let's divide 10 (by｜to) 5.

4　Two times seven is (twelve｜fourteen).

D Look, Read, and Write | 看圖並且依照提示，在空格中填入正確答案。

1

$$(4) \times (3) = 12$$

▸ the numbers that are being multiplied

_____

4

$$10 \div (2) = 5$$

▸ the number doing the dividing

_____

2

$$4 \times 3 = (12)$$

▸ the answer to a multiplication problem

_____

5

$$(10) \div 2 = 5$$

▸ the number being divided

_____

3

$$10 \div 2 = (5)$$

▸ the answer to a division problem

_____

6

▸ to add a number to itself a particular number of times

_____

E Read and Answer | 閱讀並且回答下列問題。 🔊 096

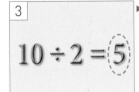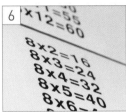

Why Do We Multiply?

Sometimes, you might want to add many groups of things together. For example, you might have five groups of apples. Each group has two apples. You could add 2 five times like this: $2 + 2 + 2 + 2 + 2 = 10$. But that's too long. Instead, use multiplication. You can write that as a multiplication problem like this: $2 \times 5 = 10$. When you multiply, you add equal groups of numbers many times. Multiplication is useful because it makes math easier. However, remember a couple of things about it. First, when you multiply any number by 1, the product is always the same as that number: $5 \times 1 = 5$. $100 \times 1 = 100$. Also, when you multiply any number by 0, the product is always 0: $2 \times 0 = 0$. $100 \times 0 = 0$.

Fill in the blanks.

1 When you multiply, you add _____ _____ of numbers many times.

2 $2 \times 5 = 10$ is a _____ problem.

3 Any number times _____ is the same as that number.

4 Any number times 0 is _____.

A

Write | 請依提示寫出正確的英文單字。

1	〔數〕加數 _____	11	三位數的 _____
2	偶數 _____	12	四捨五入 _____
3	奇數 _____	13	測量；計量 _____
4	時間軸 _____	14	計算 _____
5	秒 _____	15	刪掉；劃掉 _____
6	立體圖形 _____	16	1/4 個鐘頭；15 分鐘 _____
7	平面圖形 _____	17	邊 _____
8	〔數〕全等的 _____	18	頂點 _____
9	〔數〕乘法 _____	19	劃分；分成 _____
10	使相乘 m_____	20	〔數〕除（法） _____

B

Choose the Correct Word | 請選出與鋪底字意思相近的答案。

1　A day **passes** in 24 hours.

　　a. goes by　　　　　　b. comes　　　　　　c. measures

2　We can **measure** time with a calendar or a clock.

　　a. pass　　　　　　b. read　　　　　　c. calculate

3　It is **fifteen minutes** after 2.

　　a. half　　　　　　b. a quarter　　　　　　c. 30

4　It is **thirty minutes** after 4.

　　a. half　　　　　　b. a quarter　　　　　　c. 15

C

Complete the Sentences | 請在空格中填入最適當的答案，並視情況做適當的變化。

number sentence	calendar	three-digit	curved

1　4+5=9 is an example of a _____ _____. 4+5=9 是一個數字方程式。

2　We call numbers like 100 and 250 _____ numbers.
　　我們稱 100 和 250 這種數字為三位數。

3　A _____ shows time in days, weeks, and months.
　　日曆用日、週和月的方式表現時間。

4　The sphere has a _____ surface. 這個球體有一個曲面。

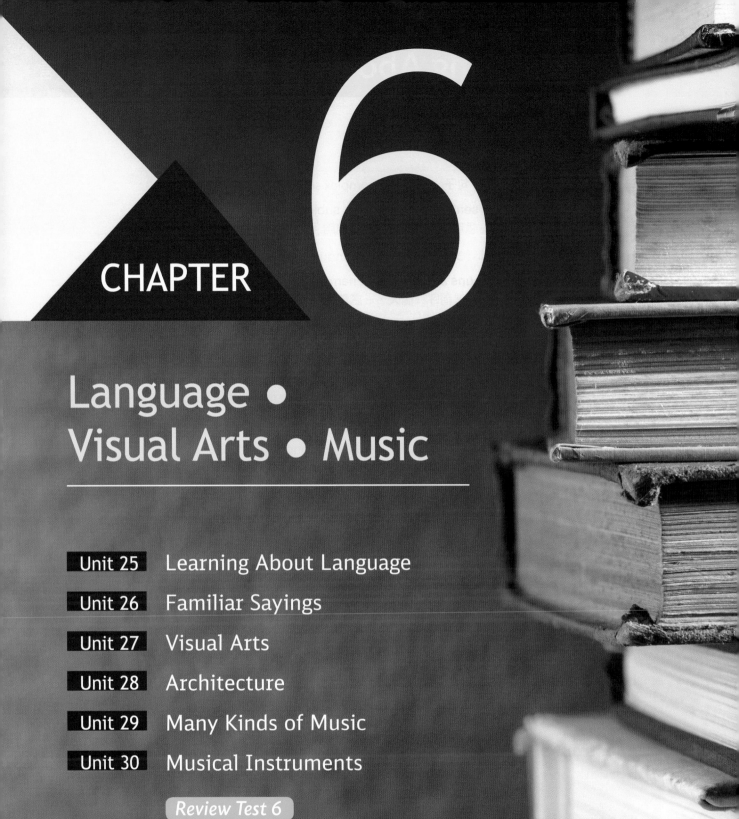

CHAPTER 6

Language •
Visual Arts • Music

Key Words 🔊 097

01 **sentence**
[ˋsɛntəns]

(n.) 句子　*simple/complex sentence【文】簡單句／複合句

A **sentence** must have a subject and a verb.
一個句子必須要有主詞和動詞。

02 **noun**
[naʊn]

(n.)〔文〕名詞　*proper noun 專有名詞　*noun phrase 名詞片語

Nouns are words that name a person, place, or thing.
名詞是稱呼一個人、一處地方或一件事物的單字。

03 **verb**
[vɝb]

(n.)〔文〕動詞　*regular/irregular verb 規則／不規則動詞
　　　　　　　 *verbal phrase 動詞片語

A **verb** describes the action in a sentence.　動詞形容一個句子中的動作。

04 **adjective**
[ˋædʒɪktɪv]

(n.)〔文〕形容詞　*adjective clause 形容詞子句

Adjectives describe nouns and pronouns.　形容詞用來形容名詞與代名詞。

05 **pronoun**
[ˋpronaʊn]

(n.)〔文〕代名詞　*reflexive pronoun 反身代名詞
　　　　　　　　 *personal pronoun 人稱代名詞

I, he, she, it, we, you, and they are all **pronouns**.
I、he、she、it、we、you 和 they 都是代名詞。

06 **preposition**
[ˌprɛpəˋzɪʃən]

(n.)〔文〕介系詞　*prepositional phrase 介系詞片語

A **preposition** is a word like in, at, and on.
介系詞是像 in、at、on 這類的字。

07 **subject**
[ˋsʌbdʒɪkt]

(n.)〔文〕主詞　*subjective case 主格

The **subject** is one of the main parts of a sentence.
主詞是一個句子中的主要部分。

08 **contraction**
[kənˋtrækʃən]

(n.)〔語〕縮短形；縮約形式

A **contraction** is a short form of two words.
縮短形是兩個字的簡寫形式。

09 **apostrophe**
[əˋpɑstrəfɪ]

(n.) 省略符號

Put an **apostrophe** between two words when you make a contraction.
將兩個字變成縮短形時，在中間加上省略符號。

10 **abbreviation**
[əˌbrivɪˋeʃən]

(n.) 縮寫

An **abbreviation** is a short form of a long word.
縮寫是長單字的縮寫形式。

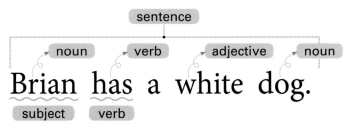

sentence

noun　verb　adjective　noun

Brian has a white dog.

subject　verb

take the place of

代替

Pronouns **take the place of** nouns.　代名詞代替名詞。

replace

[rɪ`ples]

取代

Pronouns **replace** nouns.　代名詞取代名詞。

abbreviate

[ə`brivɪˌet]

縮寫；使省略

You can **abbreviate** some long words.　你可以將某些長的單字形成縮寫。

shorten

[`ʃɔrtn̩]

縮短

You can **shorten** some long words.　你可以縮短某些長的單字。

capitalize

[`kæpətl̩ˌaɪz]

用大寫書寫

Capitalize the first letter of the first word in a sentence.
將句子中的首字母大寫。

describe

[dɪ`skraɪb]

形容；修飾

Adjectives are words that **describe** nouns and pronouns.
形容詞是用來形容名詞與代名詞的字。

Word Families ● 099

singular noun	單數名詞	A singular noun refers to just one thing.　一個單數名詞代表一件事物。
plural noun	複數名詞	A plural noun refers to more than one. 一個複數名詞代表超過一件事物。
action verb	動作動詞	*Run*, *eat*, and *sleep* are action verbs. 跑、吃和睡都是動作動詞。
linking verb	連綴動詞	*Is*, *are*, and *seem* are linking verbs. 「is」、「are」和「seem」都屬於連綴動詞。

Contractions
縮短形；縮約形式

I am = **I'm**	He is = **He's**
She is = **She's**	It is = **It's**
We are = **We're**	You are = **You're**
They are = **They're**	

Abbreviations
縮寫字；縮寫式

noun = **n.** 名詞	verb = **v.** 動詞
adjective = **adj.** 形容詞	preposition = **prep.** 介系詞
subject = **s.** 主詞	object = **o.** 受詞
abbreviation = **abbr.** 縮寫	

Checkup

A

Write | 請依提示寫出正確的英文單字。

1	句子	_____	9	省略符號	_____
2	名詞	_____	10	縮寫 (n.)	_____
3	動詞	_____	11	代替；取代	_____
4	形容詞	_____	12	連綴動詞	_____
5	代名詞	_____	13	縮寫；使省略 (v.)	_____
6	介系詞	_____	14	用大寫書寫	_____
7	主詞	_____	15	形容；修飾	_____
8	縮約形式	_____	16	單數名詞	_____

B

Complete the Sentences | 請在空格中填入最適當的答案，並視情況做適當的變化。

apostrophe	replace	adjective	plural	preposition
abbreviation	subject	contraction	sentence	pronoun

1　A _____ must have a subject and a verb.　一個句子必須要有主詞和動詞。

2　I, he, she, it, we, you, and they are all _____.
　　I、he、she、it、we、you 和 they 都是代名詞。

3　_____ are words that describe nouns and pronouns.
　　形容詞是用來形容名詞與代名詞的字。

4　A _____ noun refers to more than one.　一個複數名詞代表超過一件事物。

5　The _____ is one of the main parts of a sentence.
　　主詞是一個句子中的主要部分。

6　An _____ is a short form of a long word.　縮寫是長單字的縮寫形式。

7　A _____ is a short form of two words.　縮短形是兩個字的簡寫形式。

8　Put an _____ between two words when you make a contraction.
　　將兩個字變成縮短形時，在中間加上省略符號。

C

Read and Choose | 閱讀下列句子，並且選出最適當的答案。

1　Pronouns (describe | replace) nouns.

2　You can (abbreviate | name) some long words.

3　You can (short | shorten) some long words.

4　(Take the place of | Capitalize) the first letter of the first word in a sentence.

D Look, Read, and Write | 看圖並且依照提示，在空格中填入正確答案。

 ▸ one of the main parts of a sentence

_____

 ▸ a word like *I*, *he*, *she*, *it*, *we*, *you*, and *they*

_____

 ▸ a word that describes the action in a sentence

_____

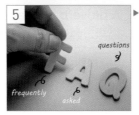 ▸ a short form of a long word

_____

 ▸ a word that describes nouns and pronouns

_____

 ▸ the symbol ' used in writing

_____

E Read and Answer | 閱讀並且回答下列問題。 🔊 100

Parts of Speech

There are many words in the English language. We use words to make sentences. But there are also many types of words. We call these "parts of speech," and we make sentences with them. Nouns, verbs, adjectives, and prepositions are all parts of speech.

Every sentence needs a subject and a verb. The subject is often a noun. Nouns are words that name a person, place, or thing. Look around your room. Think of the names of everything you see. All those words are nouns. Verbs describe actions. Think of some activities you do. The names of those activities are verbs. Sometimes we also use other parts of speech. Adjectives describe other words like nouns and pronouns. *Hot*, *cold*, *white*, *black*, *windy*, *rainy*, and *sunny* are all adjectives.

Answer the questions.

1 What do we use to make sentences? _____

2 What does every sentence need? _____

3 What do verbs do? _____

4 What do adjectives do? _____

Key Words 🔊 101

01	**saying**	(n.) 格言；諺語 *it goes without saying 不言而喻 *as the saying goes 常言道
	['seɪŋ]	There are many common **sayings** people use every day. 有許多格言人們每天都會用到。

02	**proverb**	(n.) 俗語；諺語
	['prɑvɝb]	A **proverb** is a saying with an important meaning. 俗諺是具有重要意義的格言。

03	**familiar**	(a.) 熟悉的；通曉的 *be familiar with 熟悉；精通
	[fə'mɪljɚ]	"Look before you leap" is a **familiar** saying. 「三思而後行」是一句常見的格言。

04	**meaning**	(n.) 意義；含意 *well-meaning 善意的 *meaningless 無意義的
	['minɪŋ]	What is the **meaning** of that saying? 那句格言的含意是什麼？

05	**moral**	(n.) 道德上的教訓；寓意 *on moral grounds 基於道德考量 *business morals 商業道德
	['mɔrəl]	A **moral** is an important meaning of a story. 寓意是一則故事的重要含意。

06	**knowledge**	(n.) 知識 *have a wide knowledge of sth. 在某方面知識淵博 *knowledgeable 有知識的
	['nɑlɪdʒ]	Many expressions have important **knowledge** in them. 許多語句都含有重要知識。

07	**well-known**	(a.) 出名的
	['wɛl'non]	"An apple a day keeps the doctor away" is a **well-known** saying. 「一天一蘋果，醫生遠離我」是句有名的格言。

08	**folklore**	(n.) 民間傳說 *folk religion 民間信仰 *folk song 民謠
	['fok,lor]	Some sayings come from **folklore**. 某些格言來自於民間傳說。

09	**wisdom**	(n.) 智慧；學問 *the wisdom to do sth. 做某事的智慧
	['wɪzdəm]	There is a lot of **wisdom** in many familiar sayings. 許多常見的格言中蘊含豐富的智慧。

10	**oral**	(a.) 口述的 *oral agreement 口頭協議
	['orəl]	Many sayings are passed down from the **oral** tradition. 許多格言由口述的傳統方式所流傳下來。

Familiar
Sayings

Look before you leap.

An apple a
day keeps the
doctor away.

pass on
傳遞下去
Parents pass on important sayings to their children.
父母將重要格言傳承給小孩。

transmit
[træns`mɪt]
留傳
Parents transmit important sayings to their children.
父母將重要格言傳述給小孩。

provide
[prə`vaɪd]
提供
That expression provides wisdom for people.　那句話提供了智慧給人們。

tell
講述
Some people like to tell proverbs.　有些人喜歡講述俗諺。

speak
說話
Some people like to speak by using proverbs.
有些人喜歡將俗諺運用在談話中。

definition
釋義；定義
What is the definition?　這個的定義是什麼？

explanation
解釋
Give me an explanation of this proverb.　請告訴我這個俗諺的解釋。

expression
措辭；詞句
These expressions are from Greek myths.　這些措辭表達來自希臘神話。

idiom
慣用語；成語
Idioms from other languages are hard to understand.
來自另一個語言的慣用語不好理解。

Common Sayings
常見格言

Never leave till tomorrow what you can do today.
今日事，今日畢。
Practice makes perfect.　熟能生巧。
There's no place like home.　金窩、銀窩，不如自己的狗窩。
Don't cry over spilled milk.　覆水難收。
Don't judge a book by its cover.　不要以貌取人。
Where there's a will, there's a way.　有志者事竟成。

Checkup

A

Write | 請依提示寫出正確的英文單字。

1	格言	_____	
2	俗語;諺語	_____	
3	通曉的	_____	
4	意義;含意	_____	
5	寓意	_____	
6	知識	_____	
7	出名的	_____	
8	智慧	_____	

9	民間傳說	_____
10	口述的	_____
11	傳遞下去	_____
12	留傳	_____
13	提供	_____
14	釋義;定義	_____
15	解釋	_____
16	慣用語;成語	_____

B

Complete the Sentences | 請在空格中填入最適當的答案,並視情況做適當的變化。

saying	wisdom	moral	familiar	statement
definition	folklore	oral	proverb	well-known

1 A _____ is a saying with an important meaning.
俗諺是具有重要意義的格言。

2 There are many common _____ people use every day.
有許多格言人們每天都會用到。

3 A _____ is an important meaning of a story. 寓意是一則故事的重要含意。

4 "Look before you leap" is a _____ saying. 「三思而後行」是一句常見的格言。

5 "An apple a day keeps the doctor away" is a _____ saying.
「一天一蘋果,醫生遠離我」是句有名的格言。

6 Some sayings come from _____. 某些格言來自於民間傳說。

7 Many sayings are passed down from the _____ tradition.
許多格言由口述的傳統方式所流傳下來。

8 There is a lot of _____ in many familiar sayings.
許多常見的格言中蘊含豐富的智慧。

C

Read and Choose | 閱讀下列句子,並且選出最適當的答案。

1 Parents (transmit | pass) on important sayings to their children.

2 That expression (provides | uses) wisdom for people.

3 (Idioms | Stories) from other languages are hard to understand.

4 Some people like to (understand | speak) by using proverbs.

Look, Read, and Write | 看圖並且依照提示，在空格中填入正確答案。

Complete the sayings.

 1 ▶ Practice makes _____.

 4 ▶ Don't judge a book by its _____.

 2 ▶ Look before you _____.

 5 ▶ Where there's a _____, there's a way.

 3 ▶ Don't cry over spilled _____.

 6 ▶ Never _____ till tomorrow what you can do today.

E

Read and Answer | 閱讀並且回答下列問題。 🔘 104

Some Common Sayings

Every language has common sayings. People use them in various situations. They are hard to translate into other languages. But they make sense in their own language. English has many common sayings. One is "Better late than never." This means it is better to do something late than never to do it. Another is "Two heads are better than one." This means a second person can often help one person doing something. And "An apple a day keeps the doctor away" is a common saying. It means that eating apples every day helps keep you healthy. So the person will not get sick and won't have to see a doctor.

What is true? Write T(true) or F(false).

1   Common sayings are easy to translate into other languages.   _____

2   "Better late than never" is a common saying.   _____

3   "Three heads are better than one" is a common saying.   _____

4   "An apple a day keeps the teacher away" is a common saying.   _____

Visual Arts 視覺藝術

Key Words
🔊 105

| 01 | **vertical line** [ˈvɝtɪkl̩ laɪn] | *(n.)* 垂直線 |
| | | A vertical line goes up and down. 垂直線上下發展。 |

| 02 | **horizontal line** [ˌhɑrəˈzɑntl̩ laɪn] | *(n.)* 水平線 |
| | | A horizontal line goes from left to right. 水平線由左到右。 |

| 03 | **diagonal line** [daɪˈægənl̩ laɪn] | *(n.)* 對角線 |
| | | A diagonal line moves up or down at an angle. 對角線沿對角上下移動。 |

| 04 | **close-up** [ˈklos͵ʌp] | *(a.)* 特寫的；近距離的 |
| | | The picture shows a close-up part of a landscape. 這張照片顯示景色的特寫部分。 |

| 05 | **faraway** [ˈfɑrə͵we] | *(a.)* 遠方的；遙遠的　*in faraway times/places 在遙遠的過去／地方 |
| | | The picture shows a faraway landscape. 這張照片表現了遠景。 |

| 06 | **realistic** [ˌrɪəˈlɪstɪk] | *(a.)* 逼真的；寫實的　*be realistic about sth. 對某事物切於實際 |
| | | Some artists want to make very realistic pictures. 某些藝術家希望達到寫實的畫作。 |

| 07 | **imaginary** [ɪˈmædʒə͵nɛrɪ] | *(a.)* 想像中的；虛構的 |
| | | Some artists want to make imaginary pictures. 某些藝術家希望創作出虛構的畫作。 |

| 08 | **abstract** [ˈæbstrækt] | *(a.)* 抽象的　*abstract expressionism 抽象表現主義 |
| | | Abstract paintings don't look like the real thing. 抽象的圖畫看似不像真實事物。 |

| 09 | **realistic art** [ˌrɪəˈlɪstɪk ɑrt] | *(n.)* 現實主義藝術 |
| | | Realistic art shows objects as they look in reality. 現實主義藝術呈現出物品在現實中的模樣。 |

| 10 | **abstract art** [ˈæbstrækt ɑrt] | *(n.)* 抽象主義藝術 |
| | | Abstract art shows objects different from how they look in reality. 抽象主義藝術呈現出與現實模樣相異的物品。 |

faraway landscape　　close-up landscape　　realistic painting　　abstract painting

show

顯示;表現

This picture **shows** us the imaginary world. 這張圖畫讓我們看到一個虛幻的世界。

copy

描摹;複製

Some artists don't want to **copy** objects in a lifelike way.
有些藝術家不喜歡描摹物件的寫實面。

create
[krɪˋet]

創造

Abstract paintings **create** images in a new and unusual way.
抽象畫創造了一個新穎與獨特的形象。

reflect
[rɪˋflɛkt]

反映

Art **reflects** people's thoughts and emotions. 藝術反映人們的想法與情感。

look alike

相像;相似

These two paintings **look alike**. 這兩幅畫看來相似。

differ
[ˋdɪfɚ]

相異

Those two paintings **differ**. 這兩幅畫不同。

realistic painting

寫實畫

Realistic painting was popular for many years.
寫實畫許多年來都很受歡迎。

realistic painter

寫實畫家

Rembrandt was a realistic painter.
林布蘭特是一位寫實畫家。

abstract painting

抽象畫

Abstract painting looks different from other paintings.
抽象畫看來與其他畫作不同。

abstract painter

抽象畫家

Picasso was a famous abstract painter.
畢卡索是頗負盛名的抽象畫畫家。

a self-portrait
by Rembrandt

Lines

vertical line
垂直線

horizontal line
水平線

diagonal line
對角線

wavy line
波形線

thin line
細線

thick line
粗線

Checkup

A

Write | 請依提示寫出正確的英文單字。

1	垂直線	_____	9	特寫的；近距離的	_____
2	水平線	_____	10	遠方的；遙遠的	_____
3	對角線	_____	11	顯示；表現	_____
4	寫實的	_____	12	描摹；複製	_____
5	虛構的	_____	13	反映	_____
6	抽象的	_____	14	相像；相似	_____
7	現實主義藝術	_____	15	相異	_____
8	抽象主義藝術	_____	16	抽象畫家	_____

B

Complete the Sentences | 請在空格中填入最適當的答案，並視情況做適當的變化。

differ	imaginary	close-up	abstract	realistic art
reflect	realistic	faraway	diagonal	abstract art

1 A _____ line moves up or down at an angle. 對角線沿對角上下移動。

2 Some artists want to make _____ pictures.
某些藝術家希望創作出虛構的畫作。

3 _____ paintings don't look like the real thing.
抽象的圖畫看似不像真實事物。

4 _____ _____ shows objects as they look in reality.
現實主義藝術呈現出物品在現實中的模樣。

5 _____ _____ shows objects different from how they look in reality.
抽象主義藝術呈現出與現實模樣相異的物品。

6 Art _____ people's thoughts and emotions. 藝術反映人們的想法與情感。

7 The picture shows a _____ part of a landscape.
這張照片顯示景色的特寫部分。

8 The picture shows a _____ landscape. 這張照片表現了遠景。

C

Read and Choose | 閱讀下列句子，並且選出最適當的答案。

1 These two paintings look (differ | alike).

2 This picture (shows | reflects) us the imaginary world.

3 Abstract paintings (copy | create) images in a new and unusual way.

4 Some artists don't want to (copy | differ) objects in a lifelike way.

Look, Read, and Write | 看圖並且依照提示，在空格中填入正確答案。

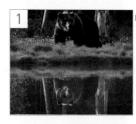 1 ▶ to show the image of (something) on a surface

_____

 2 ▶ art that shows objects in a new and unusual way

_____

 3 ▶ a line that goes up and down

_____

 4 ▶ a line that moves up or down at an angle

_____

 5 ▶ not real but only created in your mind

_____

 6 ▶ very near the subject

_____

E

Read and Answer | 閱讀並且回答下列問題。 108

Realistic Art and Abstract Art

There are two main kinds of art. They are realistic art and abstract art. Some artists like realistic art, but others prefer abstract art. Realistic art shows objects as they look in reality. For example, a realistic artist paints a picture of an apple. The picture will look exactly like an apple. Most art in the past was realistic art. Abstract art looks different than realistic art. Abstract art does not always look exactly like the real thing. For example, an abstract artist paints a picture of an apple. It will not look like an apple. It might just be a red ball. That is abstract art. Nowadays, much art is abstract.

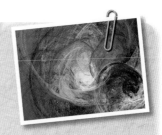

Fill in the blanks.

1   There are _____ main kinds of art.

2   _____ art shows objects that look real.

3   _____ art does not always look real.

4   In abstract art, an apple might look like a _____ ball.

Unit 28 Architecture 建築

Key Words 🔊 109

01	**architecture** [ˋɑrkəˌtɛktʃɚ]	*(n.)* 建築學　　*modern architecture 現代建築 Architecture is the art of designing, planning, and constructing buildings. 建築學是設計、規劃與建造房屋的藝術。
02	**architect** [ˋɑrkəˌtɛkt]	*(n.)* 建築設計師 An architect is a person who does architecture. 一個建築師是從事建築的人。
03	**design** [dɪˋzaɪn]	*(n.)* 設計　　*designer 設計師　　*interior design 室內設計 The **design** of a building is very important.　房屋的設計十分重要。
04	**symmetry** [ˋsɪmɪtrɪ]	*(n.)* 對稱 Buildings should have **symmetry** so that they look nice. 建築需要對稱才會有出色的外觀。
05	**column** [ˋkɑləm]	*(n.)* 圓柱　　*column 報紙欄位（sports column 體育欄） The ancient Greeks had many beautiful buildings with **columns**. 古希臘擁有許多圓柱搭建的壯麗建築。
06	**dome** [dom]	*(n.)* 圓屋頂　　*Tokyo Dome 東京巨蛋 A **dome** is a round-shaped roof.　圓頂是一個圓形屋頂。
07	**arch** [ɑrtʃ]	*(n.)* 拱門　　*triumphal arch 凱旋門　　*arch bridge 拱橋 There is a famous **arch** in St. Louis, Missouri. 密蘇里州的聖路易有一座知名的拱門。
08	**monument** [ˋmɑnjəmənt]	*(n.)* 紀念碑；紀念塔　　*ancient monument 古代遺跡 　　　　　　　　　　　　　　*a monument to sb./sth. 某人或某事物的明證 He is designing a **monument** to honor the president. 他正在設計一座紀念碑來表達對總統的尊敬。
09	**building** [ˋbɪldɪŋ]	*(n.)* 建築；建築物　　*office building 辦公大樓 Many architects design **buildings**.　許多建築師設計房屋。
10	**blueprint** [ˋbluˋprɪnt]	*(n.)* 藍圖；設計圖 The **blueprints** show what a building will look like. 這份藍圖呈現出建築未來的外觀。

column

symmetry

dome

the Gateway Arch over St. Louis, Missouri

the Washington Monument

design 設計
[dɪˋzaɪn]
An architect is a person who **designs** buildings. 建築師是設計建物的人。

plan 繪製……的平面圖
An architect **plans** a building. 建築師繪製建物的平面圖。

display 展出；陳列
[dɪˋsple]
They will **display** a model of the building before making it.
他們在興建建物前，會先陳列模型。

construct 建造
[kənˋstrʌkt]
After the blueprints are done, they must **construct** the house.
在藍圖設計好後，他們便會開始建造房屋。

build 興建
After the blueprints are done, they must **build** the house.
在藍圖設計好後，他們便會開始興建房屋。

Word Families 🔊 111

Buildings with Columns in Ancient Greece
古代希臘的圓柱建物

The Parthenon 帕德嫩神廟	The Temple of Hephaestus 海菲斯塔斯神殿	The Stoa of Attalus 阿塔勒斯柱廊
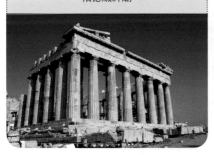		

Types of Buildings
建築的種類

skyscraper 摩天樓	**office building** 辦公室
apartment 公寓大樓	**house** 住宅
shopping mall 購物中心	**warehouse** 倉庫
hotel 飯店；旅館	**stadium** 體育場

Building Materials
建築材料

brick 磚塊	**cement** 水泥
iron 鐵	**concrete** 混凝土
steel 鋼鐵	**glass** 玻璃
wood 木頭	

Checkup

A Write | 請依提示寫出正確的英文單字。

1	建築學	_____	9	建築；建築物	_____
2	建築設計師	_____	10	對稱	_____
3	設計	_____	11	體育場	_____
4	藍圖；設計圖	_____	12	繪製……的平面圖	_____
5	圓柱	_____	13	展出；陳列	_____
6	圓屋頂	_____	14	建造	_____
7	拱門	_____	15	磚塊	_____
8	紀念碑	_____	16	摩天樓	_____

B Complete the Sentences | 請在空格中填入最適當的答案，並視情況做適當的變化。

blueprint	design	column	monument	dome
skyscraper	display	symmetry	architecture	arch

1 _____ is the art of designing, planning, and constructing buildings.
建築學是設計、規劃與建造房屋的藝術。

2 The _____ of a building is very important. 房屋的設計十分重要。

3 The ancient Greeks had many beautiful buildings with _____.
古希臘擁有許多圓柱搭建的壯麗建築。

4 Buildings should have _____ so that they look nice.
建築需要對稱才會有出色的外觀。

5 A _____ is a round-shaped roof. 圓頂是一個圓形屋頂。

6 He is designing a _____ to honor the president.
他正在設計一座紀念碑來表達對總統的尊敬。

7 There is a famous _____ in St. Louis, Missouri.
密蘇里州的聖路易有一座知名的拱門。

8 The _____ show what a building will look like.
這份藍圖呈現出建築未來的外觀。

C Read and Choose | 閱讀下列句子，並且選出最適當的答案。

1 An architect is a person who (designs | supports) buildings.

2 An architect (shows | plans) a building.

3 After the (prints | blueprints) are done, they must construct the house.

4 They will (display | honor) a model of the building before making it.

Look, Read, and Write | 看圖並且依照提示，在空格中填入正確答案。

1
▶ the fact that something has two halves that are exactly the same

_____

4
▶ a print of a detailed plan for a building

_____

2
▶ a person who designs buildings

_____

5
▶ a curved structure at the top of a door, window, or gate

_____

3
▶ a round-shaped roof

_____

6
▶ a tall, thin, round structure that is used as support and forms part of a building

_____

Read and Answer | 閱讀並且回答下列問題。　⊙ 112

What Do Architects Do?

Architects have very important jobs. They design buildings. Some design tall buildings like skyscrapers. Others design restaurants, hotels, or banks. And others just design houses. Architects need to have many skills. They must be engineers. They must be good at math. They must be able to draw. They must have a good imagination. And they must work well with the builders, too. Architects draw blueprints for their buildings. Blueprints show how the building will look. They are very detailed. When the blueprints are done, the builders can start working.

Which is NOT true?

1　Architects design buildings.

2　Skyscrapers are very tall buildings.

3　Architects must know math.

4　Architects buy blueprints.

Key Words 🔊 113

01 **classical music**
[ˈklæsɪkl̩ ˈmjuzɪk]

(n.) 古典樂

The piano and violin are important in **classical music**.
鋼琴與小提琴在古典樂扮演重要角色。

02 **folk music**
[fok ˈmjuzɪk]

(n.) 民謠

Every country has its own **folk music**.
每個國家都有自己的民謠。

03 **traditional music**
[trəˈdɪʃənl̩ ˈmjuzɪk]

(n.) 傳統樂

Traditional African **music** has some exciting drum sounds.
傳統非洲音樂會搭配一些激昂的鼓聲。

04 **patriotic music**
[ˌpetrɪˈɑtɪk ˈmjuzɪk]

(n.) 愛國音樂

Patriotic music makes people feel proud of their country.
愛國音樂讓人民對自己的國家感到驕傲。

05 **choral music**
[ˈkorəl ˈmjuzɪk]

(n.) 聖歌

Bach composed a lot of **choral music** for churches.
巴哈為教堂作了很多聖歌。

06 **symphony**
[ˈsɪmfənɪ]

(n.) 交響樂 　＊symphony orchestra 交響樂團

A **symphony** is a long piece of music for an orchestra.
交響樂是由管弦樂隊所演奏的長版樂曲。

07 **concerto**
[kənˈtʃɛrto]

(n.) 協奏曲 　＊piano concerto 鋼琴協奏曲

A **concerto** is played by an orchestra. 協奏曲由管弦樂隊演奏。

08 **solo**
[ˈsolo]

(n.) 獨奏（曲）；獨唱 　＊sing solo 獨唱 　＊play a solo 彈奏獨奏曲

The singer is performing a **solo** now. 這位歌手正在進行獨唱表演。

09 **duet**
[duˈɛt]

(n.) 二重唱；二重奏 　＊perform a duet 表演二重唱／二重奏

A piano **duet** is played by two pianists.
鋼琴二重奏由兩位鋼琴家彈奏。

10 **aria**
[ˈɑrɪə]

(n.) 詠嘆調；抒情調

An **aria** is a solo in an opera. 詠嘆調是歌劇中的獨唱曲。

solo　　　　duet　　　　trio　　　　quartet

create [krɪ`et]	創作 Beethoven **created** nine symphonies. 貝多芬創作了 9 首交響曲。	
compose [kəm`poz]	作曲 Beethoven **composed** nine symphonies. 貝多芬作了 9 首交響曲。	

write	編寫（曲子） Beethoven **wrote** nine symphonies. 貝多芬編寫了 9 首交響曲。
be written by	由……寫下 Nine symphonies **were written by** Beethoven. 有 9 首交響曲由貝多芬所寫。

record [rɪ`kɔrd]	錄製 The orchestra will **record** *The Greatest Hits* series of Mozart. 管弦樂隊將要錄製莫札特的《音樂選輯》系列。
play	演奏 The orchestra will **play** *The Greatest Hits* series of Mozart. 管弦樂隊將要演奏莫札特的《音樂選輯》系列。
be played by	由……表演 *The Greatest Hits* series of Mozart will **be played by** the orchestra. 莫札特的《音樂選輯》系列將由管弦樂隊表演。

pass down	傳下來 Folk songs are songs that have been **passed down** for many years. 民謠是多年流傳下來的歌曲。

Word Families 🔊 115

Musicians 音樂家	**Modern Popular Music** 現代流行樂	**Types of Songs** 歌曲類型
soloist 獨奏者	**rock music** 搖滾樂	**hymn** 聖歌
organist 風琴手	**pop music** 流行樂	**ballad** 民歌；抒情歌
flutist 長笛演奏者	**dance music** 舞曲	**rap** 饒舌歌
trumpeter 小號手	**rap music** 饒舌樂	**folk song** 民謠
	R&B (rhythm and blues) 節奏藍調	**children's song** 兒歌
	jazz music 爵士樂	**vocals** 聲樂

symphony orchestra

Checkup

A

Write | 請依提示寫出正確的英文單字。

1	古典樂	_____	9	愛國樂	_____
2	民謠	_____	10	聖歌	_____
3	傳統樂	_____	11	獨奏（曲）；獨唱	_____
4	交響樂	_____	12	二重唱；二重奏	_____
5	協奏曲	_____	13	由……寫下	_____
6	詠嘆調	_____	14	錄製	_____
7	創作	_____	15	由……表演	_____
8	作曲	_____	16	傳下來	_____

B

Complete the Sentences | 請在空格中填入最適當的答案，並視情況做適當的變化。

play	solo	symphony	traditional	write
folk	patriotic	concerto	classical	record

1   The piano and violin are important in _____ music.
    鋼琴與小提琴在古典樂扮演重要角色。

2   _____ African music has some exciting drum sounds.
    傳統非洲音樂會搭配一些激昂的鼓聲。

3   Every country has its own _____ music. 每個國家都有自己的民謠。

4   Nine symphonies were _____ by Beethoven. 有 9 首交響曲由貝多芬所寫。

5   A _____ is a long piece of music for an orchestra.
    交響樂是由管弦樂隊所演奏的長版樂曲。

6   The singer is performing a _____ now. 這位歌手正在進行獨唱表演。

7   _____ music makes people feel proud of their country.
    愛國音樂讓人民對自己的國家感到驕傲。

8   The orchestra will _____ *The Greatest Hits* series of Mozart.
    管弦樂隊將要演奏莫札特的《音樂選輯》系列。

C

Read and Choose | 閱讀下列句子，並且選出最適當的答案。

1   Beethoven created nine (concertos | symphonies).

2   The orchestra will (record | compose) *The Greatest Hits* series of Mozart.

3   Bach composed a lot of (symphony | choral) music for churches.

4   A (concerto | solo) is played by an orchestra.

Look, Read, and Write | 看圖並且依照提示，在空格中填入正確答案。

1 ► to write a piece of music

_____

4 ► a long piece of music for an orchestra

_____

2 ► music sung by a choir

_____

5 ► a piece of music sung or played by one person

_____

3 ► music that has been passed down for many years in a country

_____

6 ► a song that is sung by one person in an opera

_____

E

Read and Answer | 閱讀並且回答下列問題。　⦿ 116

Different Kinds of Music

People have different tastes in music. Some like slow music. Others like fast music. Some like to hear singing. Others like to hear musical instruments. So there are many different kinds of music. Classical music relies upon musical instruments. It has very little singing in it. On the other hand, folk music and traditional music use both instruments and singing. Every country has its own kind of folk music. It's usually fun to listen to. There are also many kinds of modern music. Rock music is one popular genre. So is jazz. Some people prefer rap or R&B. Overall, there is some kind of music for everyone.

What is true? Write T(true) or F(false).

1   People like different kinds of music.　_____

2   Classical music has a lot of singing in it.　_____

3   Folk music uses no instruments.　_____

4   Jazz is a popular kind of music today.　_____

Key Words 🔊 117

01 percussion instrument
[pəˋkʌʃən ˋɪnstrəmənt]
(n.) 打擊樂器
The drum is a popular percussion instrument.
鼓是一種受歡迎的打擊樂器。

02 string instrument
[strɪŋ ˋɪnstrəmənt]
(n.) 弦樂器
Guitars, violins, and cellos are all string instruments.
吉他、小提琴與大提琴全都是弦樂器。

03 wind instrument
[wɪnd ˋɪnstrəmənt]
(n.) 管樂器
The flute, clarinet, and saxophone are some wind instruments.
長笛、單簧管與薩克斯風是一些管樂器。

04 brass instrument
[bræs ˋɪnstrəmənt]
(n.) 銅管樂器
Brass instruments are made of metal called brass.
銅管樂器由稱作黃銅的金屬製造而成。

05 keyboard instrument
[ˋkiˌbord ˋɪnstrəmənt]
(n.) 鍵盤樂器
The piano is a keyboard instrument. 鋼琴是一種鍵盤樂器。

06 reed
[rid]
(n.) 〔音〕簧舌；簧片　　*reed pipe 牧笛；簧管　*double-reed 雙簧的
The clarinet and saxophone need reeds to make sounds.
單簧管與薩克斯風需要簧片才能發出聲響。

07 pitch
[pɪtʃ]
(n.) 音高　　*higher/lower pitch 音調較高／較低
The pitch is how high or low the sounds are. 音高是聲音的高低。

08 note
[not]
(n.) 音符　　*half/eighth note 二分／八分音符　　*whole note 全音符
Composers use special marks called notes.
作曲家使用的特殊記號叫作音符。

09 staff
[stæf]
(n.) 〔音〕五線譜
Composers write musical notes on the staff.
作曲家在五線譜上標上音符。

10 made of
[med ɑv]
以……為材料製造而成
Some wind instruments are made of wood.
某些管樂器由木頭製造而成。

Musical Instruments

string instruments

percussion instruments

drum

hit 打擊
The drummer is **hitting** the drum with his drumsticks.
鼓手正用鼓棒打鼓。

strike 敲擊
[straɪk]
The drummer is **striking** the drum with his drumsticks.
鼓手正用鼓棒敲鼓。

beat 擊打
The drummer is **beating** the drum with his drumsticks.
鼓手正用鼓棒打擊鼓。

drumsticks

blow 吹奏
A flutist **blows** on a flute to make a sound. 長笛手吹奏長笛使它發出聲音。

pluck 撥彈
[plʌk]
A guitarist **plucks** the strings of the guitar. 吉他手撥彈吉他的弦。

push 推（琴鍵）
The pianist **pushes** the piano keys to make music.
鋼琴手推琴鍵彈出音樂。

press 按（琴鍵）
[prɛs]
The pianist **presses** the piano keys to make music.
鋼琴手按琴鍵彈出音樂。

Word Families 🔘 119

wind instruments   brass instruments

keyboard instrument

Percussion Instruments 打擊樂器	**String Instruments** 弦樂器
drum 鼓	**violin** 小提琴
cymbals 鐃鈸	**viola** 中提琴
triangle 三角鐵	**harp** 豎琴
xylophone 木琴	**cello** 大提琴
castanets 響板	**guitar** 吉他
chime 樂鐘	**banjo** 五弦琴
tambourine 鈴鼓	**mandolin** 曼陀林

notes   staff

Checkup

A Write | 請依提示寫出正確的英文單字。

1	管樂器 _____	9	五線譜 _____
2	打擊樂器 _____	10	以……為材料製造而成 _____
3	弦樂器 _____	11	打擊；敲擊 _____
4	銅管樂器 _____	12	三角鐵 _____
5	鍵盤樂器 _____	13	大提琴 _____
6	簧片 _____	14	吹奏 _____
7	音高 _____	15	撥彈 _____
8	音符 _____	16	推（琴鍵） _____

B Complete the Sentences | 請在空格中填入最適當的答案，並視情況做適當的變化。

staff	keyboard	pitch	note	brass
reed	percussion	string	wind	made of

1 Guitars, violins, and cellos are all _____ instruments.
吉他、小提琴與大提琴全都是弦樂器。

2 The drum is a popular _____ instrument. 鼓是一種受歡迎的打擊樂器。

3 _____ instruments are made of metal called brass.
銅管樂器由稱作黃銅的金屬製造而成。

4 The flute, clarinet, and saxophone are some _____ instruments.
長笛、單簧管與薩克斯風是一些管樂器。

5 The _____ is how high or low the sounds are. 音高是聲音的高低。

6 The clarinet and saxophone need _____ to make sounds.
單簧管與薩克斯風需要簧片才能發出聲響。

7 Composers write musical notes on the _____. 作曲家在五線譜上標上音符。

8 Composers use special marks called _____.
作曲家使用的特殊記號叫作音符。

C Read and Choose | 閱讀下列句子，並且選出最適當的答案。

1 The drummer is (pushing | beating) the drum with his drumsticks.

2 A flutist (blows | plucks) on a flute to make a sound.

3 The pianist (presses | makes) the piano keys to make music.

4 A guitarist (strikes | plucks) the strings of the guitar.

D

Look, Read, and Write | 看圖並且依照提示，在空格中填入正確答案。

 ▸ instruments like the flute, clarinet, and saxophone

_____

 ▸ instruments that have keys to press

_____

 ▸ a thin piece of wood or metal in an instrument that makes a sound when you blow over it

_____

 ▸ a written symbol that indicates duration and pitch of a tone

_____

 ▸ instruments that are made of brass like the trumpet

_____

 ▸ It looks like a ladder and has 5 lines.

_____

E

Read and Answer | 閱讀並且回答下列問題。 🔊 120

Different Kinds of Musical Instruments

Some instruments look alike or have common characteristics. We can put many of these instruments into families. There are some different families of musical instruments.

Keyboard instruments have keys to press. The piano, organ, and keyboard are in the keyboard family. The violin, viola, and cello have strings. So they are called string instruments. There are two kinds of wind instruments: brass and woodwinds. Brass instruments include the trumpet, trombone, and tuba. Woodwinds are the clarinet, flute, oboe, and saxophone. Percussion instruments are fun to play. You hit or shake them with your hand or with a stick. There are many other kinds of instruments. Apart, they make lots of sounds. Together, they combine to make beautiful music.

Fill in the blanks.

1   There are many _____ of musical instruments.

2   The piano, organ, and keyboard are in the _____ family.

3   Brass and _____ are wind instruments.

4   You _____ or shake percussion instruments with your hand.

Review Test 6

A

Write | 請依提示寫出正確的英文單字。

1	主詞	_____	11	省略符號	_____
2	縮短形；縮約形式	_____	12	縮寫 (n.)	_____
3	格言	_____	13	留傳	t_____
4	出名的	_____	14	相像；相似	_____
5	現實主義藝術	_____	15	展出；陳列	_____
6	抽象主義藝術	_____	16	反映	_____
7	建築學	_____	17	協奏曲	_____
8	建築設計師	_____	18	由……表演	_____
9	民謠	_____	19	五線譜	_____
10	打擊樂器	_____	20	吹奏	_____

B

Choose the Correct Word | 請選出與鋪底字意思相近的答案。

1　Pronouns take the place of nouns.

　　a. describe　　　　　b. replace　　　　　c. capitalize

2　You can abbreviate some long words.

　　a. make　　　　　　b. describe　　　　　c. shorten

3　Parents transmit important sayings to their children.

　　a. provide　　　　　b. pass on　　　　　c. explain

4　After the blueprints are done, they must construct the house.

　　a. display　　　　　b. plan　　　　　　c. build

C

Complete the Sentences | 請在空格中填入最適當的答案，並視情況做適當的變化。

proverb	abstract art	sentence	traditional

1　A _____ must have a subject and a verb.　一個句子必須要有主詞和動詞。

2　A _____ is a saying with an important meaning.　俗諺是具有重要意義的格言。

3　_____ _____ shows objects different from how they look in reality.
抽象主義藝術呈現出與現實模樣相異的物品。

4　_____ African music has some exciting drum sounds.
傳統非洲音樂會搭配一些激昂的鼓聲。

140

Index

ANSWERS
AND
TRANSLATIONS

01 Unit ● Building Citizenship (p. 12)

A

1 respect   2 responsibility   3 fairness
4 honesty   5 courage   6 population   7 law
8 area   9 citizenship   10 caring   11 take care of
12 treat   13 live in   14 rural community
15 urban community   16 suburban community

B

1 responsibility   2 courage   3 respect
4 citizenship   5 Caring   6 located   7 treat
8 law

C

1 located   2 large   3 care   4 treat

D

1 urban community   2 courage
3 suburban community   4 fairness
5 honesty   6 law

E 形形色色的社區

　　人們住在許多不同的地方。有些人喜歡大城市，有些人偏好住在鄉間，還有些人這兩個地方都不喜歡，他們選擇小城市或市鎮居住。大城市就是都市社群，有些城市的市民高達數百萬。生活在大城市的市民居住空間擁擠，他們通常住在公寓，經常搭乘公車或地鐵。鄉村社區位於鄉間，那裡的人口較少。農夫們都住在鄉村。當地人住在平房裡，通常都是自己開車。近郊社區是鄰近大城市的小型市區。有很多家庭住在郊區，但是卻在大城市工作。居民也許是自己開車，或是搭乘公車和地鐵。

* **countryside** 鄉間　**neither** 兩者皆不　**prefer** 寧願選擇

將正確答案填入下列空格。
1 某些人住在小型市區或城鎮。(cities)
2 大城市的人口可達數百萬人。(millions)
3 鄉村位於鄉間。(Rural)
4 近郊社區鄰近大城市。(Suburban)

02 Unit ● Moving to a New Community (p. 16)

A

1 homeland   2 opportunity   3 immigrant
4 improvement   5 custom   6 culture
7 manual labor   8 low-paying   9 faraway
10 ethnic   11 immigrate   12 emigrate   13 move to
14 come from   15 seek   16 get used to

B

1 customs   2 homelands   3 faraway
4 opportunities   5 improvement   6 low-paying
7 ethnic   8 culture

C

1 get used to   2 immigrated   3 came   4 moved

D

1 homeland   2 ethnic   3 manual labor
4 immigrate   5 custom   6 improve

E 19 世紀的美國移民

　　1789 年，美利堅合眾國成為了一個國家。它的國土廣闊，而且國家規模擴張後變得更為龐大。但是在當時，很少人居住在美國。

　　美國需要移民，因此在 19 世紀時，上百萬民眾遷徙至美國，而其中大多數的人來自歐洲。其他還有來自愛爾蘭、德國、義大利、俄國和別國的人民，共有數百萬的人來到了美國。這些移民工作勤奮，但通常錢賺得卻很少。不過漸漸地，他們的生活獲得了改善。而他們也幫助美國成為了一個非凡又強大的國家。

* **expand** 擴張；擴展

將正確答案填入下列空格。
1 美國在 1789 年時成為一個國家。(1789)
2 許多外來移民於 19 世紀來到美國。(nineteenth)
3 數百萬移民來到美國。(Millions)
4 移民們一開始通常賺的錢很少。(little)

03 Unit ● Lots of Jobs (p. 20)

A

1 job   2 work   3 factory   4 company   5 trade
6 volunteer   7 work   8 learn   9 service
10 employment   11 salary   12 wage
13 earn money   14 make money   15 pay
16 get paid

B

1 job   2 service   3 employment   4 work
5 salaries   6 wages   7 earn   8 save

C

1 works   2 make   3 get   4 spend

D

1 salary   2 service job   3 volunteer   4 trade
5 factory   6 save

E 形形色色的工作

　　人們在畢業後，通常會開始找工作。人們從事各種不同的工作，但工作主要有三種類型：服務業、製造業，以及專業工作。從事服務業者，提供服務給他人，他們也許是送信人或是食物外送員。服務業者通常在餐廳工作，也會在商店裡擔任銷售員與出納。從事製造業者專門生產東西，像是電視、電腦、汽車，與其他物品。從事專業工作者通常受過專業訓練，他們會擔任醫師與工程師、律師與教師的工作。這些人也許需要去學校習得技術。

* **category** 類別　**manufacturing** 製造的
　professional 從事特定專業的

回答下列問題。
1 畢業後。(after they finish school)
2 服務業、製造業和專業工作。
(service, manufacturing, and professional)
3 生產產品。
(They make things.)
4 醫師、工程師、律師、教師。
(doctor, engineer, lawyer, teacher)

A
1 geography 2 region 3 location 4 landform
5 climate 6 environment 7 natural resource
8 natural feature 9 geographical
10 physical environment 11 form 12 make up
13 change 14 adapt 15 affect
16 Southeast region

B
1 locations 2 Geography 3 landforms
4 Climate 5 physical environment
6 natural resources 7 natural features
8 geographical

C
1 makes up 2 affect 3 adapt 4 landforms

D
1 West region 2 Alaska
3 Southwest region 4 Midwest region
5 Southeast region 6 Hawaii

E 美國的地理
　　美國是一個擁有 50 州的大國。美國每個區域擁有不同的地理特徵，東北部是新英格蘭區，包括麻薩諸塞州和康乃迪克州，地形多山丘；東南部則是另一個區域，阿拉巴馬州、田納西州和佛羅里達州都涵蓋其中。這個區域擁有一些低矮山脈，也孕有河流與湖泊。中西部是一片平坦的土地，農場綿延了好幾英里，愛荷華州和伊利諾州便座落於此。西南部天氣炎熱，擁有好幾座沙漠。大峽谷與落磯山脈都位於此區。西部包括加州與華盛頓州，這裡擁有山脈與大型森林。

將正確答案填入下列空格。
1 麻薩諸塞州位於東北部。(Northeast)
2 東南部擁有一些低矮山脈。(mountains)
3 愛荷華州和伊利諾州位於中西部。(Midwest)
4 落磯山脈座落於西南部。(Rocky)

A
1 governor 2 mayor 3 legislature
4 state capitol 5 city council 6 county
7 town 8 local 9 federal 10 national
11 govern 12 represent 13 support 14 protect
15 maintain 16 local government

B
1 legislature 2 mayor 3 local 4 federal
5 represent 6 county 7 national 8 city council

C
1 supports 2 governs 3 protect 4 maintain

D
1 town 2 governor 3 state capitol 4 fire station
5 local governments 6 represent

E 州政府與地方政府
　　聯邦政府對美國十分重要，它是美國的中央政府。每一州同時也擁有自己的政府，都市亦是如此。每州有一位州長，州長就像是總統，是一州中權力最大的人。每一州也設有立法機關，其中成員眾多，各自代表每一州的各個小區域，負責通過法案，使其形成州立法律。都市也擁有政府，而大多數的都市都擁有一位市長，有些都市還有市行政官。市行政官好比市長，而市議會就好比立法機關，不過通常只會有幾名成員而已。

回答下列問題。
1 中央政府稱為什麼？(the federal government)
2 誰是一州最有權力的人？(the governor)
3 誰負責通過法案？(the legislature)
4 市政府官就好比什麼？(a mayor)

Review Test 1

A
1 responsibility 2 fairness 3 homeland
4 immigrant 5 volunteer
6 job/work/employment 7 geography
8 natural resource 9 governor 10 legislature
11 rural community 12 urban community
13 immigrate 14 ethnic 15 earn money
16 salary/wage 17 physical environment
18 landform 19 federal 20 local government

B
1 (b) 2 (b) 3 (c) 4 (a)

C
1 courage 2 improvement 3 service
4 geographical

A
1 tribe 2 nomad 3 wilderness 4 canoe
5 bow 6 arrow 7 buffalo 8 hunt 9 tepee
10 totem pole 11 spirit 12 ancestor worship
13 wander 14 roam 15 shoot 16 believe in

B
1 tribes 2 wilderness 3 buffalo 4 tepees
5 Ancestor worship 6 canoes 7 bow and arrow
8 spirits

C
1 roamed 2 believed 3 shoot 4 hunted

D
1 totem pole 2 nomad 3 tepee 4 shoot

E 印地安人如何來到美國
　　第一批來到美國的人來自亞洲。他們橫渡連接俄國與阿拉斯加的狹長土地，也就是陸橋，而連接兩個大陸的僅是一層海面上的浮冰。接著這批人順著陸路從北美走到了南美，他們就是印地安人。在形成美國的這片國土上，住著為數眾多的印地安部落，其中一些部落十分強大，其他則不然。全數的部落都以土地為生，其中有些是游牧民，終年逐著水牛群而居，其他則是過著小團體生活或住在村落裡。這些部落族人知道如何耕作，種植各式作物，此外他們還會狩獵與捕魚。

* **cross** 橫渡　**strip** 細長的一塊　**connect** 連接
across 穿過；橫越　**live off** 住在……之外　**herd** 畜群；牧群

以下何者為「非」？ (1)
1 人們一開始從美洲來到亞洲。
2 亞洲與美洲曾經相連。
3 有許多不同的印地安部落。
4 許多印地安人是游牧民。

Unit 07 ● The Early Americans (p. 38)

A
1 ancestor　2 rainforest　3 temple　4 canal
5 legend　6 empire　7 crop　8 land bridge
9 ancient　10 nature gods　11 follow, chase
12 build　13 cut　14 carve　15 conquer　16 defeat

B
1 ancestors　2 crops　3 land bridge　4 canals
5 Legends　6 Ancient　7 empire　8 carve

C
1 (b)　2 (c)　3 (b)

D
1 Aztec Empire　2 Inca Empire　3 Maya Empire
4 rainforest　5 canal　6 land bridge

E　美洲三大帝國

　　第一批來自亞洲的美國人定居北美和南美。他們學習農業與房屋建造，興建了城鎮與都市，其中有些人甚至建立了偉大的帝國。第一個帝國由馬雅人創立。馬雅人定居於中美，生活在叢林中，不過他們的帝國仍然強大。馬雅人十分先進，他們懂得運用繪畫來替代文字書寫，同時他們的數學能力很好，還興建了壯觀的神殿與其他建築。印加人居住在南美，統治了南美大半土地，甚至在高聳的安地斯山區建立起城市。阿茲提克人居於北美，帝國的首都就在今日的墨西哥。阿茲提克族非常好戰，參與過許多戰役，而且通常都讓對手吃下敗仗。

* **settle** 定居　**advanced** 先進的　**amazing** 令人吃驚的
rule 統治　**warlike** 好戰的　**battle** 戰鬥；戰役

回答下列問題。
1 第一批的美國人來自哪裡？ (Asia)
2 馬雅人住在中美哪個區域？ (the jungle)
3 馬雅人如何書寫？
(with pictures / by drawing pictures)
4 阿茲提克人居於何處？ (North America)

Unit 08 ● The Europeans Come to the New World (p. 42)

A
1 European　2 spice　3 explorer　4 water route
5 adventure　6 attack　7 conqueror　8 warrior
9 claim　10 difference　11 set sail　12 send out
13 land in　14 explore　15 conquer　16 weapon

B
1 spices　2 Europeans　3 adventure　4 explored
5 attacked　6 conquered　7 claimed
8 differences

C
1 (b)　2 (a)　3 (c)

D
1 attack　2 water route　3 spice　4 explorer
5 warrior　6 conqueror

E　歐洲人前往美洲

　　在哥倫布（Christopher Columbus）之後，許多歐洲人航行至美洲。葡萄牙、西班牙、法國與英國，紛紛派出探險家尋找通達亞洲的水路。西班牙探險家到達了今日的佛羅里達州，還抵達了墨西哥與中美的其他地區，他們甚至踏上南美的土地。葡萄牙人主要前往南美，在巴西建立了殖民地。法國人同樣追隨西班牙與葡萄牙的腳步，抵達了今日的加拿大。法國人在加拿大奪下大塊土地並定居於當地。英國人則是來到了今日的維吉尼亞州。

以下何者為「非」？ (3)
1 歐洲探險家希望找到通往亞洲的水路。
2 西班牙人探勘中美洲。
3 法國人在巴西建立了殖民地。
4 英國人在維吉尼亞的部分地區定居。

Unit 09 ● The English Come to America (p. 46)

A
1 cross　2 colony　3 settlement　4 port city
5 independence　6 religious　7 plantation　8 tax
9 settler　10 slave　11 found　12 settle　13 plant
14 pay　15 colonist　16 colonize

B
1 crossed　2 independence　3 settlers
4 colonies　5 religious　6 port city　7 colonized
8 slaves

C
1 settled　2 founded　3 pay　4 settlement

D
1 port　2 colony　3 plantation　4 slave
5 independence　6 tax

E　在美國殖民的英國人

　　西班牙人為了黃金來到了新世界，但是英國人卻是為了別的理由踏上這裡：他們想要殖民地。英國人在北美殖民，建立了許多殖民地，其中兩個各在維吉尼亞州與麻薩諸塞州。第一個英國的殖民地是詹姆士鎮，位於維吉尼亞州。殖民地居民的生活很困苦，許多人死於飢餓與疾病，但仍然有越來越多人從英國來到這裡。許多移居者希望在美國展開新生活，他們為了宗教自由而來，這正是新教徒與英國清教徒到美國的原因。這些移居者在波士頓附近建立殖民地，定居於麻薩諸塞州。

在下列空格填入正確答案。
1 西班牙人在新世界尋找黃金。(gold)
2 英國人在維吉尼亞州與麻薩諸塞州建立殖民地。(Virginia)
3 第一個英國殖民地是詹姆士鎮。(Jamestown)
4 清教徒在美國尋找宗教自由。(freedom)

10 ● American Independence (p. 50)

A
1 revolution 2 declaration 3 rule 4 equality
5 right 6 signer 7 soldier 8 battle 9 war
10 commander 11 sign 12 fight 13 command
14 lead 15 freedom 16 liberty
B
1 Revolution 2 equality 3 ruled 4 rights
5 Declaration 6 signed 7 signer 8 battles
C
1 (b) 2 (a) 3 (c)
D
1 soldier 2 the Declaration of Independence
3 commander 4 Revolutionary War

E 殖民地獲得自由
　　在第一批英國移民抵達詹姆士鎮後，越來越多人從歐洲前往美國。這些人居住在稱為「殖民地」的地方。隨著時間過去，出現了 13 個殖民地。這些殖民地由英國國王統治，但是大多數的殖民地不希望受到英國的治理，它們想要的是自由。1776 年 7 月 4 號，殖民地大部分的領袖簽訂了獨立宣言。獨立宣言的內容表示，美國人民希望獲得自由，建立自己的國家。殖民地與英國開戰，戰爭持續了好幾年。喬治・華盛頓指揮美國士兵，帶領他們迎向勝利。戰爭結束後，殖民地成為了一個國家，就是我們所稱的美利堅合眾國 (the United States of America)。今天美國人在 7 月 4 號慶祝美國獨立紀念日。

以下題目何者為是？何者為非？請填入 T 和 F。
1 美國有 13 個殖民地。(T)
2 這些殖民地希望英國來統治它們。(F)
3 喬治・華盛頓是英國的領袖。(F)
4 美國獨立紀念日是 7 月 4 號。(T)

Review Test 2

A
1 tribe 2 nomad 3 empire 4 ancestor
5 explorer 6 water route 7 colony 8 settlement

9 revolution 10 declaration 11 spirit 12 worship
13 ancient 14 conquer 15 claim 16 set sail
17 settler 18 colonist 19 battle 20 freedom
B
1 (c) 2 (b) 3 (b) 4 (a)
C
1 tribes 2 conquered 3 colonized 4 signed

11 ● Living and Nonliving Things (p. 56)

A
1 living, alive 2 nonliving 3 oxygen 4 nutrient
5 shelter 6 growth 7 need 8 alike
9 move around 10 room 11 space 12 survive
13 stay alive 14 stay healthy 15 grow bigger
16 breathe
B
1 alike 2 living things 3 Nutrients 4 growth
5 alive 6 need 7 shelter 8 grow bigger
C
1 nonliving 2 survive 3 oxygen 4 breathe
D
1 living things 2 breathe 3 shelter 4 room
5 nutrient 6 alike

E 生物 vs. 非生物
　　所有在地球上的事物不是「生物」就是「非生物」。生物是活生生的事物，非生物則沒有生命。動物與植物兩類都屬於生物，石頭、空氣和水則是非生物。動物與植物的種類十分多樣，但兩者在某些地方具有相似性：他們都需要氧氣以維生，同樣地，他們也需要食物與水。當他們進食與喝水時，可以從中汲取養分，而養分提供了他們能量。大部分的動植物也需要陽光，他們還可以製造出跟自己一樣的新生物。非生物沒有生命，也無法移動和呼吸，他們無法製造出如同自己的新事物。

將正確答案填入下列空格。
1 地球上所有的事物不是「生物」就是「非生物」。(living)
2 動物與植物是生物。(Animals)
3 生物需要氧氣、食物與水來維持生命。(water)
4 非生物無法製造如同自己的新事物。(make)

12 ● Kinds of Animals (p . 60)

A
1 reptile 2 amphibian 3 fish 4 mammal
5 bird 6 young 7 adult 8 lungs 9 egg
10 gills 11 give birth to 12 bear 13 lay
14 hatch 15 raise 16 feed
B
1 Amphibians 2 reptiles 3 Mammals 4 birds
5 adults 6 feeds 7 hatch 8 lungs

C
1 lay 2 young 3 feed 4 gills

D
1 hatch 2 reptiles 3 amphibians 4 mammals
5 gills 6 young

E 動物的相異處

　　所有動物可以分成五類，分別是哺乳動物、鳥類、爬蟲類、兩棲動物和魚類，每一類動物都和其他動物不同。哺乳類像是狗、貓、母牛、獅子、老虎和人類。他們會產下寶寶，而媽媽們會餵母奶給自己的小寶寶。鳥類擁有羽毛，絕大部分的鳥會飛；企鵝、老鷹、麻雀都屬於鳥類。爬蟲類和兩棲動物相似度高，兩者都會生蛋。爬蟲類如蛇，而青蛙和蟾蜍則屬於兩棲動物。兩棲類動物居住在陸地和水中。魚生長在水裡，會產卵，利用鰓呼吸水中的氧氣；鯊魚、鱸魚和鯰魚都屬於魚類。

以下何者為「非」？(2)
1 動物共分為五類。
2 哺乳動物是如蛇和蜥蜴的動物。
3 魚利用鰓來呼吸。
4 鱸魚和鯊魚都屬於魚類。

13 Unit ● **The Life Cycle of an Animal (p. 64)**

A
1 life cycle 2 stage 3 birth 4 reproduction
5 death 6 maturity 7 tadpole 8 hibernate
9 growth and change 10 go through 11 be born
12 grow up 13 grow older 14 mate
15 reproduce 16 fertilize

B
1 stages 2 life cycle 3 Reproduction 4 growth
5 hibernate 6 maturity 7 go through
8 grows up

C
1 reproduce 2 born 3 mate 4 birth

D
1 cub 2 reproduction 3 tadpole
4 hibernate 5 puppy 6 caterpillar

E 貓與青蛙的生命週期

　　每種動物都擁有生命週期，一個從出生到死亡的階段。
　　貓屬於哺乳動物，能直接產下幼兒。貓寶寶被稱為小貓（kitten），貓媽媽會照顧小貓數週，用身體產生的母奶餵養自己的寶寶。當小貓越長越大時，會漸漸變得獨立。大約一年後，小貓長成成貓，便可以照顧好自己。
　　青蛙擁有不同的生命週期。青蛙從卵裡面出生，當它們被孵化時，稱作「蝌蚪」。蝌蚪有一條長尾巴，沒有長腳，它們使用鰓在水中呼吸。不久，蝌蚪長出了腳，開始用肺呼吸，之後它們便可以離開水。當這個情況發生了，它們就變成了成蛙。

回答下列問題。
1 貓寶寶又稱作什麼？(a kitten)
2 幼貓變成成貓需要多少時間？(about one year)

3 青蛙如何出生的？(in eggs)
4 青蛙何時會離開水？
(when they grow legs and breathe with lungs)

14 Unit ● **Plants (p. 68)**

A
1 seed 2 pollen 3 sprout 4 fruit 5 petal
6 energy 7 warmth 8 absorb 9 trunk 10 store
11 hold 12 germinate 13 pollinate 14 mature
15 shrub, bush 16 anchor

B
1 seed 2 fruit 3 petals 4 Pollen 5 warmth
6 stores 7 hold 8 pollinate

C
1 germinate 2 bush 3 mature 4 absorb

D
1 trunk 2 pollen 3 seed 4 petal 5 bud
6 bush, shrub

E 松樹的生命週期

　　每一棵植物，如松樹，都有自己的生命週期。松樹的生命週期從一顆種子開始。成年的松樹會結松果，松果內部全都是微小的種子。每一年都有許多松果掉落在地上，有些會停留在原本的松樹附近，但有時會有動物將它們拾起，帶到不同地方去，風和雨水也可能使松果移動。有時候，種子會從松果裡灑落，埋入泥土中。通常這些種子會開始發芽，它們也稱為幼苗（seedling）。幼苗越長越大，經過數年之後，長成了成松，又可以結成含有種子的松果。新的生命週期便又展開了。

將正確答案填入下列空格。
1 松樹有松果。(cones)
2 松果每年都會掉落地上。(ground)
3 當埋入泥土中的種子發芽時，它稱為幼苗。(seedling)
4 幼苗隨後會長成成松。(adult)

15 Unit ● **The Food Chain (p. 72)**

A
1 food chain 2 food web 3 energy pyramid
4 plant eater 5 meat eater 6 prey 7 ecosystem
8 relationship 9 depend on 10 make up
11 adapt 12 be linked to 13 be connected to
14 decay 15 decompose 16 get hunted

B
1 food chain 2 Plant 3 Ecosystems 4 food web
5 Prey 6 depend on 7 makes up
8 relationships

C
1 adapt 2 linked 3 decomposes 4 Meat

D

1 ecosystem　2 meat eaters　3 prey
4 food chain　5 decay　6 energy pyramid

E　食物鏈

　　所有的動物必須藉由進食來維生。有些動物吃植物，有些吃動物，還有些既會吃植物也會吃動物。食物鏈呈現其中每種動物和其他動物的關係。食物鏈的最底端是草食動物，他們通常也是其他動物的獵物，像松鼠和兔子之類的小型動物都屬於此類；有時如鹿這種體型較大的動物也算在內。食物鏈中層級較高的動物會以這些草食動物為食，像是貓頭鷹、蛇和浣熊；而更大型的動物如熊和狼，會吃掉上述這些動物。最後便來到了食物鏈的最頂端，也就是最危險的動物：人類。

將正確答案填入下列空格。

1 某些動物既會吃植物也會吃動物。(plants)
2 草食動物是食物鏈中的最底層。(bottom)
3 松鼠與兔子屬於獵物。(prey)
4 最危險的動物是人類。(man)

Review Test 3

A

1 living, alive　2 nonliving things　3 amphibian
4 mammal　5 life cycle　6 reproduction　7 seed
8 pollen　9 food chain　10 food web　11 breathe
12 alike　13 reptile　14 feed　15 maturity
16 go through　17 germinate　18 pollinate
19 depend on　20 get hunted

B

1 (c)　2 (a)　3 (b)　4 (a)

C

1 living things　2 lungs　3 stages　4 absorb

Unit 16 ● Insects (p. 78)

A

1 insect　2 head　3 thorax　4 abdomen　5 leg
6 antenna　7 exoskeleton　8 caterpillar　9 pupa
10 metamorphosis　11 change　12 undergo
13 go through　14 gather　15 cooperate　16 larva

B

1 head　2 insects　3 antennae　4 thorax
5 abdomen　6 caterpillar　7 metamorphosis
8 larva

C

1 caterpillar　2 undergo　3 cooperate　4 pupa

D

1 insects　2 pupa　3 abdomen　4 exoskeleton
5 metamorphosis　6 antennae

E　昆蟲的身體

　　昆蟲有許多種類，包括螞蟻、蜂、蝴蝶、蚱蜢和蟋蟀，每一種的外觀皆不相同，然而身體部分的結構卻一樣。

　　所有昆蟲的身體主要都分成三部分，分別是頭部、胸部和腹部。頭部包括昆蟲的嘴、眼睛和觸角。昆蟲利用觸角來感覺與辨識事物的味道。胸部是身體的中間部位，包含有三對腳。成蟲擁有六隻腳，有些昆蟲身體上還附有翅膀。腹部是第三個部分，也是昆蟲的最後一個部位。

以下何者為「非」？(3)

1 蟋蟀和蚱蜢都屬於昆蟲。
2 所有的昆蟲都有頭部、胸部和腹部。
3 昆蟲的觸角位於腹部。
4 成蟲擁有六隻腳。

Unit 17 ● The Solar System (p. 82)

A

1 solar system　2 planet　3 star　4 satellite
5 constellation　6 rotation　7 orbit　8 phase
9 cause　10 repeat　11 rotate　12 spin around
13 revolve　14 move around　15 cover　16 hide

B

1 solar system　2 orbit　3 rotation　4 planets
5 satellite　6 seasons　7 constellation　8 phases

C

1 (b)　2 (a)　3 (b)

D

1 satellite　2 constellation　3 phase
4 full moon　5 planets　6 orbit

E　月亮的月相

　　月亮繞行地球需要約 29 天。在此期間，月亮會改變形狀，我們便把月亮呈現的不同面貌稱為「月相」。隨著月亮繞行地球，月相也會有所改變。

　　第一個月相稱作新月（new moon），這個階段仍不顯眼，但是月亮的亮度會越變越強，形狀就如同月牙般。下一個月相稱作娥眉月（waxing crescent），英文 waxing 的意思是「越來越大」。很快地，月相就轉變成上弦月（first quarter phase），能看到一半的月亮形狀。接著滿月便出現了，這時月亮的全貌都清楚可見。之後月亮轉虧，逐漸地消失，經歷最後的下弦月相，然後變成虧眉月（waning crescent），最後又再次回到了新月。

* **invisible** 看不見的　**waxing**（月亮）漸圓的
　visible 看得見的　**wane**（月）虧；缺

以下何者為「非」？(1)

1 月亮環繞地球一圈費時 19 天。
2 月亮擁有不同的月相。
3 月亮在新月階段無法看見。
4 滿月清楚可見。

18 Unit ● The Human Body (p. 86)

A
1 cell　2 tissue　3 skin　4 organ
5 skeletal system　6 muscular system
7 circulatory system　8 digestive system
9 nervous system　10 respiratory system
11 pump　12 chew　13 swallow　14 digest
15 strengthen　16 make strong

B
1 cells　2 skin　3 Tissues　4 organs　5 nervous
6 digestive　7 circulatory　8 skeletal

C
1 strengthen　2 pumping　3 chew　4 swallow

D
1 skeletal system　2 circulatory system
3 muscular system　4 nervous system
5 digestive system　6 respiratory system

E　人體的器官
　　器官是人體非常重要的部分，它們協助進行特定的身體功能。器官有許多種，其中一個重要的器官就是心臟。心臟打出血液輸送全身，如果沒有心臟，人也無法存活。大腦控制身體的神經系統，凡是身體與心理的活動都受它主宰。人仰賴肺呼吸，一個人則擁有兩顆肺。胃部幫助消化食物，將食物分解成身體其他部分也能吸收的營養素；肝臟同樣也能幫助消化。人最重要且最大的器官是皮膚。皮膚覆蓋了人體的全身！

* **thanks to** 由於　**break down** 分解

將正確答案填入下列空格。
1 人體有許多不同的器官。(organs)
2 心臟將血液打出輸送全身。(heart)
3 人有兩顆肺臟。(two)
4 最大的器官是皮膚。(skin)

19 Unit ● Motion and Forces (p .90)

A
1 motion　2 speed　3 force　4 gravity　5 friction
6 magnet　7 attraction　8 pole　9 magnetic pole
10 magnetic field　11 compass　12 move
13 attract　14 pull　15 repel　16 push away

B
1 force　2 Motion　3 Gravity　4 Friction　5 poles
6 magnet　7 attraction　8 magnetic field

C
1 pull　2 push　3 attracts　4 north

D
1 magnet　2 gravity　3 magnetic field　4 speed
5 compass　6 friction

E　磁鐵的作用
　　某些物件會相互吸引，某些則是彼此排斥。磁鐵擁有能夠吸引或排斥其他物品的能力，不需要碰觸到鋼或鐵之類的物品，便可以使它們移動。磁鐵是如何產生磁性的呢？磁鐵是一塊帶有磁性的金屬如鐵或鎳，擁有兩個相異的磁極，一端是向著北極（稱為 N 極），另一端向著南極（稱為 S 極），兩極產生一個磁場，能夠吸引或排斥不同的金屬。假設某塊磁鐵的北極鄰近另一塊磁鐵的南極，兩塊磁鐵會互相吸引；但要是兩塊磁鐵的北極相鄰，彼此則會產生排斥。

* **magnetized** 帶有磁力的

回答下列問題。
1 磁鐵不用碰觸也能移動的物品為何？
(iron and steel things)
2 磁鐵是由什麼構成？
(magnetized metal like iron or nickel)
3 磁鐵的兩極各是什麼？(the N pole and S pole)
4 如果兩塊磁鐵的北極接近，會發生什麼事？
(They will repel each other.)

20 Unit ● Sound (p.94)

A
1 sound　2 noise　3 vibration　4 tone
5 sound wave　6 frequency　7 loudness　8 pitch
9 speed of sound　10 noise pollution　11 vibrate
12 hear　13 listen to　14 make sound
15 travel through　16 move through

B
1 Sound　2 vibrations　3 frequencies　4 tone
5 pitch　6 speed　7 loudness　8 Sound waves

C
1 vibrate　2 travel　3 hear　4 pitch

D
1 noise　2 loudness　3 solids　4 sound wave

E　電話的發明
　　在很久之前，電話還沒出現。不過那時候人們知道，藉由振動可以傳導聲音，因此有很多人嘗試發明電話，亞歷山大‧葛拉罕‧貝爾（Bell）正是其中一位。貝爾希望利用電力傳導聲音，他認為自己能夠將聲音轉為電脈衝（electric pulse），聲音便可以經由金屬線傳送。貝爾對這個計畫投入許多努力。在 1876 年的某日，貝爾在辦公室發生了一個意外，需要求助助手華森。貝爾說：「華森，快來，我需要你。」華森當時在房子的另一頭，但他卻透過電話聽到了貝爾的聲音。最終貝爾成功了，他發明了電話！

* **electric pulse** 電脈衝　**assistant** 助手

將正確答案填入下列空格。
1 亞歷山大‧葛拉罕‧貝爾想要發明電話。(telephone)
2 貝爾希望用電力傳導聲音。(electricity)
3 在 1876 年，貝爾發明了第一具電話。(1876)
4 貝爾在電話裡呼叫助手華森。(Watson)

Review Test 4

A

1 thorax 2 abdomen 3 constellation 4 rotation
5 organ 6 circulatory system 7 motion
8 friction 9 vibration 10 frequency
11 metamorphosis 12 undergo 13 rotate
14 revolve 15 skeletal system
16 respiratory system 17 magnetic pole
18 magnetic field 19 vibrate 20 travel through

B

1 (a) 2 (b) 3 (a) 4 (c)

C

1 caterpillar 2 planets 3 cells 4 Gravity

Unit 21 ● Numbers From 1 to 100 (p. 100)

A

1 number sentence 2 addend 3 even number
4 odd number 5 equation 6 number line
7 estimate 8 fraction 9 missing number
10 three-digit 11 skip-count 12 estimate
13 double 14 halve 15 round 16 tally mark

B

1 number sentence 2 estimate 3 equation
4 addends 5 tally mark 6 rounds 7 three-digit
8 tens

C

1 Estimate 2 double 3 halve 4 Round

D

1 even numbers 2 odd numbers 3 halve
4 addends 5 missing number 6 fraction

E 數字方程式

　　人們說話時會運用句子（sentence），但其實算數學也有「句子」（數學方程式）可以套用。人們要怎麼用句子來算數學呢？方法其實很簡單，只要運用數字方程式（number sentence）即可。

　　我們試想一則數學題：有四顆蘋果，然後你再多加上兩顆，總共就會得到六顆蘋果。我們用這個例子來形成一個數字方程式，就會得到 4+2=6。數字方程式可以用來相加，或是相減。例如你的朋友有 10 顆糖果，其中有 5 顆已經吃光了，所以只剩下 5 顆，用這個例子來形成數字方程式，則會得到 10-5=5。

（譯註：英文 sentence 有兩種中文解釋：「句子」和「方程式」。）

將正確答案填入下列空格。
1 人們用句子形成談話。(sentences)
2 人們算數學時會利用數字方程式。
(number sentences)
3 1+3=4 是一個數字方程式。(number)
4 你可以運用數字方程式進行加法和減法。(addition)

Unit 22 ● Time (p. 104)

A

1 time 2 calendar 3 week 4 month 5 year
6 timeline 7 second 8 minute 9 hour
10 measure 11 calculate 12 pass 13 go by
14 noon 15 midnight 16 quarter hour

B

1 time 2 calendar 3 months 4 weeks 5 year
6 seconds 7 minutes 8 timeline

C

1 measure 2 quarter 3 half 4 midnight

D

1 1) two / five 2) five / 2
2 1) six / fifteen 2) fifteen / 6
3 1) five / thirty 2) half / 5
4 1) three / forty-five 2) a quarter / 4
5 1) ten / 9 2) ten / 9
6 1) five / 10 2) five / 10

E 時間流逝

　　約翰早上七點醒來，學校上課時間是八點，他只剩下一個鐘頭要到校。約翰抵達學校是七點 45 分，再 15 分鐘課就要開始了。學校時間是八點到下午三點，總共是七個鐘頭。約翰早上的課從八點排到中午，上課時數共是四個鐘頭。接著從 12 點到 12 點 45 分，是午餐時間。接著從 12 點 45 分到下午三點，他還有其他課程，共計是兩個鐘頭又 15 分。最後下午三點是放學時間，約翰就可以回家了。

回答下列問題。
1 約翰的學校幾點開始上課？(at 8:00)
2 約翰早上要上幾小時的課？(for 4 hours)
3 午餐時間到幾點結束？(at 12:45)
4 約翰的學校幾點放學？(at 3:00)

Unit 23 ● Solid Figures and Plane Figures (p. 108)

A

1 geometry 2 figure 3 solid figure
4 plane figure 5 curved surface 6 flat surface
7 congruent 8 area 9 line of symmetry
10 perimeter 11 cross out 12 slide 13 roll
14 face 15 edge 16 vertex

B

1 geometry 2 solid figures 3 plane figures
4 flat 5 curved 6 perimeter 7 congruent
8 symmetry

C

1 Cross 2 find 3 slide 4 roll

D

1 ① triangle 2 ② square 3 ④ hexagon 4 ⑤ cone
5 ⑦ cube 6 ⑥ sphere

E 「平面圖形」與「立體圖形」

幾何學是規則形狀的研究學說。我們可以將形狀分為兩類：平面圖形與立體圖形。平面圖形有許多種，像正方形、長方形、三角形，和圓形都屬與此類。平面圖形有長與寬，因為由平面組成，所以可以將它們畫在紙上。立體圖形與平面圖形不同，它擁有長、寬與高。像一個箱子就是立體圖形，在幾何學上被稱作立方體（cube）。地球儀也是立體圖形，因為它是一個球體；三角體和圓錐體則是立體圖形的另外兩種範例。

以下何者為「非」？(4)
1 幾何學是規則形狀的研究學說。
2 形狀共有兩類。
3 正方形屬於平面圖形。
4 圓形屬於立體圖形。

24 Unit ● Multiplication and Division (p. 112)

A
1 multiplication 2 multiply 3 factor 4 product
5 multiplication table 6 division 7 divide
8 quotient 9 times 10 equal group 11 divisor
12 dividend 13 divide by 14 divide into
B
1 Multiplication 2 equal groups 3 product
4 quotient 5 factors 6 times 7 Division
8 Multiplication tables
C
1 multiply 2 divide 3 by 4 fourteen
D
1 factors 2 product 3 quotient 4 divisor
5 dividend 6 multiply

E 為什麼我們需要乘法？

有時候你或許需要將很多組事物相加，舉例來說，你有 5 袋蘋果，每一袋都有兩顆蘋果。你可以將一袋的兩顆蘋果相加 5 次，得到算式 2 ＋ 2 ＋ 2 ＋ 2 ＋ 2 ＝ 10。但是那樣的算式太長了，所以你可以改用乘法來替代。你可以把上述的加法算式寫成 2 × 5 ＝ 10 的乘法題目。當你將數字相乘，等於把等組數字進行多次相加，乘法的實用性也讓數學變得更簡單。然而，有幾件事情要謹記：第一、當你將任何數字與 1 相乘時，得到的乘積一定是那個數字本身，例如 5 × 1 ＝ 5，而 100 × 1 ＝ 100；另外當你將任何數字和 0 相乘時，乘積必定等於 0，例如 2 × 0 ＝ 0、100 × 0 ＝ 0。

將正確答案填入下列空格。
1 當你將數字相乘，等於把等組數字進行多次相加。(equal groups)
2 2×5 ＝ 10 是乘法題目。(multiplication)
3 任何數字乘以 1 等於那個數字本身。(1)
4 任何數字乘以 0 等於 0。(0)

A
1 addend 2 even number 3 odd number
4 timeline 5 second 6 solid figure
7 plane figure 8 congruent 9 multiplication
10 multiply 11 three-digit 12 round 13 measure
14 calculate 15 cross out 16 quarter hour
17 edge 18 vertex 19 divide 20 division
B
1 (a) 2 (c) 3 (b) 4 (a)
C
1 number sentence 2 three-digit 3 calendar
4 curved

25 Unit ● Learning About Language (p. 118)

A
1 sentence 2 noun 3 verb 4 adjective
5 pronoun 6 preposition 7 subject
8 contraction 9 apostrophe 10 abbreviation
11 take the place of, replace 12 linking verb
13 abbreviate 14 capitalize 15 describe
16 singular noun
B
1 sentence 2 pronouns 3 Adjectives 4 plural
5 subject 6 abbreviation 7 contraction
8 apostrophe
C
1 replace 2 abbreviate 3 shorten 4 Capitalize
D
1 subject 2 verb 3 adjective 4 pronoun
5 abbreviation 6 apostrophe

E 英語的詞類

英語中有許多單字，我們用這些單字造句。然而這些單字可分為許多類型，我們把它們稱為「詞性」（parts of speech），而我們就用這些詞性來進行造句。詞性包括名詞、動詞、形容詞和介系詞等。

每一個英文句都需要主詞和動詞，通常主詞的詞性為名詞。名詞是代指一個人、一個地方或一件事的字。看看你的房間，所有你能想出名字的事物都屬於名詞。動詞描述的是動作。想一想某些你所從事的活動，那些字都是動詞。有時候我們還會使用其他詞性，像是形容詞，其作用在形容其他如名詞和代名詞的單字：熱的（hot）、冷的（cold）、白色的（white）、黑色的（black）、風大的（windy）、下雨的（rainy）、晴天的（sunny）這些字都屬於形容詞。

回答下列問題。
1 我們用什麼來造句？(words, parts of speech)
2 每個（英文）句子都需要什麼？(a subject and a verb)
3 動詞的作用是什麼？(They describe actions.)
4 形容詞的功用是什麼？(They describe other words like nouns and pronouns.)

Unit 26 ● Familiar Sayings (p. 122)

A

1 saying　2 proverb　3 familiar　4 meaning
5 moral　6 knowledge　7 well-known　8 wisdom
9 folklore　10 oral　11 pass on　12 transmit
13 provide　14 definition　15 explanation
16 idiom

B

1 proverb　2 sayings　3 moral　4 familiar
5 well-known　6 folklore　7 oral　8 wisdom

C

1 pass　2 provides　3 Idioms　4 speak

D

1 perfect　2 leap　3 milk　4 cover　5 will
6 leave

E 常見的格言

　　每個語言都有其常見的格言諺語，經常使用於各種場合。格言很難被翻成其他語言，但在原本的語言中卻通情達意。英文中有許多常見格言，其中像「Better late than never.」（亡羊補牢），意思是即使起步晚，也勝過什麼都不做；另外還有「Two heads are better than one.」（一人計短，兩人計長），意謂第二個人的幫忙通常有所效益。「An apple a day keeps the doctor away」（一天一蘋果，醫生遠離我）也是很通俗的諺語，它表示每天吃蘋果有助健康，不生病也就不需要去看醫生。

* translate into 翻譯成

以下題目何者為是？何者為非？請填入 T 和 F。
1　常見俗語可以很容易翻譯成其他語言。(F)
2　「Better late than never.」（亡羊補牢）是句常見俗語。(T)
3　「Three heads are better than one.」（一人計短，三人計長）是一句常用俗語。(F)
4　「An apple a day keeps the teacher away.」（一天一蘋果，老師遠離我）也是一句常用俗語。(F)

Unit 27 ● Visual Arts (p. 126)

A

1 vertical line　2 horizontal line　3 diagonal line
4 realistic　5 imaginary　6 abstract　7 realistic art
8 abstract art　9 close-up　10 faraway　11 show
12 copy　13 reflect　14 look alike　15 differ
16 abstract painter

B

1 diagonal　2 imaginary　3 Abstract
4 Realistic art　5 Abstract art　6 reflects
7 close-up　8 faraway

C

1 alike　2 shows　3 create　4 copy

D

1 reflect　2 abstract art　3 vertical line

E 「寫實主義」與「抽象主義」藝術

　　藝術主要可分為兩類，分別是寫實主義與抽象主義。某些藝術家走寫實主義路線，但有些則是選擇抽象主義藝術。寫實主義呈現事物在現實中的樣貌，如果說一位寫實藝術家要畫一幅蘋果的畫作，它看起來就會像一顆真的蘋果。過去大多數的畫作都屬於寫實藝術。抽象主義跟寫實主義藝術不同，抽象藝術不一定會呈現事物的真實性。以先前的例子來說，一個抽象藝術家畫的蘋果，看起來不會像是一顆蘋果，可能會像是一顆紅色的球，這就是所謂的抽象主義。現在非常多的藝術都屬於抽象主義的創作。

將正確答案填入下列空格。
1　藝術主要可分為兩種。(two)
2　寫實主義呈現事物在現實中的樣貌。(Realistic)
3　抽象主義看起來不一定是真實的。(Abstract)
4　在抽象藝術中，一顆蘋果或許看起來會像一顆紅色的球。(red)

Unit 28 ● Architecture (p. 130)

A

1 architecture　2 architect　3 design　4 blueprint
5 column　6 dome　7 arch　8 monument
9 building　10 symmetry　11 stadium　12 plan
13 display　14 build, construct　15 brick
16 skyscraper

B

1 Architecture　2 design　3 columns
4 symmetry　5 dome　6 monument
7 arch　8 blueprints

C

1 designs　2 plans　3 blueprints　4 display

D

1 symmetry　2 architect　3 dome　4 blueprint
5 arch　6 column

E 建築師的工作

　　建築師的工作相當重要，他們負責設計建築物。有些建築師設計像摩天樓的高樓，有些設計餐廳、飯店或銀行，而有些只負責設計房屋。建築師必須要擁有很多本領，他們同時也要是工程師、有很強的數學能力、能夠繪圖、運用良好的想像力，還要能和建商合作無間。建築師會替建物繪製藍圖，用來展示其樣貌。藍圖涵蓋複雜的細節，當藍圖繪製完畢，建商便可以開始興建工程。

以下何者為「非」？(4)
1　建築師設計建物。
2　摩天樓是高樓建築。
3　建築師必須熟悉數學。
4　建築師購買藍圖。

Unit 29 ● Many Kinds of Music (p. 134)

A
1 classical music   2 folk music
3 traditional music   4 symphony   5 concerto
6 aria   7 create   8 compose   9 patriotic music
10 choral music   11 solo   12 duet
13 be written by   14 record   15 be played by
16 pass down

B
1 classical   2 Traditional   3 folk   4 written
5 symphony   6 solo   7 Patriotic   8 play

C
1 symphonies   2 record   3 choral   4 concerto

D
1 compose   2 choral music   3 folk music
4 symphony   5 solo   6 aria

E 不同的音樂種類

　　人們對於音樂有不同的喜好。有些人喜歡輕音樂，有些人喜歡快的旋律。有些人習慣聽加上歌聲的曲子，有些人偏好樂器演奏。音樂有許多不同的種類，像古典音樂就是以樂器演奏為主，旋律中很少會出現歌聲。另一方面，民謠與傳統樂同時使用了樂器搭配上歌聲。每個國家都有自己的民謠音樂，通常它們都富有趣味。現代樂也分為許多種類，其中的搖滾樂很受歡迎，爵士樂同樣也是。有些人則喜愛饒舌樂或節奏藍調。整體說來，每個人都能找到自己喜歡的音樂。

以下題目何者為是？何者為非？請填入 T 和 F。
1 人們喜歡不同種類的音樂。(T)
2 古典音樂中加入了很多唱歌的橋段。(F)
3 民謠不使用樂器搭配。(F)
4 爵士樂在今日是很流行的音樂。(T)

Unit 30 ● Musical Instruments (p. 138)

A
1 wind instrument   2 percussion instrument
3 string instrument   4 brass instrument
5 keyboard instrument   6 reed   7 pitch   8 note
9 staff   10 made of   11 hit, strike, beat   12 triangle
13 cello   14 blow   15 pluck   16 push

B
1 string   2 percussion   3 Brass   4 wind   5 pitch
6 reeds   7 staff   8 notes

C
1 beating   2 blows   3 presses   4 plucks

D
1 wind instruments   2 reed
3 brass instruments   4 keyboard instruments
5 note   6 staff

E 各種樂器

　　某些樂器看似相像，或是擁有共同的特徵。我們可以把這些樂器分門歸類，根據這些種類，有各種類型的樂器。

　　鍵盤樂器有鍵能彈，包括鋼琴、風琴和電子琴，都是這個鍵盤樂器中的一員。小提琴、中提琴和大提琴擁有弦，因此被稱為弦樂器。管樂器分為兩類：銅管樂器和木管樂器。銅管樂器有小號、長號和大號；單簧管、長笛、雙簧管和薩克斯風則是屬於木管樂器。打擊樂器演奏時很有樂趣，你可以用手或拿棒子敲擊、震動樂器。除此之外，還有很多樂器項目。這些樂器分開演奏時，會製造出很大的聲響，但合奏時，它們卻結合譜出美妙的樂音。

將正確答案填入下列空格。
1 有各種類別的樂器。(families)
2 鋼琴、風琴和電子琴，都屬於鍵盤樂器。(keyboard)
3 銅管樂器和木管樂器都是管樂器。(woodwinds)
4 你可以用手敲擊或震動打擊樂器。(hit)

Review Test 6

A
1 subject   2 contraction   3 saying, proverb
4 well-known   5 realistic art   6 abstract art
7 architecture   8 architect   9 folk music
10 percussion instrument   11 apostrophe
12 abbreviation   13 transmit   14 look alike
15 display   16 reflect   17 concerto
18 be played by   19 staff   20 blow

B
1 (b)   2 (c)   3 (b)   4 (c)

C
1 sentence   2 proverb   3 Abstract art
4 Traditional